THE DREAM JUMPER'S PURSUIT

KIM HORNSBY

PRESS

Seattle~Maui

Cover design by Top Ten Press

TOP
PRESS

Paperback ISBN-13: 978-0-9962973-1-8

Book 3 of The Dream Jumper
Series

"Your work is to discover your world and then with all your heart give yourself to it."

Buddha

CHAPTER 1

Jamey pulled his truck into what used to be his wife Tina's parking spot at her Maui dive shop. *Her* dive shop. He needed to talk to her about ordering a new sign for the store, one that included his name. Being petty wasn't a quality he wanted to embrace, but still.

Obi, Tina's dog, jumped out of the truck and led the way through the alleyway door and into the backroom office. Tina's former desk was hardly recognizable these days with everything in neat piles and file folders, now that it was his. He was a meticulous person. He had to be because he had so little control in other areas. Entering dreams, reading minds, had always left him with the need to keep order.

Dropping the truck keys in a box labeled KEYS, Jamey thought about the upcoming afternoon dive with Tina. They planned to anchor between Maui and Lanai and go deep enough to see the Hawaiian Black Coral—a rare species that had only been discovered in Hawaii fifty years ago. It was only found at depths of more than a hundred feet down, and although he wasn't scared about the depth, he was hesitant about something. Since he'd woken that morning, something hovered like one of those dark rainclouds that sometimes swept in from beyond Molokai. On days like this, he kept his guard up.

As he walked through to the shop, his niece, Katie, was ringing up a group of customers buying snorkel gear. "I'm going for smoothies," he whispered to her. This had become their routine when he came to work; he'd check in, then cross the street to the Sunrise Cafe. He and Tina were off coffee these days. Him, because he drank way too much, and Tina because she was breastfeeding their six-month-old son and didn't want anything to taint the breast milk.

"The usual," Katie called to him.

Jamey whistled for Obi to follow and the brindled pit-mix scooted out the door with him. Having always wanted a dog of his own, this relationship was satisfying even if Obi was firstly loyal to Tina. Lahaina's downtown was already busy at nine a.m. and Jamey wasn't taking any chances with the traffic. "Heel boy," he said as they crossed the main street.

Months ago, before Jamey had taken over running the dive shop, Obi had independently wandered the block of stores off Lahaina's main street at whim. As a former street dog, Obi knew how to navigate the downtown of Maui's historic whaling town better than most locals. "Wait outside," Jamey told him at the café's door, then slid in to the early morning lineup.

Tina's friend Pepper was going to babysit Kai that afternoon, to give them time away from being new parents. This was a first and something they hadn't indulged in since Kai was born. Maybe they'd have enough time to fool around after the dive. Turn it into a real date. It'd been awhile. Then Jamey remembered that Katie was along to satisfy a new Coast Guard law about keeping a licensed captain on board during dives.

From the line, he watched Obi run around the Lahaina Library grounds sniffing and backtracking when he got a scent. West Maui's homeless hung out on the vast lawn with their dogs and shopping carts full of belongings. The smells were probably pretty good judging from how dirty some of these guys looked.

Living on Maui and working in Lahaina was a sweet life in so many ways. Certainly better than living on base in Afghanistan and entering the dreams of prisoners for the military. He didn't miss life in the sandbox one bit. What he did miss, although he didn't want to admit it to Tina, was being the Dream Jumper. His whole existence, as long as he could remember, was tied up in being able to enter people's dreams. Now Tina had that ability, although she wasn't pleased to have it. The only way he could jump now was if Tina took him along. A nagging feeling of being emasculated by losing the talent that defined him, coupled with the fact that he was living Tina's life, picked at him these days. Maui was Tina's world; he ran her dive shop, hung out with her dog, lived in her house, and jumped her dreams. And when it came to Kai, she was the main caregiver because of breastfeeding.

Recently he'd let a nasty thought worm its way into his mind that did not sit well. A thought that needled him in his most insecure moments. He and Tina's first husband, Hank, had something in common. Dependency on Tina. He was now in a position similar to Hank's when Tina married him. Hank lived in Tina's house, shared the business, the dog, the Maui life. Jamey had to remind himself that, unlike Hank, he wasn't trying to con her out of money or the valuable paintings she kept in airtight boxes in the garage. He kept telling himself that unlike Hank, he and Tina had a child and a solid marriage based on love and respect. And, unlike Hank, he had given up a pretty good life to be with Tina. Before he'd found Tina again, over a year ago, he was perfectly happy to settle down in Carnation, Washington where his daughters lived with their mother. Now, he wanted to fit into Tina's life, to make her happy, not to steal from her, and not because he had nowhere else to go in the world.

He just had to figure out who he was now, without jumping. For the last few days, he'd been toying with the idea of creating some type of sideline that was all his idea, something that Tina didn't have a hand in. Something to call his own and be proud of. But what? Damned if he knew.

With smoothies in hand, Jamey whistled for Obi and they started back to the shop. Yup, it was a good life. He couldn't complain. Or at least he shouldn't. Not after living in the Sandbox. He never wanted to return to Afghanistan, even though he hadn't been officially discharged yet. Sergeant Milton, his commander, hadn't been in touch lately and that was good news. The man knew Jamey was now useless as the dream jumper and hopefully Milton was losing interest.

"What's shakin', Blondie?" Jamey kissed Katie's curly head, set the drinks on the counter, and approached a group of customers over by the wall of mask samples. "Hi Folks," he said, "Are you heading out to do some snorkeling today? I recommend Airport Beach, then we can take you over to Lanai on the boat to do an introductory scuba dive."

"It's easier than snorkeling," Katie said, "and super fun!"

"How much is diving?" the taller man asked, even though his wife looked worried.

Jamey turned to Katie who was ready to do her sales job on them. *Good girl.* Now to fill some tanks, do paperwork, and then get over to the Maala Boat ramp at noon to meet Tina's boat. They'd do a dive led by her, with dive equipment from her shop.

He had to stop this analytical bullshit about his tailcoat-riding life before he drove himself nuts.

***

Tina glanced up to the surface of the water, over a hundred feet away. Up top, it was a calm day in the channel between Maui and Lanai, but then it was mid-summer. The amount of water between her and the atmosphere was mind boggling, not to mention the weight. The anxiety that had once crippled her underwater and kept her from earning a living as a diving instructor, was long gone. Instead, her thoughts were of how much air her buddy, the heavier breather, had used already from his tank. She looked to her husband, Jamey, who was leading them down to the black coral garden twenty feet below. He was an accomplished diver, but at this depth they had to keep an eye on each other in case nitrogen narcosis set in and one of them did something stupid.

She signaled to ask if Jamey was okay. He was, and they angled down to the grouping of coral below. Jamey shone his dive light on the spindly black coral bushes bringing out the ebony hue and all other colors in the light's beam. Most everything was blue, the last color to be lost at this depth until you used a light.

Then, like a fire drill, the buzzer from their boat above them broke through the silence of the dive. Looking up, she saw the *Maui Dream*—a faint shadow that was matchbox-sized. Jamey heard the call too and they started back to the anchor. The buzz continued. This was the signal to abort the dive. They'd have to ascend slowly after being at almost one hundred and thirty feet. Or risk decompression sickness. And nobody wanted to fly to Honolulu to sit in a hyperbaric chamber for a week.

Once back at the trident stuck in the sand, Tina noticed a shadow off to their left and glanced over. A large tiger shark swam only thirty feet from Jamey's left side. This wasn't an emergency even though tigers hold the record for the most bites in Hawaiian waters. Would Katie sound the alarm for a shark?

The ascent on the slanted anchor line was slow, as needed, and Tina kept her eye on the shark circling behind them. He seemed simply curious. Tina couldn't help but remember that her dead husband's totem and dream form had been the tiger shark. Hank had turned into this form in her premonitory dreams. But Hank was dead and gone now. His spirit that lingered in their house was long gone since they'd found his body off Molokai a year earlier. Still, why did the shark linger?

She looked up the anchor line to where she'd left a scuba tank tied at the decompression stop. And there it was, fifteen feet from the surface with two regulators. Because the dive's duration had been cut short, they might not need the extra air for their breathing stop. They'd have plenty air in their own tanks.

The alarm signal stopped and Tina felt instant relief from the incessant buzzing. She looked over to the shark and wished she hadn't left her knife back on the boat. Why hadn't she strapped it to her leg before she got in the water?

Jamey pointed to the boat where Katie's wavy form could be seen at the swim step, most likely waiting to tell them a huge shark was in the area. Tina nodded at her husband and looked around to see the shark had disappeared. Probably lost interest. Jamey's eyes were set in that focused way and she wondered if her husband, whose intuition was exceptionally good, knew already what the emergency was.

Then it hit her. Maybe the emergency had something to do with Kai. Maybe Pepper dropped her baby on his head, or he choked, or got his foot stuck in the crib railings. Or crib death. He'd been asleep when she'd left the house today.

Oh God.

Tina's heart went to panic mode in two seconds and the adrenaline shooting through her nerve endings made her want to rush to the surface. She had to think this through before she risked paralysis and possible death.

Katie wouldn't have called them up for a shark, would she? Tina untied the extra tank to prepare to surface. Then, she looked at Jamey, making a gesture as though holding a baby. He grabbed her arm and shook his head. Was he saying don't rush to the surface or no, it's not Kai? Jamey's intuition was better than hers. They both looked up to where Katie stood waiting on the swim step, her neon green T-shirt visible. She wasn't sitting with her legs in the water, so maybe the shark *was* the emergency. After a very long two minutes at the stop with Jamey still holding her arm, they surfaced. Tina's heart beat hard enough to feel it pounding through her wetsuit.

Breaking through to the air, she spit out the regulator. "Is it Kai?"

Katie looked extremely agitated. "No."

Tina handed her the extra tank and Kati hoisted it onto the boat.

"There's a shark behind you. You might want to get out of the water." Katie grabbed their weight belts.

A dorsal fin headed their way, sixty feet off. Not necessarily bad news but they couldn't risk it. "Get the knife in my bag!" She hoisted her tank and jacket onto the swim step. Jamey wasn't wearing a full wetsuit to cushion a shark bite. Not like her. "You go first, I have a suit," she said to Jamey.

"You first. I'll punch it in the gills." He turned and faced the shark.

Tina scrambled up the ladder. "Out, Jamey!" She lay down on her belly with the knife, her head and arms submerged, ready to thrust the weapon into the shark if it tried to grab Jamey but he was out in two steps and safely standing on the swim step. Tina pulled her arms out of the water and the shark passed under the boat. "What the hell was that?" she said ripping off her mask.

"Do you think it would've taken a bite?"

"Not sure, but it got too close for comfort," she said. Katie had a frozen look of horror on her face. "It's okay, Katie. We're out."

"I didn't call you up because of the shark," she said, looking over to Jamey. "I answered your phone Uncle Jamey. I saw it was Carrie." Katie's expression sent a shiver down Tina's spine. "You need to call her back."

Carrie was Jamey's ex-wife back in Washington State, the mother of Jamey's twin girls.

"Are the girls okay?" Jamey asked, reaching for the phone in Katie's hand.

"They are, but Wyatt isn't." Tears filled her eyes and her face crumpled.

Wyatt was Jamey's twins' beloved half-brother. Only seven-years-old. Tina put her arm around Katie while Jamey dialed.

"What happened, Carrie?" Jamey said.

The silence was difficult, waiting, watching Jamey. "When?" His eyebrows were knit together, his mouth set in a grim line.

Tina rubbed Katie's back and looked to her for a hint that Wyatt wasn't dead. She got nothing. Katie's gaze was fixed on her uncle, her hand covering her mouth in horror.

"I'll get the first flight out."

Tina's heart jumped. It must be serious if Jamey was headed to Seattle. "Is Wyatt okay?" she whispered to Katie, who shook her head.

Jamey looked at his wife and niece. "I need to get to Carnation immediately. Pull anchor, Katie." He looked directly at Tina who was thinking the worst, whatever that was.

"Wyatt's been abducted."

CHAPTER 2

They rushed back to the house from the boat launch. Katie drove the truck and boat back to the dive shop in Lahaina while Tina drove her truck the opposite way to the house. Jamey booked a ticket for the next flight to Seattle, estimating that they had just enough time to go home, grab a few things, including the baby and take off for the other side of Maui to get to the airport in time.

On that forty-minute drive to the Kahului airport Jamey sat in the back seat with Kai, who was strapped in to his rear-facing baby seat. Passing the Pali Cliffs and heading inland to the airport, Jamey phoned Carrie one last time to get more details on the situation. From her end, behind the wheel, Tina heard a lot of Carrie talking but not discernable words and waited until Jamey hung up to find out the details. The boy's birth father, Kevin, a dad when it suited him, had his son for the weekend. But he didn't return him as planned. When Carrie finally got in touch with Kevin, he'd told her that he wanted the week with his son to go on a road trip. It was Kevin's birthday and he thought he deserved this.

"Long story short," Jamey said, "Carrie and Kevin fought, words were exchanged, and Carrie was furious. Kevin finally hung up on her, but not before threatening that she'd never see her son again."

"He shouldn't have said that." Tina said. "Any mother would freak out. He's only seven." Tina couldn't imagine how panicked those words would make her feel if it was Kai who'd been taken. "Did she drive over to Kevin's house to get Wyatt?"

"Yup. But there was no one home. Today too. The house is shut up tight, like no one's been there for days. So she wants me there to try to get a feeling from the house, or outside. Chris is on a business trip trying to get home."

Carrie's husband Chris was probably in Japan, a business trip he did twice a year. He's be frantic too. Tina sped along the coastal road to Kahului, the traffic heavy, as usual. "How long since that phone conversation between Carrie and Kevin?" Tina asked.

"Twenty-five hours by now." Jamey rattled a lion toy in the backseat for Kai. "Carrie's biggest fear is that Kevin's gone somewhere with Wyatt to wait this out, make her miserable. And he's with Looney Tunes, Rose."

"I thought Kevin and Rose broke up after her last miscarriage." Tina didn't like Kevin all that much, but she really didn't like the girlfriend who was manipulative and bitchy in a quiet, dangerous way.

"Guess they are back together. I told Carrie to call the police even though there's no formal custody agreement that she can refer to, but she wanted to give them another day or two. Then she got the text from Rose saying that Wyatt was hers now."

"That's horrible of Rose to send Carrie a text like that. She's got something wrong with her." Tina couldn't imagine what it would feel like to have another woman gloating over abducting your child. It would be horrific to lose Kai. "Wyatt is such a Mama's boy, always hanging off Carrie. Hopefully he has no idea what's going on and thinks he's just on a long weekend." They pulled up to the airport drop-off; Jamey kissed her goodbye, and was gone.

The next morning, Tina woke and immediately tried to recall dreams. She grabbed her notebook on the bedside table, something she and Jamey decided had to become a part of their strange life now. Seeing they both dreamed vividly, and she was prone to traveling into other people's dreams while sleeping, sometimes taking him with her, keeping account of her dreams had become something more than interesting data. She might have dreamed something revealing about Wyatt's situation.

Her dog Obi, raised his head to verify she wasn't getting out of bed and then settled his blocky, brindle-striped head on her leg while she wrote. *Normal.* This meant the dream didn't look like a premonition or what they called a *Remembrance*. In those, the colors were faded, the scenes usually blurry.

"Nothing unusual, Obi," she said to the still morning air in her bedroom. Obi's eyes were closed. She hadn't said any of the words he wanted to hear, like walk, treat, truck, shop, go. Tina had dreamed of her father, a man she missed terribly since his passing a year earlier.

Dad and I driving in car along a coastal road, maybe Oregon, talking- Dad so serious. Wanted to me to pay attention to driving. Kept saying "look around you. See the road?"

Thinking about the dream, she verified it was a Normal and lay back on her pillows. Nothing to help find Wyatt. No dream jump into Kevin's subconscious, which is what she was really hoping for. It was a longshot, but still. Jamey couldn't dream jump without her anymore. Something she detested about this ability she'd inherited from him. She could only take him along on dreams. Tina hoped this ability of hers was temporary. Until then, it was her responsibility to treat dream jumping, and her intuition, very seriously.

The birds in Tina's front yard began their morning ritual. Doves cooed and then the myna birds joined the cacophony, raising the noise level higher. Kai's little baby voice broke through on the baby monitor. Obi jumped off the bed and trotted down the hall to the nursery. Obi and Kai had a cute little relationship already. A delighted sigh came from the monitor. Kai had recently mastered rolling over and was probably on his tummy looking through the railings. The handbook on parenting suggested you not run to your baby every time they vocalized, so she forced herself to wait. It was hard.

The best-case scenario for Carrie would be that Wyatt would come home this morning. At the very least, Jamey would have a visit with his daughters, Jade and Jasmine, before he flew back to Maui. He missed his eleven-year-old girls on a daily basis, but kept in touch more than tweenager girls actually wanted from a parent. These days. Up until last year, he'd been stationed in Afghanistan, coming and going in their lives. Carrie and Chris had five kids between them, in a big house nestled in the small town of Carnation, outside Seattle and the girls belonged there. Now Wyatt was gone.

"When I spoke with Carrie from the boat, I had a flash of something," Jamey had said on the way to the airport. "Kevin won't be returning Wyatt anytime soon. I think it might be months. Unless I can change the future."

When Tina asked specifically what he'd seen, Jamey explained it was a long, sandy beach. "With palm trees. That rules out Seattle. Wyatt was playing in the sand with Kevin and Looney Tunes." Rose had earned this nickname at their wedding reception by toasting the "knocked-up bride" then pouring her champagne on Kevin and storming off.

"If I had to guess, I'd say California. I saw a pelican." Jamey said. "Looks like they'll take Wyatt south. If they cross to Mexico, Carrie's fucked." Jamey was sure it was a premonition. "To change the future," he'd said, "I'll have to find Wyatt and get him home before they get to that beach in California."

From her bed, Tina stared out the window at the cloudless sky, now brightening to a deep blue. She had a bad feeling about all this. If Kevin and Rose went into Mexico, it would be difficult to use the authorities. From what she knew, thousands of kids go missing every year in America, and abduction by parents wasn't even serious enough to get a manhunt underway in this country. And Wyatt was taken by a biological parent. If Kevin and Rose crossed the border to Mexico with Wyatt, they'd be traveling away from American intervention to a country that favored men. Jamey's mission, he'd said yesterday, was to find them before they left Seattle.

"And if that doesn't work, I'll have to find them before they leave the U.S.A. or it's going to be one helluva job to find Wyatt in a strange country, especially without my abilities firing on all ten cylinders."

***

If he and Tina could dream jump with 2,000 miles between them, he might finally get a clue where Wyatt was. He'd spent all morning with Carrie, talking, reassuring his daughters that Daddy would find their brother and bring him home. He needed to pick up on something useful. At Kevin's house the roommate wasn't home, but Jamey left a note on the door saying that he was Wyatt's Uncle looking for the boy and needed information on Kevin.

Then, he'd laid his hands on the driveway where Kevin usually kept his new truck. Jamey breathed slowly, thinking of Wyatt and his skinny little frame, too small for seven. He got nothing. Standing by both the front and back doorways didn't reveal anything except that Kevin lived there. Jamey sat on the backdoor step for a few minutes, trying to pull something in, but all he got was that Kevin hated the backyard and mowing the lawn.

Walking back to Carrie's minivan, he noticed a toy in the grass that he guessed was Wyatt's. Carrie had said that the roommate, who was a young mechanic in town, didn't have children. Jamey recognized the toy as a Star Wars character, Boba Fett. He picked it up and thought of the little boy who loved to play Star Wars. Like digging with a shovel, Jamey imagined going deeper and was rewarded.

He got a flash that Wyatt was going to a party somewhere. There'd be a pool, and Wyatt could go swimming. Wyatt loved to swim. Kevin had bought him a new pair of swimming trunks. Jamey had a clear feeling that Wyatt felt bad calling his bio-dad Kevin, but Mama said it was okay. His real dad was called Chris by everyone else. Chris deserved to be called Daddy, not Kevin. He loved Mama's story about how Chris married Mama and sang to her big tummy until Wyatt finally popped out. The day he was born, Daddy cried because he was so happy. Wyatt loved Daddy. And he loved Kevin a bit too. Off to the party!

Jamey put the toy in his pocket and tried a few more things before driving to pick up the twins at school. He'd call Tina later with an update. Maybe tonight, they could jump together, give it a try from this long distance. Tina was much better at jumping than he ever was. She'd jumped long distance when he was in Afghanistan. For that reason, Jamey was glad his wife was now the jumper and not him. That and the fact that if he was still jumping, he'd be in Afghanistan fighting insurgents and trying to find weapons caches in dreams.

When Jamey landed in the dream that night, Tina was there waiting. He noticed immediately that the colors were faded and the edges of the scene were blurry. "Premonition," Jamey whispered glancing around at the surrounding beach. Tina would have tried to summon something from Kevin or Wyatt's mind as she fell asleep. This was how it worked for her.

"Was this the beach?" Tina's mouth was turned down, her expression grim. "I feel something wrong. Something tricky. You?"

Jamey nodded. The beach was alongside a busy road. A parking lot separated the traffic from the sand and in the distance jammed-together houses filled in the real estate. Palm trees lined the parking lot and a smattering of kids ran around with a kite behind them. The sand was coarse, light brown, and the ocean was deep blue with a surf line rolling in. A beginner surfer fell off a board and some teenagers on shore cheered. Jamey took Tina's hand and they started walking towards the houses a quarter mile away where he'd seen Wyatt digging. The setting that time was the same. "What do you think? It's Kevin's or Wyatt's?"

"From Kevin, I'm sure of that." She looked around.

Up ahead, three bodies materialized on the beach, one of them small. Wyatt. With his curly blonde hair and his slight frame, the little guy was easy to spot. When Jamey and Tina got as close as they dared without being recognized, the boy laughed at Kevin and plunked down on the sand. He dug a hole, then gathered water to put in the hole. Tina opened a beach umbrella that had appeared in her hand and pulled Jamey to sit. From behind the umbrella, they quietly observed the seemingly happy family building something in the sand.

Months ago, Kevin had told Carrie he was worried about Rose, worried and afraid of things she'd said. For that reason he'd broken things off. At the time, Jamey thought that was a good move, but now he wondered if they'd ever parted ways. They looked so happy playing with Wyatt on the beach. He whispered to Tina. "I wish we could figure out the logistics of this dream, like when and where."

Tina looked around. "I'm pretty sure it's California. From what I remember, it looks like Malibu." She stood up and walked over to the group of teenagers watching a surfer. "Hi there." They looked up. "Sorry to disturb you but do you know the time?" Then Jamey heard her say something about the date.

This was a damn good idea if the beach was an exact premonition. He'd always wondered if people in these dreams were real, if they could see him. As Tina walked back towards him, he stood.

"August fifth. Tomorrow at 3:20. I couldn't ask the year in case I looked like a crazy lady who thinks she's time traveling." Tina didn't smile but fixed her gaze on the family who were now at the water's edge getting pails full of water and laughing. "At least Wyatt looks the same age. And he looks like he's having fun."

"If they took him, and are headed to California, he's going to start missing his family soon. Moments of playing in the sand are fleeting."

"Agreed." She looked at the sky. "I'd say they were right about 3:20. I'm not sure if dream people would know the date. Another thing to put on our list to test someday. We don't know if they are actually going to be on this beach on the day that Kevin and Wyatt show up here."

He nodded. "3:20, you say." Tina was good at this stuff. Estimating time by the sun, gauging weather patterns, something Jamey also prided himself on. He usually agreed with her guesses. It was foolish to find that sexy, but he did. It was one of the many things that set Tina apart from every other woman he'd ever known, including Carrie. "I wonder what would happen if I went up to them and took Wyatt? What if we tried to jump out of the dream with him?"

"Dangerous," she said.

"Agreed, but I still wonder." Never having tried that, Jamey couldn't risk a botched jump. Maybe he'd wake up with Wyatt in his arms, but probably not. And would it hurt the real Wyatt somehow or change the future? Who knew what the rules were for this weird shit? Not him, and not Tina who looked to him for advice even though now she was technically the jumper. He'd never asserted himself in these dreams, not even when he'd seen Tina marry another man. He'd been warned by his uncle to stay on the sidelines, be invisible, don't try to change the future. Was Uncle Don right in telling him this? Jamey had already changed the future for Tina when he intervened and told her parents that Hank was a crook, out for their daughter's money. And look where that landed him. Smack dab in the middle of looking for Hank's dead body. No, he wouldn't grab Wyatt on the beach or try to connect with him. Even though Tina was clearly visible to the teens on the beach, he didn't want to take the chance that jumping out might hurt Wyatt. Or not work. Those teenagers might not even be real people but a figment of Kevin's thoughts. This was Kevin's premonition.

Gathering Tina in his arms, Jamey hugged her close. "I fear this isn't looking good for Carrie."

"Or Wyatt."

"Let's just stay long enough to see the vehicle." He kissed the top of her head as they pretended to look out to sea. "I guess I'm flying from Seattle to L.A. tomorrow morning."

Jamey sat in a rental car in the parking lot at LAX, the main terminal in view, his cell phone on the seat beside him. Having seen the beach in the dream yesterday, he had a good idea of where to look today. Tina didn't need to join him in California. Chris had re-routed his business trip and would be landing in Los Angeles any minute. Together, they'd drive out to Malibu, confirm the beach, and wait for three people to start digging in the sand. Jamey itched for retribution and it was impossible to not rehearse a scathing speech about what a dirt bag Kevin was to do this to Carrie and Chris, but it wasn't Jamey's speech to make. He'd follow Chris's lead because Chris was the real father to Wyatt, having been there for the birth, sat up nights with baby Wyatt, took photos of him at his first steps, first day of preschool, first time he caught a fish. Everything. Kevin just blew into town last year, wanting to be a part of his biological child's life after blowing off Carrie's requests for years.

Chris's flight was scheduled to arrive at 10:12. Once Jamey got him in the car, they'd take off on the Pacific Coast highway for Malibu. It was a glorious summer day in southern California, just like the dream, with few clouds in the vibrant blue sky. The temperature was cooler than Maui, but wasn't most of the northern hemisphere cooler in August?

When he'd spoken to Chris on the phone last night, he was reminded why they shouldn't call the police. "If we can take care of this ourselves, we can call the shots, not wait for the cops to tell us how they did it months after they find Wyatt. Remember, Jamey, you were the police. It takes forever to get things approved. There's channels they have to work through and paperwork. Carrie and I both feel with your ESP, you can get more done than they can." Carrie's usually calm husband sounded quietly furious, like he might want to wring Kevin's neck himself, not caring if he'd get away with it. Jamey understood that feeling. If anyone took Jade, Jasmine, or Kai, he'd be tempted to do serious damage to the abductor. Hell, he was ready to wring Kevin's neck himself.

Chris was Wyatt's father and he loved the boy unconditionally. Jamey was a close second in that love. As Jamey sat waiting in the car for Chris's phone call, he thought about those days after his divorce from Carrie. When Carrie discovered she was pregnant, the baby's father beat a hasty retreat. Jamey agreed to help raise the child that wasn't his, right alongside his twin daughters. He wasn't going to reconcile with Carrie, because they both knew that would never work, but he'd stick around and be Daddy. But then, Chris came into the picture in Carrie's final months of her pregnancy. He'd asked Carrie to marry him, taking the Daddy spot. Chris named the child—Wyatt Christopher, his final claim on the baby complete. Jamey didn't want to admit it, but he was heartbroken when he lost the opportunity to parent that child, the baby he'd imagined as his. Turning that disappointment into something better, he vowed to watch over the little guy in his own way. And he had. Jamey had always felt a soft spot for Wyatt. Being able to get into dreams, premonitions and remembrances was how he could best serve Wyatt now. That, and by being in Los Angeles, maybe he'd keep Chris from killing Kevin and going to prison.

Jamey's phone rang and he picked it up.

"Thanks, Jamey, for doing this."

"Sure, Chris. Where are you?"

"I'm at the curb." Chris was a man of few words, but this morning's words sounded like a man on a mission.

Jamey swung the white rental car out of the lot and found Chris pacing at the curb's edge. He put the car in park and threw open the door. "Your ride has arrived." He got a look at Chris's face. With narrowed eyes, set jaw and a nod of the head, the man looked ready for a manhunt.

Throwing a small duffel in the back, Chris slid into the passenger seat. "Let's get out to Malibu and find

Wyatt." He buckled in. "Do you think they flew here or drove?"

"Drove. I saw Kevin's shiny, new, black truck."

"Kevin picked him up Friday after school. So four days of driving. Lots of time to get to Los Angeles."

Jamey agreed. It was early morning still, when they reached the stretch of beach that matched the dream. Surfers came and went from the parking lot, their boards tucked under their arms. The two men had time to develop a plan about how they'd first grab Wyatt and secondly deal with Kevin and Rose. With hours until that sun was in the three o'clock position, Jamey tried to talk Chris out of anything foolish. He wasn't sure if Chris would attempt murder, but had to argue on the side of caution, in case Chris had that in the back of his mind.

"Don't do anything serious to Kevin, as much as you want to."

"I'll try not to."

"It's not worth abandoning your kids to go to prison." Jamey wasn't sure if that's why they were leaving the police out of this situation.

They stayed on that Malibu beach until the sun was low in the sky and sinking fast. No Wyatt. No Kevin. No Rose. No shiny black truck. Chris and Jamey had walked up and down the beach all day searching for the threesome. Today was August fifth, just like in the dream. More than once Jamey wondered if asking the date in a premonition might not be accurate. What if the person Tina asked had the date wrong? What if some other detail of the premonition was wrong? Kevin, Rose, and Wyatt never came here on that day, never planted themselves in the sand just off to the side of the blue house. For most of the day, he'd watched the stretch of beach where Wyatt would've built the castle. Finally Jamey tried to get a reading by standing in the area where Wyatt had been digging with his red pail, but nothing came to him.

At dark, Chris and Jamey got a motel room just down the road and lay on their beds talking about what to do.

"Every minute he's with Kevin, he could be getting further away," Chris said, his voice full of worry.

"I have to think it hasn't happened yet. I didn't feel anything out there today, and even though I'm not jumping these days, there's nothing wrong with my intuition." Chris was silent and Jamey continued. "I got nothing on that beach today. Nothing."

"Wrong beach?"

"Nope. The house, the parking lot, the curve of the beach, the view, all the same." After a few minutes of silence, Jamey continued. "Let's try tomorrow. Surveillance is not for the impatient, I'm sorry to say. Tomorrow, we'll hang out there all day, see if anyone shows. In the meantime I'll see if Tina can find anything tonight." It was nine o'clock, six in Hawaii. She and Kai wouldn't go to sleep for another few hours. He'd call her before bed. See if she could jump.

"I wish we could ask the police to help, but we just can't. Not yet," Chris finally said. "For one thing, we have something we can't reveal." He looked at Jamey. "Your intuition. And for another, Kevin isn't some stranger. Carrie is convinced he'll realize this is foolish and bring him home in a few days. He just wants to make her suffer. God, I hope she's right."

Jamey disagreed. If Kevin was in California with Wyatt, this disappearance had become a much larger problem. Kevin, who supposedly loved his son, was now an abductor. Not just making Carrie mad. If Kevin was trying to get back at Carrie, he wouldn't have driven all the way to Southern California. Jamey wasn't sure he should point this fact out to Chris.

This was Carrie and Chris's call. Not his. And he had to remember that bringing in the authorities didn't always work. With his abilities, he'd never been one to use the conventional channels to solve a legal problem. His supply of information was unexplainable, and if he tried, it would be discounted immediately.

"We'll figure it out, man. We don't need the police poking around in Carnation. They won't do much right away anyhow. Kids go missing every minute in this country. I'm sure we're farther ahead this way."

The motel room was dark, lights from the minimart across the street slanted in. Jamey reached over to turn on a light. And as the light illuminated the small room, a flash of something invaded Jamey's consciousness, like a photo in a slide show, and then it was gone. "What the hell?" he whispered. He looked at Chris on the other bed. "I saw something."

CHAPTER 3

The scene was brief, tenuous, barely there, and Jamey tried to recall every single detail.

Chris knew enough to stay quiet. To wait.

As hard as Jamey focused, nothing more came to him. Finally, he looked over at Chris whose face was wracked with worry. "Okay, all I got was this. Wyatt was playing with a new truck, on a blue carpet," he said. "He was wearing his Spiderman T-shirt, making those noises he makes when he plays with trucks. Kevin and Rose were watching TV, lying on a bed in what looked like a hotel room. Patterned bed covering, queen bed, drapes, a window."

Chris looked to the window. "Here?"

"Dunno." Jamey looked at the carpet. "I couldn't tell." He closed his eyes again. "Not this room, if it was here. The carpet was blue. The window was on the bed's right. The configuration of the room was different, the walls were white, not paneled like here." It had been such a quick flash, he couldn't be sure of any more details.

The two men walked to the door and Chris opened it. Outside, a hot summer night hit them. They'd had the air conditioning on in the room and this Los Angeles weather was steamy. "What are we looking for?"

"Maybe nothing but best case scenario would be all three of them leaving from one of these motel rooms, preferably in the next few minutes so we can grab Wyatt and be done with this. Maybe I'll walk up and down in front of these doors to see if I get anything," Jamey said.

Chris's face held an expression Jamey'd never seen before. "If we find them I'm going to take Kevin somewhere private and explain to him with my fists that he's never to come near my family again."

Jamey was almost glad to hear Chris get mad. His quiet anger all day had been troubling.

Jamey and Tina decided to try to dream jump long distance. With the phone on speaker and Chris outside watching the motel, they attempted to fall in to a dream together but after a few minutes with nothing happening, agreed to try later after they both fell asleep. During the night, the men took shifts, each staying awake to watch the motel parking lot, hopeful that if Wyatt was there somewhere, Kevin would leave their room to prove it. No luck. And no shiny truck anywhere close. Jamey hadn't jumped a dream either and just before dawn Jamey figured they'd better get back to the beach. Kevin could be anywhere in any motel room in California. It didn't have to be this one, just because Jamey saw something when he turned on the light.

The beach was cold at four a.m. and the two men sat in the car watching the parking lot and beach, talking about Carrie's kids, Jamey's kids, and Chris's kids. Between them, there were six children and Chris parented five of them. He was birthfather to two, Jamey to three, but that meant little because they all helped out and loved all six. Chris took most of the load. Because they shared Dad duties with Jade and Jasmine, talking about the girls was a good distraction. Chris mentioned that the girls were starting to notice boys, and Jamey felt a twinge of sadness to think that they were leaving their childhoods behind.

At ten, Chris fell asleep in the car while Jamey watched the beach from a picnic table and downed a glazed donut in four big bites. Pulling out his phone, he called Tina to say good morning and see if she'd had any success dreaming.

"Nothing. I'm sorry."

Jamey could hear Kai making that humming noise in the background, the sound of him happily drinking. He missed that little body in his arms, the smell of him, those goofy-looking toothless smiles. Today, they'd catch Kevin and he'd be home by tomorrow.

"I only had a normal dream," she said. "About me and Kai in a hotel room and I was trying to find diapers in a duffle bag to go to a parade. You had a beard."

"What's your take on what I saw last night in the premonition?" He'd come to rely on his wife to help him decipher the weirdness, something he couldn't imagine now doing without.

"I'd say that they were holed up in a hotel room like you guys, watching TV, but where that is, would be hard to tell. Did you check the beach for the remains of that castle they were building?"

He looked over to the spot where they'd seen the threesome digging in the sand. "There's nothing there, like it hasn't happened yet."

Tina blew out a breath she'd been holding. "You might be right. If you don't see them today, maybe I should come there and try jumping with you."

Maybe Tina couldn't get anything on her own because he was the connection to Wyatt. Trying to gather information to develop rules for this dream phenomenon never seemed to work. Just when he thought that they only jumped into a future glimpse when Tina was tired, they were proven wrong. And they'd once had a premonition that didn't have the telltale signs of fuzziness. Dream jumping rules were always changing, something that kept them on their toes and in a state of perpetual frustration. But one thing was holding true. For some reason their ability to get into premonitory dreams worked better when they tried to jump together, like all the puzzle pieces were in place.

"We could try over the phone, I suppose. Would that work?" she asked.

"It might." They'd never tried that before. But, Tina had the uncanny ability to jump from anywhere. Not him. Before he'd lost the ability to jump dreams, he'd always needed to be touching the dreamer. Now, he only jumped with Tina, no one else. They'd been successful doing a tandem jump separated by thousands of miles before, when Tina was in America and he was in Afghanistan.

"I can't try until I get someone to watch Kai. Do you want me to phone you back when I'm free?"

"Yeah, hang on." Jamey had walked to the exact spot where he'd seen Wyatt playing. "Feel anything right now?" He knelt and shoved one hand into the sand, brought it up and smoothed the surface of the patch of beach. He probably looked like a crazy person to the sunbathers nearby, but continued to run his hands along the sand, going six feet in both directions.

"Oh, my God, Jamey!" Tina shouted. "We're too late. They've come and gone!"

He shot to his feet. "Are you sure?"

"They went south. Down the coast. What did you do just now? I had a flash of something."

"I stuck my hand in the sand. Do you think they're going to Mexico?" He laid both hands on the hot sand, holding the phone between his shoulder and his ear.

"I feel like that's where they wanted to go. Is it possible to get into Mexico without a passport for Wyatt?" All the emotion had drained from her voice.

"It is if they hide him when they cross the border."

Tina phoned her next-door neighbor, Sharon, to watch Kai for thirty minutes. "I just need to run an errand and I don't want to tromp around with him in my arms. Not when he's so close to his nap." Little did the neighbor know that if Kai was anywhere close to going to sleep, she wouldn't need a babysitter. If Kai went to sleep, she could jump.

The cane field road was bumpy and summertime dusty but Tina needed someplace extremely private and couldn't very well lock herself in her bathroom while Sharon watched the baby in the next room. Or park in a public parking lot while she slept in the car. Driving along the red dirt road, she turned the truck and pulled off to the side of a smaller track. With the A/C running, she went over the plan. Worst-case scenario, if she didn't wake with Jamey and was still in this car in an hour, at least she wouldn't die of heat stroke. Dreams were usually no more than a few minutes.

She and Jamey had made a careful plan, knowing she needed to wake up right after the dream ended. On his end, Chris would wake Jamey after twenty minutes, and that would wake her as well. The likelihood of oversleeping in this sugarcane field was highly unlikely. Regardless of that fact, now that Tina was a mother, every thought was filled with innumerable what if's and backup plans.

She lay down on the bench seat of her truck. It took only a few deep breaths and the intense focus Tina was becoming good at, to get in to the dream with Jamey. They stood on the beach at midday, exactly where they'd seen Wyatt. Chris was not there, but then this was Jamey's dream. She hadn't actually joined Jamey in Malibu. Even though Chris was probably sitting beside Jamey in reality, she and Jamey were where they called *down below.*

She gave her husband a look of hope and sank to the sand to try something. "Is this the exact spot?"

"Yes. I'm actually lying on this spot up above."

She laid her palms on the sand and dug her fingers into the warmth. She then swirled her hands, digging them in and disrupting an area of about eight square feet. A dizziness overcame her and she closed her eyes to concentrate on what she felt. Very briefly, Tina was grateful to have this unbelievable ability. So far, the premonitions had been incredibly accurate. Then, a clear thought washed over her, accompanied by an explanation, almost like a photo with a caption.

Kevin and Rose had been here with Wyatt and were headed to the Mexican border with the distinct plan to keep Wyatt with them as their son. The emotion of their mission was clear to Tina. Rose had recently miscarried again, and she was grieving for the loss of her baby. Kevin's baby. There was something off-center, slightly wild about Rose in what Tina felt. This was a woman who wasn't thinking rationally. She'd always been quietly controlling and suspicious of people but now she'd taken on a feeling of power. Rose had convinced Kevin that a father should raise his son, not a mother. Carrie had too many children to give Wyatt the attention he deserved. Rose, Kevin and Wyatt would become a family, living off the beaten path in Mexico and never look back. It was the best thing for Kevin's boy who was being neglected at home. Wyatt had recently complained that his mom and dad were too busy with the new baby and Mama told him to go play with the twins. She didn't have time for him anymore. Wyatt was heartbroken.

Tina got a clear picture that Wyatt's shyness and insecurities had been troubling Kevin lately and he'd agreed that this might be the best thing for his son to give him the attention and love that an only child gets.

In the dream, she opened her eyes to see Jamey watching her. "Rose wants Wyatt. Kevin too. They're headed for Mexico to build a life with him. They think Wyatt needs more attention than Carrie and Chris can give him and that's why Wyatt is so insecure." The words spilled from her lips. "I think they've changed Wyatt's name to Luke or Nick. It looks like they're driving a black truck and they're going to hide him when they cross the border."

"When?"

"I don't know." She tried to get more by sticking her hands back in the sand. "I don't get a sense of when. It's only a feeling. Rose is desperate. And Kevin hates Carrie right now and blames her for Wyatt's social problems." She put her hands in the sand and tried to pull something out of the moment, but nothing more came.

"How's Wyatt doing? Is he scared?"

"He thinks they're playing a game. Maybe something to do with Star Wars."

"That's why they're calling him Luke." Jamey looked down the beach to the south. "No idea if they crossed yet?"

"No. All I got was the plan. No idea if it worked. What if we try to go to the border crossing in this dream? See if anything comes through."

Jamey reached for her hand and pulled her to stand. "The border at Tijuana, right?"

She nodded. This process sometimes involved changing locations within the dream. If they could fly around in dreams for their own entertainment, they'd probably be able to turn up at the Tijuana border.

"Let's see if it works." He grabbed her hand.

There was no traveling time, no flying through the air over Southern California. They stood outside a green border guard hut on the Mexican side. The only time Tina had been to Mexico, she'd flown and had never seen the border. The scene was incredibly complete. She was surprised at the traffic and number of lanes of cars waiting to cross into Mexico. "Does it look like this?"

"It does. Just like this," Jamey said as he looked around. "Lots of trucks here. See anything that might be them?"

She scanned the sea of traffic. "No." It might not even be the real border. "This is needle in haystack difficult. I don't feel anything, but remember this is just a dream. Maybe if we actually went to the border, we could both get a sense."

He nodded. "I hate to say this, but can you leave Kai with anyone and get to California tonight?"

Her heart sank at the thought of leaving her baby, but the trail to Wyatt would only be hot for another little while. The first forty-eight hours were critical. Same with psychic readings.

"I'll book the next flight to San Diego."

***

At the San Diego airport Chris caught a flight home to Seattle, within an hour of Tina's plane landing from Maui. Jamey had finally convinced Chris he was needed at home and there was little he could do in this hunt for Wyatt that Tina couldn't do. The search wouldn't involve muscle and manpower, but a psychic thread that Jamey and Tina had together. Chris was hesitant to leave California until Wyatt was found, but Carrie asked him to leave the pursuit to Jamey and Tina, and come home. There was a trust involved in this decision that Jamey didn't take lightly and told him so before saying goodbye. "I'm going to find your son."

"Make sure you do. Let me know if there is anything I can do to help. And, constant phone contact," Chris specified.

While waiting for Tina's plane to land, Jamey called Milton. His superior officer had been leaving cryptic messages to call for days. The last thing Jamey wanted was to get involved in a Sixth Force situation, especially when he was searching for an abducted family member. Trouble was, until he was dismissed from the military officially, Jamey was under oath to stay in contact. He was still a Forcer.

"What's up?" he said to Milton's hello.

"We got a Forcer over here who says you are faking it."

"Faking what?" His heart rate sped up slightly.

"You're jumping and telling us you aren't."

"Sounds like bad information." He looked around the San Diego airport. "Check your source."

"We need you here if you're jumping. Don't lie to me on this one."

"I swear, Milton; I swear on my life; I am not able to jump into dreams. Don't you think I'd love to help catch Geronimo? I'd be on that search like a hungry tiger, but I can't get into dreams." He chose his words carefully; Tina was the jumper and that was a secret that had to be kept. Especially from his superior officer in Afghanistan.

Milton took a long drag on his cigarette and blew out the smoke, a sound that Jamey had become familiar with over the years. "Why do we have someone who said he saw you in a dream?"

"Is he a jumper? Maybe he's jumping my dreams."

"With Sitting Duck?" Milton used Tina's code name. "You were with her in a dream."

Milton must not find out they jumped, or he'd drag his wife's pretty ass over to the Sandbox and make her life hell. "I dream about my sexy wife almost every night. Of course, I was in a dream with the Duck. The good news is that it sounds like you got yourself another jumper. I'm surprised, and my feelings are a little bit hurt." Maybe dream jumping wasn't so rare after all. Milton was known for long pauses on the phone, but when he didn't speak after almost a minute, Jamey took charge. Something strange was going on. Milton sounded different. "Got someone listening in? Good idea. Check this out on your psychic lie detector test. I'm. Not. Jumping. Into. Dreams."

"We'll see." Milton was distracted.

"Okay. Well, enjoy your new jumper. And a long distance jumper, it sounds like. Just what you always wanted, Milton. You should be celebrating, not phoning me."

"Don't lose touch, Freud. And call me back when I leave you a message. That's an order." The line went dead.

Jamey headed to where Tina's flight would empty from the restricted area into the main airport and wondered if Milton actually had someone listening in to the call from his end. Probably. Most likely the same guy who entered his dream was right now assessing the conversation, telling Milton that Jamey was or wasn't a jumper. Had Tina jumped the dream of a Forcer? Geography meant nothing to her talent. Maybe. Which dream would it be? Not the beach dream with Wyatt. He knew that for sure because the beach was almost deserted both times they'd accessed the premonition. Then he remembered the homeless guy sleeping on the beach by the rest rooms, covered in a ratty sleeping bag.

Jamey would be glad when Sixth Force stopped hoping he regained his ability and moved on. Having them breathing down his neck for years was fine when he was a free agent, but with a wife and new baby, Jamey wanted out from under the scrutiny of Sixth Force. Having a new jumper would be great news.

CHAPTER 4

Tina had to bring Kai with her to California, and Jamey understood why. She was still breastfeeding. She told him on the phone before she booked the flight that she couldn't leave Kai but it was more than feeding. Tina was so in love with her baby, she could hardly leave him for an hour. Jamey didn't begrudge her that. He was in love himself and as soon as he saw his gorgeous wife and sweet baby come through the set of airport doors, his heart filled with love. It was a sappy way to feel but he loved it.

After a big kiss for both Kai and Tina, the three got into his rental car and drove south to the Mexican border. Desperate for any clue to where Kevin and Rose would go with Wyatt, they hoped to pick up something, namely if they'd made it out of America. He and Tina walked up and down the lanes and even crossed the border to Tijuana on foot with Kai in his stroller. They took a taxi through the town, stopping at every little store, and all the shopping malls to show photos of Kevin, Rose and Wyatt, but came up empty every time.

The only hint of Kevin in Mexico was Tina's reading that they wanted to cross. And that had been in less than perfect circumstances—with her hands in the sand on

Malibu through a dream, over the phone. It didn't verify that they successfully made it into Mexico.

On the second day, he and Tina concentrated their search on the U.S. side, their hours dictated by a baby's schedule. Kai could sleep in the stroller or car seat, but when he needed to feed, they had to stop everything. It was frustrating for Jamey. The search would be much quicker on his own but he needed her for dreaming.

It wasn't until the second night at a Best Western in San Diego that he and Tina jumped a premonition and got a hint of something that might or might not be a clue. They'd gone to sleep in their hotel room after Kai went down for the night and immediately fell into a dream together. At first, it seemed like they were only sharing a dream about Carrie entering a singing contest on TV, but then the dream took a turn and suddenly they found themselves on a wide, paved promenade around a picturesque marina. Expensive boats floated around a grid of docks. Palm trees and sunshine dotted the scene. They assumed it was San Diego until they noticed the Mexican flag flying over a burger restaurant. The signs were in Spanish. The souvenirs touted the town of Puerto Vallarta. The shopkeeper verified this district was called simply the marina of Puerto Vallarta.

They were in Mexico in Jalisco County? Shit. Was Kevin here?

They walked around, eyes peeled for a hint. The dream's edges were fuzzy, the colors pale. It was a good sign. The dream continued for an unusual amount of time until Jamey stopped, grabbed Tina's arm and pulled her behind a pillar outside a T-shirt shop. He put a finger to his lips to indicate silence and mouthed, "Kevin."

Even though this was a glimpse into the future, they couldn't take the chance that real Kevin wasn't cognizant, or wouldn't actually be having this dream in his sub-conscious, only to wake in a few minutes and remember seeing Jamey.

For Wyatt's sake, they had to take every precaution and remain hidden.

***

Jamey hugged his wife, shifting them around the pillar, presumably as Kevin walked by. Then he let go, moved her aside, and watched Kevin walk away. Just Kevin. Jamey nodded to her and they took off, following. He took advantage of any cover, and Tina trailed behind, watching ahead in case Kevin turned around. She hadn't seen Kevin since their wedding a year earlier and was surprised at how much weight he'd gained. His lean frame now supported a beer belly. She'd guess twenty pounds. His blonde hair was now pulled back in a scraggly ponytail. He looked rough. For a guy who did extreme sports, Tina wondered what happened. Ordinarily Tina would feel badly for him, but this was a man who had stolen Wyatt away from his family; she had no soft feelings for him now.

Kevin stopped at a clock tower and waited. Looking around, he checked his watch and shifted from foot to foot anxiously. Then, he was gone. Where he'd stood, no person or clue remained.

"Shit," Jamey said. "Dude woke up."

"Or could he be in another dream? Should we try to follow him?"

"Try it." They walked over to the spot where they'd last seen Kevin. Tina closed her eyes to pick up a clue. She knelt and laid her hands on the pavement, but got nothing.

Just then, they heard a baby's cry from far off. Kai was awake up top. "Time to go," she said, grabbing Jamey's hand. She couldn't leave dreams without him anymore. Deserting Jamey in a jump resulted in him being lost down below, unable to get out on his own. This fact made her husband feel inadequate after a lifetime of jumping, but she couldn't worry about that now. With his hand in hers, they crouched and jumped out, immediately disappearing from the Puerto Vallarta Marina. It wasn't until they woke that Tina realized she'd forgotten to check the time on the clock. Damn!

The next morning, they caught a plane for Mexico. By the end of the morning they'd rented a condo facing the clock. Once inside their place, they dropped off their few belongings and went to wander the Marina, cursing that their condo didn't have an elevator and they'd brought a stroller instead of a backpack baby holder.

They'd expected to get something like a feeling or clue when they arrived at the clock but neither Tina nor Jamey got anything when they stood at the place where

Kevin would linger. Hopefully it meant that they'd arrived in Puerto Vallarta before Kevin and Rose.

After buying a video camera and tripod for their stakeout, they went back to the condo to take turns watching the clock, again cursing that neither of them had noticed the time on that clock in the dream.

***

Jamey was eating steamed tortillas and fried eggs on the balcony overlooking the marina when Milton called. He swallowed a mouthful of eggs and picked up the phone hoping his hunch was accurate. Maybe the old guy was releasing him from the army.

"I need to talk to you," Milton said.

"So talk. I'm in Mexico. I take it you're in the Sandbox." There was none of the usual formality that usually came with the military and higher ranking officers. They were way beyond that now.

"Affirmative. It's been nine months since we met at Fort Lewis. You're becoming more of a civilian every day, Freud." Milton sounded weary. Something was not right and Jamey kept his guard up.

"Suits me. Nothing's changed since Fort Lewis." He'd met Milton at the military base near Seattle just before Kai was born. Milton wanted him to do a series of tests. The psychological tests, mixed in with checking his psychic abilities were tedious and time-consuming, but he'd understood that Sixth Force needed to know his exact status. That day Milton had him try to jump a dream, but Jamey couldn't get in. He didn't want to. He'd been hoping he'd fail, and he did.

"When are you back stateside?"

"I'm hoping within the week." Should he tell Milton what was going on?

"You and I need to sit down to talk. Specifically, we need to have a talk about what you can still offer Sixth Force."

Shit. There was a pause long enough for Jamey to finally add his two cents. "Which isn't much. I have to think you have better than my piddly intuition." If Sixth Force was stacked with psychics, and they only needed him for dream jumping, Jamey might be off the hook with this new guy.

"No jumps still?" Milton knew Jamey had to answer truthfully.

Jamey had to word this carefully. "I think you know the answer. Aren't I under obligation to tell you if anything changes?"

"You are, Freud."

"And have I contacted you to say otherwise?" After their last phone call, someone must've confirmed that Jamey wasn't jumping. Or, at least, telling the truth.

"Negative. You have not contacted me." Milton paused, said something off the phone that Jamey couldn't hear and cleared his throat. It sounded like he had the speaker covered with his hand, a trick that seemed beneath the head of a Special Forces unit at war. "Get in touch with me again as soon as you hit American soil. I need to set up another meeting with you. This time, in Virginia."

"Will do." Sixth Force was based out of Virginia. Maybe he was getting discharged. This could be his ticket out of the army. Jamey hung up the phone. Milton could be bluffing. He often began or ended conversations like this— with a tentative hint at discharge. Nine months ago they'd talked about Jamey's abilities for what seemed like hours and although his superior officer wanted him to regain his dream jumping ability, that didn't make it so. Heck, Jamey wanted to get back to jumping too, if he was being honest. He didn't like Tina being the one with the ability any more than she did. It scared her. Although she seemed to be getting more used to the strangeness of being able to have this alternative life while asleep. She was adapting to increased abilities and he felt like a smaller version of who he'd always been. It felt shitty most of the time, like he'd lost the most interesting thing about him.

When he and Tina had left Afghanistan over a year ago, Milton refused to discharge him, regardless of his last jump. He'd tried to jump into a dream that ended with him in a coma for a week and Tina having to fly to Afghanistan from Seattle to rescue him. Sixth Force had not been able to bring him out of the dream. Tina had. Milton wanted the two of them as a team of jumpers, but luckily Jamey convinced Milton that Tina couldn't enter other people's dreams. Only his. She didn't jump on her own and wouldn't be cooperative if they drafted her. Then he'd told Milton the other real reason Tina couldn't come to war. The one that kept her from being forcibly drafted. She was pregnant. Sixth Force wouldn't get her. Even a top-secret organization with a lot of clout, like the Force, couldn't draft a pregnant woman.

Ever since Kai was born, he'd been hoping that Milton wouldn't come for them. Drafting her now was a possibility, and the thought often made Jamey break out in a cold sweat when he looked at his son in Tina's arms. They'd have to give the baby to someone to look after and go to war if that happened. That's why Jamey let Tina lie to Milton about not jumping. She wasn't under oath and gladly fibbed to his superior officer about not being a "bat-shit, crazy-assed, psycho, lunatic dreamer." Jeez, he loved her acting skills.

In some respects, he'd accepted the fact he'd never initiate dream jumps again. And although Milton suspected something was up between these two, he didn't know that Tina was initiating jumps or that her jumping was as powerful and far reaching as it was. If Milton knew Tina had ten times what Jamey had, he'd figure out some way to get her.

Hearing Milton say they needed to talk made Jamey wonder if the man was going to try to recruit his wife again. If he didn't need to contact Milton until they were back in the U.S., he had some time to consider what he'd do if Milton found out about Tina. Jamey had to think of how to keep his wife from that life, keep Kai from growing up with parents in the army or at the very least keep Tina from jumping dreams of crazy insurgents in the Middle East.

***

The day grew almost boring with one of them constantly aimed at the clock, watching for Kevin. "All we need is that one moment when Kevin walks along here and stops at the clock," Jamey kept saying. That night, he and his wife went to sleep after talking about his conversation with Milton. He'd revealed that Milton wanted to meet him in Virginia when they got back to the U.S. and of course, Tina was suspicious and nervous. "I don't like the sound of it," she said.

When Jamey fell asleep, Tina pulled him into her dream. This one didn't have the signs of a premonition and it could have just been a dream born from Tina's hindbrain. Not a jump into someone's dream. They'd shared harmless dreams countless times over the last year. They now called them normals. When he landed, Tina and Milton were sitting at a table, not unlike the one where he'd interrogated them in Afghanistan. Tina wore civvies, a good sign. Him too. She looked up to see him walk over to the table and then he knew.

"He's sick." Tina looked over to Milton. "He thinks it's lung cancer."

Milton nodded and shrugged. "Serves me right for all that smoking."

If this was Milton's dream that Tina entered, not a normal, Jamey didn't want to reveal that the real Jamey and Tina jumped in. Milton needed to think he'd simply dreamed of Freud and Duck.

"That sucks," Jamey said.

"You two jump in together, or what?" Milton's eyes narrowed.

"What do you mean jump?" Tina asked.

Good girl. She realized she had to play dumb. He looked at Milton. "I think I know what he means, Duck. He thinks we jumped in the sack." Jamey stared blankly between Tina and Milton.

"Let's just ask you a few questions then," Milton leaned forward, looking like he was having fun now. "What are your full names?"

Jamey led. "Freud and Duck." He was trying to think about Milton's knowledge of them. He never called Jamey anything but Freud.

"Full names."

"James Dunn and Tina Greenly, or Green, or Dunn. Wait. Green, but maybe now Dunn. They got married. We got married. Let's say Dunn because I'm an old fashioned guy." He looked at Tina, who nodded her agreement.

Milton looked at them suspiciously, then leaned back in his chair, his eyes narrow. "Let's try this. Freud, we don't need you anymore. I have better people now who delve deeper with no risks. And before I die, I want headquarters to take out the tracking device we have in you."

What the fuck? Milton had a tracking device on him? He had to play it cool in case Milton remembered this dream when he woke. "Affirmative." Milton often said this, having been a soldier all his life.

"It's right here." Milton reached across the table and pushed on Jamey's shoulder. "Somewhere in there. In case we needed to know where you went." He looked like he was still looking for a reaction.

Just as Jamey was going to say something innocuous, Tina interrupted them. "And now it's time to go outside for a smoke, Freud." She stood, pulled Jamey to stand, and looked at Milton. "You can't smoke because you have cancer." With a vague look on her face, she led Jamey to the door. They were now over the portal where he came in just after Tina. She contemplated jumping out but he gave a tiny shake of the head when Milton looked away. They mustn't leave the dream until Milton did. If they left now, Milton would guess their bluff. "Let's dance." Jamey said, taking Tina in his arms to slow dance away from the portal.

From the corner of his eye, he watched Milton cross to the window, his back to them. His shoulders shook as though he was crying and his right hand came up to wipe his face. Then he was gone.

When they woke, Tina reached for her husband's shoulder and felt around. "Do you think it's true about the tracking device?"

He pursed his lips. "Maybe. I can't see how having a tracking device would benefit anyone. I'm not trying to skip out on my military career. He took a deep breath and thought about how owned he felt by the army already. Even before this. "I can't exactly ask them about it, seeing we don't dream jump."

She ran her hand along his arm. "And Milton has lung cancer. I sensed it was serious. Should we warn him?"

"He knows. The dream wasn't a premonition, remember?"

"I'd rather you talked to him about it, make sure he remembers the news. Hasn't buried it in his subconscious," she said.

That was Tina. Honorable and innocent. "And risk him knowing we jumped? Absolutely not."

CHAPTER 5

When Tina recognized the lumbering walk of Kevin, he was already near the clock. She almost screamed at the startling realization that their mark had actually arrived. She grabbed her phone from the deck table and speed dialed Jamey, but it went immediately to voice mail. "No!" She left a quick message and hung up. He was down there somewhere in the Marina. Maybe following Kevin. She checked that the camera was filming and waited for Jamey to call back.

Where was he?

Just like in the dream, Kevin was on his way to the clock tower, but in this instance, without the possibility of disappearing into the afternoon sunshine, he just might stand around for ten minutes. They didn't know how long he'd be there, or what happened next, because Kevin had left the dream, presumably waking. She tried Jamey's phone again and it went to message. "Jamey, pickup. Pickup. Pickup."

Hopefully her husband would be in the shadows, watching Kevin with his phone turned off. There was no way she could run down to the marina, not with Kai napping in the bedroom. And even if she did get down three flights and over to the clock, what then? She couldn't take him down. Or secretly follow him. That was Jamey's department. The plan was for Jamey to follow Kevin back to Wyatt.

Tina held the phone in her hand chanting, *call me call me call me* when suddenly the phone rang. She jumped. "He's almost at the clock tower," she said.

"No!" Jamey said. "I'm on the other side of the marina."

"Hurry!" Tina searched for Jamey in the distance, but didn't see him. Briefly wondering what he was wearing, she remembered he'd be in the same thing he'd been wearing for the last four days since leaving Maui—cargo shorts and a white T-shirt. Nike runners. He'd be running at full speed by now. And Jamey was really fast. She'd seen him run in dreams but that was different. He had physical capabilities there that he didn't have in real life, like jumping thirty feet. However, she'd seen him run on the beach, racing with Obi and he was speedy for a forty year old.

Keeping Kevin in the camera cross hairs, Tina looked up to check out the far end of the marina. It looked like a bazaar or craft fair was taking up most of the free pavement space. Was Jamey caught in that? Damn. His journey to the clock might be slow with the dense crowd. Leaning into the camera again, she noticed Kevin look at his watch. He seemed frustrated as he looked around the marina. Was he meeting someone? Rose and Wyatt? Who else would he be rendezvousing with in a foreign country? Kevin smoked weed, but she hoped he wasn't trying to score some here in Mexico. Or maybe an arrest would be a good thing if he got caught.

After checking his phone again, Kevin turned to leave. "Oh no! Kevin no!" She started to phone Jamey but realized he hadn't hung up the phone. Could he hear her? "Kevin is leaving," she shouted. Kevin was now walking in the opposite direction from the crowded end of the marina. He moved quicker, like whoever he was meeting at the clock tower might be somewhere else. Like he had the place wrong and he needed to get to another location fast. Tina kept him in the camera lens, filming, and watching. He walked toward the road behind the marina and turned right at the sidewalk. "Come on, Jamey!" She waited for Kevin to materialize on the other side of the building. There was a clear view of the space between the white condo complex and the next building.

Kai was awake. He made little noises in the baby monitor that she had clipped on her pocket. These sounds were a prelude to his agitated wake-up cry. The muttering quickly turned to muffled fretting as Tina imagined him looking around for his mommy. He probably wondered where Obi was too. He'd been such a champion with all the strangeness of being on the run. Sleeping well, eating regularly.

Tina heard a muffled crash in the phone speaker and then Jamey's voice. "Sorry, be right back..." What just happened on Jamey's end?

Watching the building, there was no renewed sign of Kevin, Rose, or Wyatt. Tina scanned the area with the telephoto lens and made note of the traffic, hoping to see the familiar black truck drive off in a direction that would be easy for Jamey to follow in a taxi. In the monitor, Kai's crying escalated. "Come on, Jamey," she whispered, searching the Marina.

"Tina? Where is he?" Jamey's voice broke through, sounding out of breath.

"He walked toward the main road beside the white apartment building, to the right of the clock, behind the restaurant. Maybe ninety seconds ago. He hasn't shown up again."

She heard thumping and breathing like Jamey was running—loud enough to be heard in the phone over Kai's crying. Then Tina heard shouts in the phone. In the other room, Kai's cry had an edge to it that made Tina wonder if his foot was stuck in a railing or if he'd climbed over the side of the crib and fallen. She'd heard tales of babies doing things like this. She could hardly stay watching the building while her baby was hysterical. "Mommy's coming," she shouted, inching from the viewpoint. Did she need to keep watching for a sign of Kevin or could she grab Kai, if she was quick? Then, she heard Jamey's voice in the phone say, "Please man. I'll go back. Swear I will. I'm looking for a child."

Oh no! Had Jamey done something and the police thought he was running away from his crime?

The shouting was muffled now, like he'd stuck the phone in his pocket. "Jamey? Jamey?"

Kai was so agitated now that Tina had no choice but to go to him. Her breast pads were soaked through and a new thought had crept into her mother's mind. Maybe he'd hurt himself, had his head stuck or couldn't breathe. Flying through the door, she saw her poor little baby red-faced with tears staining his pudgy red cheeks. No foot stuck. No safety issue. Just terribly unhappy. Or maybe scared because this place was unfamiliar to his little memory. Her heart cringed and she scooped him up in her arms. "Oh Boo-Boo. Mommy's here. Are you hungry?" Tina hugged him to her as she hurried back to the balcony. Settling in to a patio chair, she lifted her top, pulled aside her nursing bra and held Kai to the nipple. He latched on with a fierceness that made her cry out. Still no sign of Kevin out there.

"Tina? Where'd he go? Did we lose him?" Jamey's voice shouted from her phone on the table.

She leaned over and spoke. "I never saw him again. I'm nursing Kai now. Kevin didn't reappear."

"We lost him. God damn it!" Jamey hung up abruptly, then called back to say he was going to check out the area. "Call if you see him. Keep watching!"

Almost an hour later Jamey walked out to the balcony while his son was playing with a toy on Tina's lap. Hearing his father made Kai look up, all smiley-faced.

"What happened down there?" she asked.

"I knocked over someone's knitting stand, and her grandsons took off after me, thinking I stole some knitting." He reached for the baby. "Hello Kai Kai."

Tina handed Jamey a thin blanket, just in case Kai spit up on his Daddy's shoulder. "Did you ever see Kevin?"

"No. No I did not." His voice was pinched, clipped. "And after I convinced these guys to come look with me, I had to go back to fix Grannie's table and booth."

Jamey kissed his son's head. "At least we know that Kevin is in the area."

Tina scanned the marina with the camera's zoom.

"I can't believe after looking for two days, he turned up and we didn't get him." Jamey sounded pissed. "Our big hope, down the drain."

She was disappointed too, but Jamey's reaction was something more.

"And I can't believe that you left your post to get Kai when he woke. I mean come on, Tina." The look on his face was unfamiliar to her. He wasn't just mad. He was furious, and it was with her.

She felt like he'd slapped her face. "Kai was screaming. I let him cry for a while. Honestly, I did. When I finally went to get him he was hysterical. I thought he might be hurt."

"In a crib?" He looked at her reproachfully. "Looks like he's okay now." His tone implied he didn't believe her. Didn't he think she took this seriously? Kai had Jamey's T-shirt fumbling the edge in his fingers. "Tina, Wyatt has been abducted. I think Kai can scream for five minutes." Jamey's mouth was set in a hard line, and for the first time in their marriage, he was so mad at her he looked like he might spit.

"I have put Wyatt's needs first. I'm here, aren't I? I've been watching the marina for hours and hours, trying to amuse a six-month-old baby on my lap while on a stakeout. Every chance I get I try to pull in something. Every time I'm tired, I hope for a premonition. I'm trying to find Wyatt too." She took a deep breath. If anyone knew what it felt like when a child died, it was her. Her twin brother was only four when he drowned, and that was something she lived with every day. She calmed her voice to speak rationally. "You don't know what it feels like as a mother, Jamey. I didn't rush off to get Kai. I left him until I thought I'd explode with worry. Until I realized that this was a different sort of a cry. It sounded like our baby was hurt. I read about these babies that have a rat in the crib or get their heads stuck and I made a decision based on the fact that I didn't see Kevin out there anymore. It isn't like I left while I was tracking him in the camera. And I didn't know what was going on with you. For all I knew, you were wrestling with Kevin, not grandsons of some knitter." Her heart was thumping hard. She got it. They were both disappointed. More than that. They'd let down everyone by not being able to follow Kevin.

Jamey handed the baby back to Tina. "I'm going to look at the footage," he said, taking the camera and tripod inside the condo. "But if there's nothing on there, we might be dead in the water, Tina." There was no mistaking the

tone of his voice that was full of both disappointment and
fury at her.

Or at himself.

***

Jamey still felt like throwing something against the
wall and watching it smash. They'd seen Kevin and lost
him yesterday. The film footage showed nothing after
Kevin walked around the corner of the building. He didn't
reappear, not that Jamey could see, but then part of the
building overlapped another building and Kevin could've
headed away from the marina and remained undetected for
several blocks. The truck didn't appear in the ten minutes of
film after they lost him. Hearing Kai crying and Tina
fretting about going to him, reminded him over and over
that if she'd stayed to watch, maybe something out of the
camera's eye would've presented itself. She'd told him that
it only took twenty seconds to grab Kai, but those were
precious seconds. Kevin might have walked out of the
camera's range behind the apartment buildings. Tina had
kept filming but the camera was focused on the spot where
Kevin disappeared along the sidewalk. Shit. A lot could
have happened in that short amount of time, including
Kevin showing up right below them off their third-floor
balcony.

Then it hit him. When Kevin rounded the building
near the clock, maybe he'd walked into the building and

that's why he disappeared. Maybe Kevin, Rose, and Wyatt were in a condo in the white building. Why hadn't he thought of that before?

"Tina?" He shouted from the balcony. He needed to get over there, check the underground parking, and look for the truck.

"Shhh." She appeared from the bedroom, all sleepy-eyed. She'd been lying down with the baby while Jamey was on watch. Her eyes widened. "See something?"

"Can you watch now? I'm going over to that building." He nodded across the marina, "I'm going to look in the parking lot for the truck." Now that he had a new idea, he felt bad about taking this out on Tina.

The underground parking for the white building was gated and locked but Jamey knew how to break into all kinds of locks. What former cop or soldier hadn't learned a few things like that? Soon he was inside the door to the garage and walking the rows, scanning the vast cavern of a parking lot for the black truck. At this hour of the day there were lots of empty spaces. Damn. Kevin, Rose, and Wyatt could be gone for the day. Coming up empty, he vowed to return later tonight, maybe check the other garages along the marina. Why hadn't he thought of this before? Walking out through the metal door, he squinted into the bright midafternoon sunshine. Like Afghanistan, he was temporarily blinded when he first went outside.

The squeal of tires on the street in front of him made him shade his eyes from the direct sun. And there it was. Kevin's truck was less than fifty feet away, frantically turning around to get out of this dead-end road. Kevin was at the wheel having obviously recognized Jamey coming out of the parking garage. Jamey ran towards the truck as it turned. Rose's face at the passenger window was haunting as she screamed something inside the truck. Was Wyatt in the back seat of the cab wondering what was going on?

"Kevin! Just a minute, Kevin." Jamey took off running at full speed down the center of the street after the truck heading towards the stop sign at the corner. They'd have to turn right, towards town. Jamey cut the corner in hopes of catching up. They had to hit a stoplight at some point. He was grateful that he'd kept up his fitness regime when he left Afghanistan. But the truck did not stop at the ALTO sign on the corner. It spun around to the right and took off. Jamey had a good chance of catching up if he cut across a few lawns. Then what? Get in the cab and wrestle Kevin to stop? Throw everyone out except Wyatt? He'd face that when and if he could get in the truck bed. The truck turned again and Jamey almost groaned to see what was ahead. The street was long and straight and his lead dropped back to four car lengths, then five, six, and more. He'd never catch them like this.

Then, Wyatt's little face appeared at the back window. His blonde head was visible even though Jamey couldn't see the look on the boy's face. Jamey ran faster. At the stoplight, the truck sped around to the right, ignoring the law, and Jamey scanned the area to try to second guess where they were headed. He cut through a parking lot, watching Kevin's truck turn the opposite way even though it looked like the slower route by car. Jamey needed a car, or a cab, but luck wasn't with him. There were no cabs in sight. Jamey flagged down a red sedan and begged the driver to help him. "My child has been stolen!" he said in broken Spanish. The middle-aged woman looked frightened and rolled up the window. He tried to flag down another car, but it didn't stop. The third vehicle was a dirty pickup truck and the blonde driver told him in English to hop in.

He did.

"Which way? And who're we chasing?" the twenty-something guy asked.

"Left at the corner. Black truck, about a minute ahead of us. They have my friends' kid."

They took the corner fast and sped up to fifty on the main thoroughfare. Jamey searched every side street for the truck. "Thanks, Man. This guy recognized me and took off."

"You a bounty hunter?"

"No. I wish I was about now." Jamey's intuition told him nothing as they sped along, but then, in an agitated situation like this, it often let him down. He wished he had Tina with him. Her intuition was good too. Sometimes stronger than his in an emergency. She picked up on the second ring. "I saw the truck, three minutes ago. They recognized me and took off. Now I'm looking for them. I flagged someone down. Can you get anything?"

"Oh God. Okay. Wait." There was a pause while Jamey covered the mouthpiece and spoke to the driver.

"Thanks, Man. We've been looking for days."

"Is that it?" The driver asked pointing.

Ahead was an old black truck parked on a side street, not Kevin's, and Jamey shook his head. "Nope. It's a new truck. Double cab. Dodge."

Tina spoke. "I'm not getting anything, but I can head over to the building and see if I pick up something."

He told her the route the truck had taken and hung up.

After a half hour of driving around, the guy at the wheel, whose name was Butch, said he had to get to work.

"I really appreciate you trying to help me."

"I hope you find the kid."

Jamey took Butch's business card for renting windsurfing gear at the Marriott Hotel, and promised to let him know when they found Wyatt.

"You should call the policia," Butch said as Jamey stepped onto the sidewalk in front of an electronic store in the Marina.

"I will. Thanks." Carrie didn't want the police involved, but maybe it was time.

CHAPTER 6

When Milton called that night, Jamey had already thought about what to say if his superior officer accused him of jumping his dream about having cancer. Play stupid. They were never in Milton's dream. But instead of using any of the rehearsed banter, the conversation went a completely different way. Before Milton got in much more than a hello, Jamey spoke.

"Milton. You're sick. You have lung cancer, did you know?" Jamey had realized in a split second that he could reveal this because of his intuition. It didn't have to include a dream jump.

"Pretty sure you're right."

"Which means you haven't gone to a doctor yet?" Jamey said.

"Right again."

"Time is important. I can feel that."

"Freud, I run a fucking psychic unit. You think I haven't been warned about this by every Forcer here?"

"Just wanted to make sure you knew." Okay, he'd done his part. Tina would be proud of him.

"The reason I called is to tell you that I'll be in Seattle next week and I need to see you."

"I told you, I'm in Mexico. I'm chasing a child abductor. I won't be back unless we find the kid."

Milton paused and Jamey had a flash of something sinister. A kid was abducted long ago. Someone Milton knew. The little girl died. Was it Milton's kid?

"You're chasing a child abductor?" Milton sounded more interested in this news than anything Jamey had ever said to him before. "Are you closing in?"

"We're trying."

"You and Tina?'

"Me and the kid's family." Milton didn't need to know anything about Tina being with him. "The child is my godson. Only seven years old. I'm in Puerto Vallarta. Ask around with the Forcers, if you can. See if anyone can get a feel for something and let me know, will you?"

"Hang on. A Forcer just walked in." Milton spoke to someone, then was back on the line. "If you want to talk to my latest recruit, he says he'll see if he can get anything."

So it was true what Milton said in the dream. He had new people. Maybe people who were more reliable than Jamey, seeing he only had intuition to offer. "Put him on."

"What's the kid's full name?" a husky voice asked.

"Wyatt Christopher Humphries." Jamey looked at Tina who had just walked in with a freshly bathed baby in her arms.

The person on the end of the phone line took a deep breath, and then let it out with a long hum. Finally, he spoke in a high voice. "Curly hair. Skinny. Big smile." He hummed again. "He's with his father."

"That's right. His birthfather." So far, Jamey wasn't impressed.

The man cleared his throat. "I see sailboats in the distance. Sunshine." He made a clicking sound like he had a Tourette's thing going on. "You're close. The boy was near you recently but now he's not." He hummed for another few seconds. "I see tragedy if you don't act quickly." He made the clicking noise again, cleared his throat, and he guessed the phone was passing to Milton.

Milton came back on the line. "That's it. Think it will help?"

"I don't know." Tragedy? Shit. What did that mean? If this guy was right, Jamey was now impressed that Milton's new guy saw a marina. Not if tragedy was up ahead. "Do you know what kind of tragedy?"

He asked the new recruit and then spoke. "Negative. No information on that." Milton sounded invested in Jamey's mission and Jamey was confused.

"How do we avoid tragedy?" This was useless.

"Keep looking, follow every lead, Freud." Milton's voice sounded softer than usual. Maybe Milton lost a child to murder. That's the feeling he was getting from the man on the other end of the phone call. "I'll take his advice, if you take my advice. Go see the Doctor. Get treatment. You'll probably save your life. And don't tell me that it's your time to go because that's bullshit."

"How did you know that's what I was thinking?" Milton said.

"No hocus pocus needed. I know how you think. And remember this on your way to the base doctor. There is no such thing as someone's time to go. The future is changed all the time. If anyone knows that, it's me."

Two days of driving around Puerto Vallarta, searching every parking lot, side street, beach, restaurant and hotel had turned up nothing. Tina and Jamey posted photos of Kevin, Rose, and Wyatt all over town, offering a reward for information leading to the safe delivery of the child. According to the two phone calls that came in, they were last spotted days ago. It looked like if they'd been staying in the white apartment building, they hadn't returned.

On the third day, Tina convinced the superintendent of the building to admit they'd been staying there. "Not here today but they paid to the end of the week," the man said in broken English. Tina told him that they had a medical emergency and the woman had to fly back to the United States with her husband and son. "If you can let me in, I'll get everything they left," she said.

He looked at her questioningly as if to size up her truthfulness.

"Okay. But I go with you," he said.

They took the elevator to the fourth floor and down an outdoor hall to the end. The Super knocked like he wasn't sure the place was empty, then opened the door with his key. With Kai in a stroller, Tina entered the sparse apartment and looked around. They hadn't left much. Maybe because she was nervous with the Super standing there watching her, but Tina didn't get any reading except the verification that Kevin, Rose, and Wyatt had been here.

Jamey was waiting downstairs by the clock, not trusting that she and the baby were entirely safe without him. They'd agreed that a woman with a baby was more likely to gain entrance to the apartment than just Jamey, and even though he hated being left out of the foraging mission, he'd agreed Tina's plan was better.

The only indications a child had been with Kevin and Rose was a transformer toy that changed from a truck into a robot and a few pieces of clothing. There wasn't even a child-sized toothbrush in the bathroom. It all made her wonder how they treated Wyatt. Not just making sure he brushed his teeth, but caring for him, loving him, and making him feel wanted, not just filling some woman's crazy need for a child.

For a week now, she and Jamey had placated themselves by saying Kevin loved the boy and he'd be well taken care of. But what if he wasn't? What if Kevin was only using him to get back at Carrie's threat to cut him out of Wyatt's life? In the small bedroom a book lay open on the bedside table, a thriller, and Tina put it in the bag. There was also a pen that advertised a local restaurant but not much else that wasn't clothing. Brochures touting local attractions littered the living room coffee table and Tina threw those in the bag. When the Super wasn't looking, she even emptied the garbage into the bag. With a black garbage bag hanging from her baby's stroller, she thanked the man, took the elevator downstairs and met Jamey at the clock.

Back at their condo, they sorted through everything, trying to get a feeling for what went on in the lives of these three before they took off. Their bathroom garbage looked maddeningly normal—some food wrappers, dirty Kleenexes, a candy bar wrapper. Then she saw it in the bottom. Picking up the stick the first thing she noticed was that there were two minus signs. No positive. Not pregnant. Rose was trying again. She found the box double-bagged in the kitchen garbage.

When Kai went down for a nap, Tina sat in the quiet bedroom and tried to summon something from the personal belongings she'd collected. When she held a blue cotton top to her face and inhaled, a clear picture of Rose presented itself. A wisp of something sad drifted through Tina's consciousness. Rose desperately wanted to be a mother and was heartbroken after her last miscarriage. That wasn't news to her, but Tina also picked up a feeling of power; Rose was manipulating Kevin with this tragedy. She was pleased that she'd been able to convince him to claim Wyatt as their own. Rose's justification was that Carrie had many children and they had none. It was only fair that she share.

Next, Tina held the toy truck and thought of the little boy with the strawberry blonde curls and fondness for all things Star Wars. Breathing in and out she pictured Wyatt the last day she'd seen him after their wedding a year ago. He'd been playing with Jamey's daughters, Jade and Jasmine, at Pops' house on the Tolt River. Tina was walking with Pops, talking about her pregnancy and how excited she was to have Jamey's baby. Wyatt was angry that the girls wouldn't throw the ball to him. "I'm telling Mama," he'd said storming off until Jade ran up to him with the ball. Tina and Pops had stopped to watch the three children work this out on their own. Jade was the more patient of the twins, always eager to smooth things over. And she loved her little brother with a protectiveness that reminded Tina of Jamey. That day Jade had appeased Wyatt and prevented Carrie's intervention. When both girls made Wyatt giggle at something, Tina and Pops headed for the house marveling at how sweet all the children were.

That summer, Wyatt had been particularly needy, especially where Carrie was concerned. He was always a mama's boy, clinging to his mother, holding her hand, not a fan of playing at anyone else's house. The family joked about how attached he was to Carrie, but according to Jamey, Wyatt was starting to branch out having found a new best friend. Even Pops said on a phone call a month earlier that Wyatt was doing better, gaining a bit of independence. Not complaining as much when he went for sleepovers with Kevin. He no longer needed Carrie in his sight as much. Tina cringed at the thought of how Wyatt must be adjusting to life without his Mama these days.

She took the toy truck and attempted to transform it into the robot. It took a minute to figure out but when she completed the task an idea popped into her head. Or rather a feeling. It was a clear emotion that Wyatt didn't particularly like Rose. He wanted his Mama, but he had to be patient. Kevin had told him that soon they'd all be together at a hotel with a big swimming pool. It would be a special surprise for Mama and Daddy and his sisters Jade, Jasmine, Mango, and even the new baby, Harley. Tina was sure that Wyatt had been told his family was at a hotel. They'd left without him when he was with Kevin and forgot to buy him a plane ticket. That's why he and Kevin had to drive so much. All these thoughts swirled through Tina's mind as she fingered the toy, concentrating on Wyatt. When Wyatt saw his Mama, he was going to be so mad that she forgot him. He wasn't going to speak to her for one whole day. This thought of Wyatt being told his family forgot him made Tina's heart hurt. Poor little kid.

She tried to get more from the toy, but came up empty. What in God's name were Kevin and Rose going to do when Wyatt finally figured out that there was no family vacation, no hotel with his parents and siblings, and no hope of ever seeing those people again?

Tina left Kai sleeping on the bed and went out to join Jamey on the patio. She sat in the Papasan chair and told him everything she felt about Wyatt and the lie Kevin had told to appease him.

Jamey watched the marina intently, listening to the story about everyone meeting for a party, then stood and turned to her. "I just hope we didn't have our only two chances 'cause we sure screwed those up."

"Me too."

He paced the length of the patio, watching. "I feel so fricking guilty about not getting to the clock."

She did too.

"And for not catching the truck. Letting them get away. I've been taking that out on you and I'm sorry."

"It's okay."

They hugged, held each other for longer than usual, and Jamey kissed the side of her head. This was a good start to getting back to where they usually were with each other.

Jamey felt terrible about Kevin's disappearance and about not having the dream jumping abilities he'd once had, especially now that he needed them most. Did he think he'd be able to summon more if he was the jumper? Tina *had* assured him that she tried all the time to get into the dreams of any one of the three. What drove Jamey crazy was that he wasn't in control. And that he didn't entirely trust his wife to get the job done. Trust was his nemesis. Ever since his mother had deserted the family, trust had barely made an appearance in James Dunn's life.

Tina had to remind herself of this fact, constantly. As they broke from the hug, she whispered, "I love you, Big Guy."

"Me too." Jamey continued pacing and watching the Marina. "They probably aren't in Puerto Vallarta anymore. I'm sure after seeing me, they're long gone." The sun was setting behind the set of high rises that lined the coast. "We need a dream." He looked at her intently. "We need a dream tonight, Baby. If you think you have any control over that, try to summon something."

She nodded. "I'll give it everything I have." Earlier, she'd tried to fall off into some type of slumber but hadn't been able to lose consciousness. Not while she could hear Kai chattering away with Jamey in the next room. Instead, she'd lay there wondering if she could've done anything differently the day they saw Kevin at the clock, and if she had, would they be comforting Wyatt right now. She hoped he had his Star Wars sword with him. Or at least the Luke Skywalker costume he wore everywhere. What comforted her was the fact that Kevin was Wyatt's father, Wyatt played with him, there was a genuine fondness there, if not love, and it wasn't like the child had been taken by a stranger. He'd been taken by his birth father who he'd known for almost two years now. Ever since Kevin had come back into Carrie's life and demanded to have visitation with his son, things had gone fairly well. Sure, Kevin had drifted in and out of Wyatt's life at leisure and was gone for months here and there, but he had become a person Wyatt knew and trusted. Hopefully Wyatt had no idea that if Kevin went deep undercover with him, they might never be able to reunite him with his family again.

At dark, Jamey left his posting and called Carrie to report for the day. "Tina cleared out their condo and found a transformer. She got a sense from it that he's fine, he's happy to be traveling with Kevin, like he's on an adventure."

Tina was feeding Kai from a small bowl of carrots and peas that she'd pureed. She looked over to see Jamey struggling with this half-truth.

"I got a feeling that he's enjoying swimming in hotel pools. He's not worried or lonely that I can tell. And Tina got the impression he thinks he's on his way to meet everyone on a big family vacation."

As expected, Carrie sounded frantic on the speakerphone. "Oh God, Jamey. What will we do if we can't find him?"

"We'll find him, Carrie. It's just a matter of when." Next, Jamey spoke to his daughters to reassure them he was hot on the trail and would have their brother back to them soon. They had no idea that their father, or Tina, had a secret weapon to aid in the search. And as far as Jamey knew, neither girl had strange dreams themselves. He'd been watching them for years, looking for signs, but so far, nothing. "I'm hoping to get Wyatt back for your next soccer game," he said.

His words sounded so confident, Tina wanted to cry. No one knew better than her how inconsistent and unreliable dream jumping was. Sometimes the dreams were actual reenactments of reality. Sometimes they were only sketchy ideas with concepts. And sometimes they were just dreams. Premonitions had pale colors, blurry edges and that's what they were waiting for now. Where the hell was Kevin?

When Jamey got off the phone, he took over feeding Kai and cleaned him up while Tina did the dishes in the condo's small kitchen. "Tina, your ability to jump is so far beyond mine. Anything seems possible," he said. "I'm thinking tonight we'll get something."

She nodded, hoping to encourage him. "I think you might be right."

***

But nothing came that night. Nothing but a brief dream about prancing horses. Jamey was beginning to wonder if they'd ever pick up on a glimpse of the tragedy that was coming Wyatt's way. What the hell was Kevin thinking? Where had he gone with Wyatt?

Kevin would know he had to get out of town with Jamey on his tail and had probably headed away from the coast to a less populated area. If it had been him, Jamey would've kept driving for days. What kind of man would steal a child from his loving family? To take a young boy from everything and everyone he knows and loves was absolutely selfish. Sure Carrie had threatened to cut him out of Wyatt's life and get full custody, but Kevin had been dealing with her for two years now. She'd been calling the shots ever since Kevin showed up back in town and wanted to play Dad.

Jamey had to wonder if Kevin now had misgivings about taking Wyatt. Was he nervous that this horrible plan was going to blow up in his face? If he realized the gravity of his actions, thought about international parental kidnapping, he'd probably be looking for a hideout. And that meant leaving Puerto Vallarta. But where? He and Tina couldn't just drive all over Mexico in hopes of picking up a clue. It was a big country.

Clues led Jamey and Tina to believe Kevin drove straight out of town the day they were discovered. South. But they could've rounded and gone north and farther inland. They spent the day wandering, waiting and researching clues, finally ending up at a little Formica table at a taco stand. Tina looked determined across the table while they ate in silence. Finally she spoke. "Tonight we have to dream. We just have to. Why isn't it coming?"

He shook his head and shoved the last bite of his dripping carnita into his mouth.

"Maybe changing locations would help. Maybe we should try to rent the apartment they were in."

"It's worth a try," he said. "Tomorrow, let's see if the place is still available." He took a swig of his beer. "That Super will think you're crazy. Did he see you empty the garbage and take it with you?"

Tina laughed. First laugh in days. "Probably. I don't care if he thinks I'm crazy if he agrees to rent it to us."

Just then Kai woke and they turned their attention to the sweet baby in the stroller who provided the grounding to this very strange and frustrating situation.

Walking back to the condo, along the marina promenade, Jamey's phone rang. Carrie.

"I just got a call from Kevin," she said, skipping any preamble. Her voice was full of nervous energy like she hadn't slept since this started. "He told me to call you off and he'd bring back Wyatt."

"What did you tell him?"

"I said I would, but he had to tell me where Wyatt was and Chris would come get him. No driving home with Wyatt. "

Jamey wasn't sure Kevin would simply hand over Wyatt. Not after what Tina got from Looney Tune's feelings about motherhood and how she felt justified in keeping the boy for their own. And, why would Kevin be worried about Jamey? He didn't know Jamey was anything but a former soldier and cop. He had no idea how capable Jamey was. "So where is he dropping off Wyatt?"

"I can't tell you. I swore I wouldn't. Chris is on his way to the airport now."

Tina spoke. "Let's think about ulterior motives before Chris gets on that plane. What if Kevin's bluffing?"

"Why would he be bluffing?" Carrie asked. "Make us go all the way down there and not give us Wyatt? To what purpose?"

Jamey wasn't sure. "To hurt you?"

"No. Kevin sounded genuinely sorry he started this whole mess and I believe him. We apologized to each other. I sucked it up and told him how sorry I was to threaten him."

Something told him not to trust Kevin's offer. "Does Chris have a rendezvous point and time?"

"Yes. And even if you guess where he's going Jamey, please stay away. For Wyatt's sake."

Tina was listening in on the call. She nodded her agreement to stay away but the look on her face told him that she didn't trust this plan either.

***

Tina woke before the sky lightened and thought briefly about how she'd had a tough time falling asleep last night. There was a Japanese proverb, told to her by her former neighbor, Mr. Takeshimi, that said when you couldn't sleep it was because you were awake in someone else's dream. She'd lain there wondering who. Finally, she'd fallen. And dreamed. Lately she'd been dreaming of her father, someone she missed with such passion, it hurt. She remembered snippets of the dream with her father at a restaurant table in a quaint village that looked like Spain. Sipping what looked like cappuccinos, Tina told her Dad how much she missed him.

"Me too, Krissy." He used his pet name for her, which made her all the more wistful.

She looked around for Jamey, but he wasn't there. It wasn't one of those dreams and she didn't feel a need to call him into the scene. "Mom is taking care of Mr. Boo."

"That's good," he smiled widely at her. "Do you like this place?" he looked around the restaurant.

"I do. The coffee here is good."

"This country is known for its coffee," he said, winking, and then was gone. His chair in the restaurant remained empty and Tina regretted that she hadn't had enough time to say more. She stood, walked out of the restaurant and took a horse-drawn carriage around a city park where she got out at a church. Inside the church, people carried a casket down a long aisle to the front. And then she was out, trying to remember the loving warmth of being with her father again.

Jamey opened his eyes and looked over. "Hi Gorgeous," he whispered. "Is our son letting us sleep in?' He shifted to his side and feathered his fingers down her exposed left arm.

She smiled at her handsome husband, just as sexy when he woke as always. Maybe more so because he seemed more vulnerable and sweet in these first moments awake.

They lay in bed whispering, touching each other, teasing about the possibility of something more until they shifted in, pressing hips together and then kissed. Long and deep. Jamey was rock hard and her excitement escalated. She pulled her panties off, slid on top of him and eased herself onto his erection. Bliss. The feeling of him entering her was so satisfying, so delicious that her eyes rolled back in her head and she had to stifle a moan.

Jamey grabbed her buttocks and shoved into her as deep as he could go. Their lovemaking got rough, desperate, and both knew why.

***

After they showered and Kai was fed, changed, and burped, they proceeded to wait out the hours until Kevin would rendezvous with Chris.

"Any good dreams?" Jamey asked from the floor where he played with Kai and a small assortment of toys to rattle, beep, and buzz.

"Just a normal about my father. We drank cappuccino, and then he was gone." She looked at her husband who'd gone back to drinking coffee a few days ago. "I miss coffee."

"You're a good mother," he smiled at her, sympathetically.

"I miss my Dad too."

"I'm sure you do, Darlin'." He looked up. "Your father loved you so much."

She didn't want to cry so she changed the subject. "If Kevin doesn't show today, what do you think he's doing?"

"Probably getting as far away as possible. Maybe sell the truck," Jamey said, playing peek-a-boo with Kai.

She agreed. Kevin had to know he was in serious trouble and might now be ready to give up Wyatt. Maybe he could see that the life they were carving for themselves as fugitives wasn't worth it.

Jamey's phone rang and he grabbed it up from the low table. "Chris. He'll be in Mexico now."

It was their habit now to put their phones on speaker so if either of them got a feeling from the conversation, they'd know the whole story.

"Hey Chris."

"I'm in a cab. Do you have any news?"

"Sorry," Jamey said. "I just wanted to warn you that this might be a decoy to keep Tina and me off their backs. I'm not sure why they'd do that, but we both have a bad feeling about Kevin showing up."

"What do you think he might do if he doesn't show?"

"Go to some remote area, rent a house, and only go to town for supplies."

"I hope not, but thanks for the warning," Chris said.

When Jamey hung up, he suggested they get out of the condo, go to town for breakfast. "Let's leave the Marina while we wait this out, go to a place on the Malecon that Butch suggested."

Tina packed the diaper bag and they were off to town. The day was hot. Mexico in the summer was difficult with the humidity and they rushed from the car to the air conditioning of the restaurant. Kai loved all the piñatas hanging from the ceiling and tried to reach for one, calling to them as they were seated.

They were just digging in to plates of omelets with salsa and tortillas when a waiter passed the table and bumped Kai's stroller by accident.

"Oops."

Jamey grabbed the waiter's arm. "Watch where you're going, amigo."

The young waiter looked apologetically at the baby sleeping in the stroller. "Lo Ciento," he said.

When the man was out of earshot, Jamey looked at Tina. "He served Wyatt a hamburger recently, I'm sure of it. I got something."

"Go ask him." Tina dug the photo of Wyatt, Kevin, and Rose out of her bag and handed it to Jamey across the table. Neil Diamond sang *Kentucky Woman* in the background.

When Jamey returned to the table, his eyes looked hard, his mouth a grim line. "They were here the day I chased the truck. They had lunch at one of these tables, the waiter said. Kevin yelled at Wyatt for spilling his coke and Wyatt cried." Jamey's angry eyes pierced through her. "God damn it! If Kevin doesn't give Wyatt to Chris today, I'm gonna rearrange Kevin's face when I get my hands on him. Make *him* cry—for his life."

After breakfast, they asked for their bill, and Jamey said waiting to hear from Chris was killing him. They hadn't heard anything. The rendezvous was set to happen over an hour ago, and they were both hoping that Wyatt was in the arms of Chris by now. "He'll probably drop off Wyatt someplace public and take off, then phone Chris to tell him a change of venue. He won't want to risk Chris bringing police with him," Jamey said, as he dialed and put the phone on speaker between him and Tina.

It was just after 11:30, an hour after the rendezvous time.

"They didn't show, not yet anyhow." Chris said. "I'm still waiting. I'm sitting here in a Mazatlán restaurant watching for them."

"Maybe they're late, driving to make the rendezvous."

"He has my cell number and the signal is good. I'll be here all day, waiting." Chris's voice was filled with a mix of worry and anger.

"Can you phone him on the number they used last night?"

"No one picked up."

But by sunset, when they still hadn't shown, Jamey was vowing to catch this "fucker and make him pay." And Tina had two problems. Wyatt's disappearance took precedence, but Jamey's anger was concerning. Of course she didn't want Jamey to get bogged down in feelings of revenge, but she understood his rage at making Chris fly all the way to Mexico for nothing.

"I'll try again tomorrow," Chris said. "I know you think he won't show, but I have to hope, Jamey."

"I know, man. Anything could've happened. It's true. It just feels fishy to me." When Jamey hung up, Tina got a clear idea that Kevin had no intention of giving up Wyatt. She now agreed with Jamey. All day they'd kept coming back to the same conversation—where the threesome was actually headed. It wouldn't be north of Puerto Vallarta or they wouldn't have led Chris to Mazatlán. They'd gone the opposite way--south.

With very little else to do, they walked around the marina. Kai was thoroughly amused by the people and the mariachi music coming from restaurants. Tina wanted to make a plan, figure out what to do if the dreams didn't come back. They couldn't stay here indefinitely. "What next?" she asked her husband as they wandered into a restaurant for dinner.

He shook his head and asked the waitress for a table outside. "I'd say go south—start driving and see if we get anything. If not, head to Mexico City. It's a large enough place for three people to get lost."

She didn't want to admit it, running around Mexico for weeks was not what she wanted to hear, but there was very little else that could be done.

After eating tortilla salads and tacos, they returned to the condo. Sitting on the balcony, Jamey voiced that he should call Carrie. She'd be disappointed and furious with Kevin that he hadn't shown. Jamey wanted to give her hope, tell her they had a plan.

"Hi Carrie. I guess you've spoken to Chris by now." He listened for a full minute, then continued. "If you want my take on it, I think Kevin has run in the opposite direction."

Kai started to fuss and Tina lifted him from the stroller to go to the bedroom. She didn't need to be in on this call. Judging by the look on Jamey's face when he joined them in the bedroom, the call to Carrie had been a difficult one.

He scrubbed his whiskers with both hands and sighed. "She still feels terrible about her fight with Kevin over custody. Blames herself. Even though she apologized to him on the phone yesterday, she thinks she drove him to do this. I told her we were heading south, still trying to dream something helpful."

When Kai passed out on the bed between them an hour later, Tina moved him to the crib and slipped in, under the covers beside Jamey. "I don't understand why Kevin wants Wyatt this badly."

"I think this plan was originally Rose's idea, then once they crossed to Mexico and realized how deep they were in, they couldn't turn back. They can't let him go now." He lay on his back, thinking, staring at the ceiling. "The hold that Rose has over Kevin must be something. I wonder if she has something on Kevin to emotionally blackmail him."

"Who knows what she's said to make Kevin agree to this. He wasn't such a standup guy to begin with, but this isn't really in character to mastermind a plan to be a parent at all costs."

"Come here, you." Jamey held out his arms.

Tina scooted over and burrowed into her husband. "I'd feel sick to think of Kai being taken away from me."

"Me too. Or the twins. And I feel sick thinking about Wyatt. We're going to find them. We just need to keep trying to dream jump, Honey."

"I hope so. Up until now I haven't even thought about what might happen if we don't find them." They didn't talk about what would happen if they were still wandering around Mexico in another few weeks. That idea was not inconceivable, but too painful to voice.

CHAPTER 7

Tina fell into a dream sometime during the night. She landed in a Hollywood party at the home of the world-renowned rock star, Goldy. Her friend, Pepper, was in the dream, which seemed appropriate because in reality Pepper had just finished touring with Goldy's band as a backup singer. She'd told Tina when she got home from the tour that Goldy had unexpectedly retired from the spotlight and everyone was shocked.

Tina and Pepper wore sparkly cocktail dresses with stilettos, something they used to do as single girls when they got invitations to Hollywood-type parties on Maui. Pepper was the semi-celebrity as a singer in the hotels and usually took Tina as her date. The two ladies stood near a bar in a vast living room, nursing pink drinks with fruit wedged onto the rim. Rock music blared throughout the house, above the din of conversations. Tina turned around to see who was calling her name very close to her and recognized the actor Brad Pitt.

Tina had developed a crush on Brad, ever since she'd seen him in Meet Joe Black, a few years ago and when he approached, she felt herself blushing.

"I've been looking for you, Tina," he said. "We need to talk." He leaned in so close that his lips brushed her ear. "I want you to consider giving us another chance." He stroked her arm and Pepper shot Tina a look of disapproval. Then she remembered. Brad was madly in love with her, but she'd recently told him they could never be a couple. It was tragic, really.

"I'm married now," she said as sweetly as she could. Apparently she and Brad had dated before Jamey, but she'd had to cut him free. This was the problem with lucid dreaming. You couldn't fully enjoy the story because you knew it wasn't true.

"Tina, we are meant for each other." His look implored her.

"Sorry, Brad." She turned to Pepper, who was sipping her drink, no doubt trying to keep quiet about Brad Pitt. "Have you seen Jamey?" Tina asked her. Hadn't her husband followed her into the dream? When they went to bed these days, he always waited to jump in, just in case it had anything to do with Wyatt. "Excuse me, Brad. Have you met Pepper? I'm going to look for my husband."

Tina wound her way through the house and outside to the beautifully lit turquoise swimming pool. Searching faces as she passed, she came up empty. After making a circle around the pool's deck, she tried to summon Jamey with no success. Then, she was in the pool swimming with Brad, still wearing her sequined cocktail dress. When he cornered her at the shallow end, she couldn't help notice what a handsome man he was, but still managed to hop out. She summoned a fluffy towel and wrapped it around her body. "Jamey?" she said loudly.

"Jamey's with Goldy in her bedroom." A tall man with a goatee and tailcoat smirked and pulled off Tina's towel to reveal that she was naked underneath.

Okay, she told herself, it's just one of those naked dreams. She summoned a long winter coat, her first thought, and after buttoning it, trudged off into the house to see if Jamey had arrived. Down here, they had a whole other world to use as they pleased. And had, especially before Kai was born. They'd been to Paris for a glass of champagne, gone diving on the Great Barrier Reef, taken a cooking class in Provence. It wasn't like the real thing because these dreams were only based on the sum total of what they knew or was in their imaginations, but still it was a fabulous adventure. It didn't work every night but when they found themselves together in a dream like this, it was fun to create their own adventures. Tina told Jamey it was like the Holodeck on Star Trek but, not being a Star Trek fan like her, he didn't know what she was talking about.

Finding herself in front of a closed door, she reached for the knob but the goateed man reappeared and opened it. "He's in here," he said with theatrical flourish.

Inside was a movie star-looking bedroom with a heart-shaped bed on a rotating platform. Tangled in the red satin sheets was the blonde bombshell, the rock star, Goldy, pinning Jamey to the bed with her long, tan limbs.

"Don't let me interrupt you two," Tina said. She and Jamey had a rule about dreams and finding each other in compromising situations. More like a guideline. No coming to jealous conclusions, especially if the person in the dream wasn't the real version who'd jumped in. Jamey turned to look at her, his knee up to prevent any closeness from Goldy. Guilt was plastered all over his face.

"Excuse me, Lady. This is my wife." Jamey moved her off him.

"This lady is Goldy, the rock star, Sherlock." Tina laughed. "Don't tell me you didn't know." She moved closer to the bed. "Sorry, Goldy, no offense." Goldy disappeared and it was only Jamey and Tina left in the bedroom. She looked to the door and slammed it on the tall man. She moved on to the rotating platform and sat on the bed. "Secret phrase?"

"Chocolate chip cookies go better with milk," he said. They'd made a habit of doing this check every time they met in dreams to make sure it was Jamey, not her idea of Jamey. "It's me, Darlin' and guess what? I'm horny as hell after that romp with the rock star. Wanna have some dream sex?" He pointed to his crotch where a sizeable erection pressed against his jeans.

Since Kai was born, their sex life had slowed down considerably to once or twice a week, and even then sex wasn't the slow, delicious fun it had been. Many times it was rip the clothes off in case the baby wakes and climax quickly. In dreams though, they had time. One hour down here was like a minute up top. Even though they were supposed to be looking for Wyatt, this wasn't one of those dreams that helped with clues, and making love would take less than a few real minutes, thereby not taking much away from the pursuit of Wyatt. "Take your pants off, Soldier Boy." Tina dropped the coat and slinked on to the bed.

"Naked under a coat," he exclaimed. "Nice touch."

She slid across the satin sheets. "Like that?" she whispered.

"You, take my pants off." Jamey lay back, his arms out, his expression predatory, like he was setting a trap for the poor little prey.

She unzipped his jeans, tugged on the top, and suddenly the pants were gone. His erection sprang to life. "You're very good at that," he said.

She nodded to his erection. "And you are very good at that." She slithered on top of him, her breasts rubbing on his need. She summoned her favorite sexy music, Marvin Gaye's Sexual Healing. Hearing the song, Jamey chuckled against her waiting mouth.

"Nice choice, Mrs. Dunn."

"When I get that feeling," she sang against his lips, then bit lightly. "Sexual healing."

He flipped her over to his favorite position—him on top. "We might not have much time and if it turns out that we do," he growled, "we'll do it again."

By the time the song played twice, they lay panting in a tangle on the bed, both satisfied and exhausted. "That was amazing," Tina whispered into his neck. "Even if it is a dream. We should do this more often." Before Jamey could answer, they were walking down a street in Mexico, arm in arm. Pastel-colored buildings lined a cobblestone street, thick with people watching a parade. Decorated horses pranced down the street, a costumed mariachi band played, and the crowd cheered. At the end of the block were trees, more festivities, and horses. She and Jamey were fully dressed in shorts and T-shirts as they walked along the outside edge of the parade watchers. Prancing horses again. Then they were gone.

When she woke from the dream, a sweet satisfaction still dwelt in her body. She hadn't imagined her physical reaction then. At least something had been real, even if Brad Pitt wasn't. She looked over to see that Jamey hadn't woken. She propped up on her elbow and watched him. "Are you faking it or still sleeping?"

He didn't answer.

They always woke together. Reaching under the covers, she felt him. His erection was dissipating and his boxers were damp. It had been real for him too. Strange but even touching him there didn't wake him. "Jamey?" Now she was worried. They hadn't been holding hands when she was taken from the dream. She hadn't jumped out deliberately.

Jamey didn't stir when she shook his shoulder.

She needed to get him out before something bad happened. Or before he'd been stuck in there for weeks. Closing her eyes, she willed herself back into the dream, slowing her breathing, counting, relaxing every part of her body. Take me back, take me back...

She was in a crowded marketplace. Same type of scene she'd just jumped out of. Music played loudly.

Spanish music. Sirens sounded. Police ran by her. The crowd was frantic, shouting, screaming, a few women wept nearby. There'd been an accident. Children clung to their parents. Huge horses nearby were restrained by a group of men in fancy Mexican dress garb. "Jamey?" she shouted. "Where are you?"

Jamey forced his way through the crowd in front of her, the look on his face horrifying.

"Jamey, what happened? Are you okay?" She shouted over the noise of the crowd. Something had sent this parade into a frenzied commotion.

"Let's jump out." His sweaty hand grabbed hers and she led him twenty feet back to the portal where she'd entered.

"Right here." She nodded, and together they jumped out. Tina's eyes flew open. She looked over to see Jamey sit up in bed. His breathing was coming fast and hard.

"Oh my God! Oh my God! We have to find Wyatt. His life is in danger."

Then she remembered that the dream had been pale with blurred edges.

They spent the next hour trying to find the parade online, with no luck. Tina was exhausted and had to get some sleep. Sometime around one o'clock, she nodded off.

The next morning, although they'd planned to leave for Mexico City, the trip was temporarily postponed, this new turn of events was too important for them to go off on a wild goose chase now. They had to find the parade.

Luckily Tina had noticed more detail. The horses, the market square at the end of the block, the architecture, a church spire. And Tina was a better artist than Jamey. While Jamey spooned cereal into Kai, she went downstairs to the store below their building and bought some paper and colored pencils to draw what she remembered of the scene. The pastel-colored buildings, the white pillars in front of a hotel, the parade float advertising beer, the high-stepping horses shaking their heads, manes dancing. There'd been a stage set up near a group of trees, and young women wearing bikini tops, jeans, and cowboy hats did a dance that resembled a cross between belly dancing, hula, and line dancing. This wasn't Hawaii though. It definitely looked like Mexico with mariachi music, trumpets blaring in tinny staccato sounds.

As she drew the scene, Tina remembered more details. After they'd woken, Jamey had only told her that Wyatt was killed, but hadn't added the details. And she hadn't asked. He was busy on the internet, trying to find out about local celebrations and parades.

Tina made them tortillas with rice and beans sprinkled with queso while Jamey watched Kai roll from his tummy to his back on a floor blanket. When she set breakfast down on the blanket, Jamey looked up appreciatively. "We have to try to jump again when Kai goes down for his morning nap. We need more details."

She agreed and smiled at her adorable son who was content watching the ceiling fan go around and around, his little arms flung out in front of him as if he could catch the ceiling's toy.

Jamey took a deep breath and stared off into space. "Here's what I saw. One of the horses, a white one with grey speckles and a long mane, was high stepping to the music and had just stepped down on his own hoof. Wyatt stood with Kevin watching the horses. But when the horse got alongside them, a firecracker went off close by and a dark horse on the far side got spooked and started to take off, making the white one try to get out of the way. Kevin had turned away and didn't see any of this until the horse tripped on the curb and fell on Wyatt. Only Wyatt's legs hung out. He was crushed." He choked on his sob, took a minute to collect himself and then continued. "And when the horse got up, Wyatt's head had been smashed under the weight of the horse's hind end. There was blood everywhere." Jamey squeezed the bridge of his nose and tried to get past the moment of recall.

By now Tina was watching him with horror.

"He was dead, along with an old lady." Jamey bit his lips. "I don't think it's happened yet but we have to get to them before it does."

"What town was this? That's what we need to find out. We have to get there before this actually happens."

"That's the thing. I'm not sure it's even Mexico."

***

Tina was resourceful. When the moment called for it, she had ideas on how to find this place. Once they'd eaten, she'd go downstairs to ask around about parades, wandering the marina while Jamey tried searching the internet. She went in and out of shops asking about horse parades and if there was one this month anywhere nearby. One lady told her that Mexico City had hipicas, horse parades. Tina called Jamey's phone to tell him that he might want to try researching the word hipica.

She continued on to the real estate office next door where a woman, whose name badge said Florencia, looked interested in her question about a horse parade this month.

"I don't know," she said with an accent that didn't sound Spanish. "But I have a friend who breeds horses. Come in. I'll make a few calls, see what she knows."

Tina told Florencia that they were searching for a child who was abducted, and had reason to believe they were headed to a hipica. The woman didn't ask any more questions. She made a few calls and finally Tina had what she believed was the answer. It made sense. This was August, and soon the town of Granada, in the Central American country of Nicaragua, would celebrate their patron saint, La Virgen de La Asuncion, with a festival and hipica. Tina thanked the woman profusely and hurried back to the condo.

"I think the parade is in Nicaragua," she said, running through the living room to the balcony where Jamey sat with his laptop. "They're headed to Granada."

"What makes you so sure?"

"There's a hipica this Sunday, and I feel something. Like we're moving closer to the answer." She gestured to the laptop. "Look it up. It's the only hipica near here this week, this horse lover said."

***

Once Jamey stopped concentrating on Mexico City, the clues fell into place. Nicaragua was famous for Andalusian horses, high-stepping animals known for their fancy footwork. Seeing photos of Hotel Plaza Colón on the internet made Tina's skin prickle in recognition, she said. "Look at my arm. Chicken skin. This is it." Even a church spire fit the one in the dream.

Probably a good sign. He hadn't noted much in the dream besides Wyatt's death but Tina had an eye for detail. The scene in their dream was in Granada. "No doubt about it," she said. And the beer logo they'd seen on the parade float—˜—was Nicaraguan beer.

They had to get to Nicaragua as soon as possible. There wasn't time to drive through Mexico, Guatemala, Honduras, and into Nicaragua. Flying was the only option. The horse parade was in four days.

They phoned the airlines, booked tickets on the next flight to Managua for that night. Having a concrete plan gave them hope. The relief in the room swirled around them that afternoon, even Kai seemed happier.

"We'll get on the six o'clock flight, land at nine, catch a cab to Granada, an hour away, and check in to the hotel." Jamey sounded focused. "We probably won't get anything tonight, but tomorrow we can verify the location and see if we pick up on anything."

"Walk around, find the accident site, try to summon something," Tina added.

"I'm not going to leave it until parade day," he said. "If I have to hire someone to stand in front of those shops all week to keep Wyatt from falling under that horse, I will."

For Wyatt, Jamey would try to change the course of the future one more time, if he could.

***

Kai slept the whole flight to Managua and woke when they landed. He was such a great little traveler, considering that back on Maui they had him in a definite routine that never swayed. Tina had to wonder how much easier it would be to not have Kai on this journey, but how could they give him to someone to take care of during all this? Where would he go while they ran around Central

America looking for Wyatt? Not her mother's house who loved her little grandson but wasn't young enough to handle a baby's schedule or carry around a sixteen pound baby all day. Babies were a lot of work and hard on the arms, not to mention how a baby disrupted one's sleep schedule and good mood. Carrie had offered to take Kai to free them up to search for her child, and Tina had considered the possibility, but Carrie had a baby too. Little Harley was only eight months old and colicky, according to Jamey. And Carrie had three other children to manage. She didn't want Carrie trying to add Kai to her daily schedule.

So far, traveling with Kai had been doable. He was just starting to show the beginning signs of wanting to crawl and she hoped he held off for another month. He'd been getting up on his hands and knees, rocking back and forth as though he was warming up to take off. Soon he'd figure out that if he moved his knee and then his hand, he could travel around. Knowing her baby like she did, she had to believe that once he started moving, it would be difficult to contain him.

At the Managua Airport, they avoided baggage claim with only a small duffel bag that fit in the overhead compartment. Kai had more stuff on this trip than the two adults. Both she and Jamey wore backpacks as well. When they stepped out into the steamy air of the Central American city from their immigration checkpoint a throng of taxi drivers offered to help with their bags. Jamey waved over a young guy to take the duffle bag and Kai's diaper bag. He spoke what sounded like fluent Spanish to the taxi driver and added "Por favor." Tina was always impressed when she learned something new about her husband. He seemed to pull rabbits out of his hat on a daily basis. She hadn't known until this month that he spoke Spanish. She'd heard him speak the local dialect in Afghanistan and had been impressed then, as well.

"Granada?" Jamey asked.

The young man nodded. "Si."

Tina locked eyes with her husband. "Here we go, Jamey."

CHAPTER 8

On the plane, Jamey had broached the unthinkable. He wasn't as confident as he let on. He'd admitted that it might be remotely possible the day, the vision, were wrong, and Wyatt was already dead. "What if?" he'd worried. But Tina assured him that he'd seen Wyatt in the truck only a week ago, and there hadn't been a hipica in Granada for months. And, that the dream they'd shared of the horse parade was a premonition with the telltale look of the future, not a dream of the past. "It was a glimpse, Honey." Her husband fell asleep shortly after that with his mouth pulled taut, his forehead furrowed. Rarely did she take on the role of reassuring him, and rarely did he show weakness or doubt with her. Not since she'd taught him to dive ten years ago had she'd been in charge like this, with him leaning on her confidence. But sitting in those close seats, with her voice at his shoulder, he'd needed her reassurance. "We'll get Wyatt this week. I feel it," she said.

Once out of the airport, Jamey lifted Kai from Tina's arms, kissed Tina's cheek, and carried the wide-eyed baby along the sidewalk to the yellow cab. Like her son, Tina was wide awake and very aware that they were in unfamiliar territory. It seemed unreal and not just because it was late at night, and they were tired. Had she ever thought about going to Central America before? She doubted it. Up until yesterday, she wasn't even sure where Nicaragua was on the map, except possibly south of Mexico, a few countries away. She was exhausted, but tried to pick up on a feeling that Kevin and Rose had been here recently. Nothing yet.

The air was hotter than Maui in August, drenched with humidity, even different from Puerto Vallarta. They were much closer to the equator now.

Kai fussed to be put in the car seat, but Tina distracted him by pretending to sneeze and the little baby soon was belly laughing at his Mama. That sound was the most precious thing she'd ever heard, the rumbly jumble of pleasure that came from deep in his little belly.

Jamey spoke with the taxi driver most of the way out of Managua, chatting presumably about the country.

Even at this hour of night, traffic was thick to get out of the capital city. "I wonder what Wyatt thought of all the traffic," she said.

"Probably not impressed," Jamey turned around. "I'm imagining Wyatt covering his ears but that could be just because he does it so much."

Wyatt did not like loud noises, heavy traffic and crowds, and that was the reason Carrie left him home if they went to the Science Center, or Space Needle in Seattle. He wasn't a fan of loud music and often clapped his hands over his ears if his sisters turned the car radio up. Wyatt never went to the state fair or even his sister's piano recitals. Soccer games were tolerable because they were outside, but not the Seattle Sounders soccer games because the crowd noise was intolerable to the little guy.

Tina amused Kai with his toys and caught glimpses of Managua out the window. The route out of town ran through poverty-stricken neighborhoods with tin shacks and dirt yards, past Coca Cola signs, along a four-lane road with a grassy center median that periodically had a cow or pig grazing. If there was a super highway to Granada, they weren't taking it. At this hour, there were very few people out and about. "Ask the driver about the hipica," she said, leaning forward touching her husband's shoulder. "See if we can get some information."

Jamey spoke in Spanish, quite fluently, and nodded casually like the information—date, time down to the minute—wasn't of the utmost importance. The driver nodded in return, apparently verifying the festival was on Sunday. Today was Wednesday. "Ask him if there's a rehearsal with the horses." She'd been worrying they might have the day wrong.

"I did. How's our boy?" Jamey swiveled and touched Kai's head over the top of the car seat. When the baby looked up at his father and smiled, Jamey smiled back. "Hola, Kai." He looked at her. "No hipica rehearsal. Looks like we have four days to find Wyatt." He shifted in his seat to see Tina better. "There's an American ex-pat community in Granada that might have seen them." Jamey nodded at the driver. "He gave me a couple of restaurants where the local Americans hang out. We'll check on those tomorrow, ask around, show Wyatt's photo, and check out a playground that's popular. The town isn't huge, the driver says, and it would be hard for a family to hide in the American community. The bad news is that we don't have a lot of time to wait for them to surface. We have to dig."

Tina nodded. "I'm ready to dig." Jamey looked more confident that this was going to work than he had on the plane. This was the closest they'd felt to finding Wyatt since this nightmare began. "And with a little luck, I'll dream tonight," she added.

The plan they'd made on the flight included combing the town for the next three days, asking everyone they met, visiting the grocery store, toy store, and the surf shop if there was one. Kevin loved surfing and might be thinking of surfers' paradise down south near Costa Rica. It was a small town called San Juan del Sur. Jamey said Kevin wouldn't be in this country without wanting to ride some of the world famous waves off the Pacific Coast. Kevin loved extreme sports, lived for extreme sports, and was probably in this country because of the surfing. Was their plan to leave inland Granada for the coast eventually? "Did we check if San Juan del Sur has Hipicas?" She worried that somehow they might have the wrong day and Wyatt's life would end sooner than they could get to him.

"They don't." Jamey said. "Just Granada and Managua, and we'll know soon if the church and hotel are from the dream."

Within a half hour, the church spires on the cathedral came into view and soon after that they drove past the white pillars of the church, the exact ones from the dream. As the taxi swung in to a parking space in front of the hotel, Tina made a positive verification. "This is it. Thank God."

Granada was quiet at this hour of the late night. Only two horse-drawn carriages remained on the street. Recently, she'd seen photos of the carriages lined up around the park square. How picturesque the town was with its colonial architecture, colored buildings, tree-filled market square, and spired buildings. Very Spanish. Her mother might like it here as long as the hotel had decent amenities. Come to think of it, this might have been the town from her dream about having coffee with her father. Hadn't she taken a brief ride in one of these carriages? The thought that her father might have actually entered the dream to lead them to Nicaragua left her feeling both happy to have contact with him, and sad that she hadn't picked up on the hint. Had she been in touch in her dreams?

After they got out of the taxi and stretched, she and Jamey exchanged a look that meant they both thought the town was pretty, but neither wanted to treat this visit like a vacation. A stray dog skulked away from the taxi when the driver lunged and made a hissing noise. Tina recalled her sweet dog, Obi, back on Maui, in the care of Katie. Jamey's niece had been happy to move into a 3,000 square foot house while her uncle, aunt, and new baby cousin took off after Wyatt. And Obi loved Katie. He'd spent many months in the dive shop with her so they were used to each other. He probably loved her more these days. On a recent business phone call, Katie told Tina that she'd been taking Obie to Airport Beach on days off and remarked how much he loved to watch the water for turtles.

Jamey lifted Kai out of the car seat, and Tina transformed the stroller/car seat that was turning out to be the handiest thing they had on this journey. They didn't have much with them, only a few essentials for themselves, but a baby seemed to need a lot of paraphernalia. Traveling light wasn't possible with diapers, a car seat, stroller attachment, and enough baby clothes to avoid doing laundry every day. For a moment, standing on the steps of the Hotel Plaza Colón, Tina could almost imagine they were on vacation, but quickly tamped down any enthusiasm for that. Ahead of them were four full days of searching. The backup plan to be in front of the juice bar on Sunday, all day, if they hadn't found him by then, was still in place. She hoped it didn't come to that.

Jamey called Carrie from their palatial hotel room. "We're in Granada," he said, while Tina changed Kai's diaper on the bed.

"Did you get any feeling yet?" Her voice was heavy with anxiety.

"No feelings, but we saw the church from the dream, the hotel, the park across from the hotel." Of course, Jamey hadn't told her that Wyatt would be killed on Sunday, only that he'd seen Wyatt clearly at the parade. Carrie didn't need to know the ugly particulars especially because he intended to prevent the horse from falling.

"Alright. Thanks. I might even get a good night's sleep."

"You try to do that. Both of you." Jamey included Chris, knowing his life was in the same turmoil.

A young man arrived at the door with a crib for Kai. After wheeling it in, Jamey thanked him and gave him an American dollar, even though they'd been told that a dollar was too much for a tip here. The room was white-walled with dark wood trim and hardwood floors, very large with a king size bed and a lovely balcony overlooking what they called the Parque Central. Tina took off her running shoes, wanting to feel the floor on her tired, warm feet, then asked Jamey if he thought it was safe to go without shoes.

"This place looks spotless, but let's not take any chances. If a scorpion bites one of us, we're screwed. Even flip flops in the shower, Darlin'." He was right. They had to take every precaution in the next few days to stay on top of things and healthy.

Later, when Tina finished nursing Kai and finally laid her sleeping baby in the crib, she heaved a sigh of relief for the day. Jamey had brought up four Toňa beers from the hotel bar before it closed for the day, and he sat waiting on the room's balcony that overlooked the market square. The rattan chair crackled as she sat down. "I'll have one of those," she said. Now that Kai was down for the night and she wouldn't nurse for eight hours, she had time to drink a beer and get it out of her system.

Jamey flipped the cap off and handed her the frosty bottle. She took a much-needed swig and looked around. All the balconies co-joined, separated by wrought iron fencing and it was a little disconcerting to see another couple two rooms down, holding hands and talking. With the park sprawled in front of them, it might be a noisy room, but they had a great view of the center of Granada. And they had air conditioning that made a whirring noise inside the room. Here, on the second-floor balcony, they'd take turns watching the square during the day when they weren't out wandering the town. Like Puerto Vallarta except they might not be able to use the video camera here.

They drank their beers in silence, Tina breathing out the worry of the day. Jamey had been able to sleep on the plane, and earlier had promised to be on duty that night with Kai if he woke so she could get some sleep. "I'll stay up for a bit, watch the square, listen for Kai, watch you sleep," he'd said. If she started dreaming, Jamey would jump in to see if they could get another read on where Kevin was hiding out with Wyatt.

"It's nice here. Pretty." The colonial architecture of the city center was stunningly beautiful and she imagined the history of the town was fascinating. She liked that each building was a different color like sunshine yellow, sky blue, even pale pink. Jamey liked history and would probably drop some information into their conversations in the next few days. Tina looked at her husband whose face looked more relaxed than on the plane. "We'll find him tomorrow."

"Yup."

Wyatt would be asleep at this hour, but tourists still wandered the town. Faint music floated from a restaurant around the corner to the right, and a horse whinnied in front of them. The frigid beer went down smooth as Tina wondered how hard it would be to find a Caucasian child in this town.

"I'll go out at dawn to pinpoint the accident site," Jamey said wiping his sweaty brow on his T-shirt.

Tina cooled her face with the beer. "Then we'll walk around with the photos to ask around."

Jamey nodded. "First, I'll take you to the site, see if you get anything, then we begin the search."

Tina hoped her intuition, her psychic connection, was as strong as Jamey said it was. If so, she might get a clue while walking around tomorrow. "We can go in and out of all the hotels too. See if we pick up anything. Then the grocery stores and see if there's a toy store." Their conversations all day had been peppered with ideas of where to look and what to do.

"Gas stations too," Jamey added, grabbing her hand. "I feel close to the end of this. How 'bout you?"

Had her husband forgiven her for leaving her balcony post in Puerto Vallarta to rescue a crying Kai? Things had been tense between them for days. "I do too, almost like I can breathe now."

Jamey kissed her hand and she got that familiar tingle in her belly that presented itself any time her sexy husband had that look on his face. "I love you, Tina. I know I haven't said it recently, but I do." She felt her insides weaken. He was just so damned sexy.

"You could prove that you know, Soldier Boy." She gave him her most provocative smile.

His look pinned her to the chair. "I'll take that as an invitation. Don't have to ask me twice." He gulped the last of his beer and slid to the edge of his chair.

"Oh, look who's ready to go!" she teased.

"Hey, Darlin'. It's been too long. And that dream sex the other night doesn't count before you say anything about ravaging my subconscious self."

She laughed. "But, in a strange way, it works when we're too tired to do it consciously." They grinned at each other.

"Agreed. Just don't leave me down there, jumper." He reached over and rubbed his thumb across her jaw. Since this search for Wyatt began, they'd been so preoccupied and exhausted that giving each other pleasure had been the last thing on their minds when they fell into bed at night.

"I won't leave you. Promise." Tina remembered another dream where Jamey couldn't get out or wake up. He'd been stuck down below for days. She'd almost lost him to the dream as his real body lay in Kandahar, comatose. Now, he relied on his wife to get out of the dream, a skill she didn't really relish. Not only was it too much responsibility, but she wasn't the expert on getting in and out of dreams. Jamey was. She still hoped that one day they'd wake up to find that Jamey was the jumper again and she'd lost everything.

When they slipped out of their clothes and quietly got into bed, Jamey's kisses moved down the length of her warm body. *Oh yes.* The room was air-conditioned but the kissing heated things up quickly and it wasn't looking like cooling off for a while. She threaded her fingers through Jamey's hair, which was barely long enough to do this. His touch was intoxicating to her needy body and she melted into the moment. "Oh yes, like that," she said. His tongue teased her inner thigh then his mouth found the center.

She grabbed handfuls of sheet on either side of her and writhed under Jamey.

"Like this?" he whispered.

She didn't need to answer in words. Her husband knew exactly what she wanted, where, and how.

CHAPTER 9

The feeling of pending doom and then tragedy was as strong as if the horse was now lying on top of Wyatt's small body. Jamey leaned against the small cafe's pink wall. It was here where the speckled white horse would be scared by another horse and would stumble on the curb. The chain reaction would begin with a firecracker noise, and end with Wyatt's death. Today was Thursday and he had until Sunday to find Wyatt.

Hotel Granada was across the street, just like Tina said. He had a slight recollection of the building front in his dream but his wife noticed details. The sign hadn't been readable for either, but now was. The windows, the color. Two skinny dogs scrounged the street for anything to eat, keeping a wide berth from Jamey who stood at the road's edge. Two women passed by, calling a friendly good morning to him. They wouldn't know his pulse pounded in his ears with the intensity of the premonition in front of him. On Sunday, two people wouldn't see the horse falling. The smaller, younger one wouldn't see the accident unfold because he'd be turned around looking at Kevin who would be buying a beer from a vender.

In the dream, Kevin had let go of Wyatt's hand and turned away to approach the vendor behind him. He'd never see what happened until it was too late. Wyatt's small body would be crushed by the thousand-pound monster. Someone would try to pull the old lady out of the way, but she'd fall and only her head and shoulders would escape the weight of the giant horse, the rider falling clear of the grizzly scene. Wyatt wouldn't hear the commotion, the cries, because he had his hands clapped over his ears.

Jamey hurried along the cracked sidewalk back to the park. He needed to calm down before he returned to Tina and Kai who were still asleep in their hotel room. He'd seen a lot of dead bodies in his day as a police officer, and then as a soldier in Afghanistan, but the memory of Wyatt's little limp body still lying on the ground, made him lean over and retch in the gutter of the cobblestoned street. He straightened, wiped his sweaty forehead, and continued on. The street was empty. It was still early. A taxi pulled up behind him, rolled down his window, and asked if he needed a ride. Probably thought he was hung over and heading home.

"No, gracias," Jamey said. He wished that he'd brought the photos of Kevin, Rose, and Wyatt to show the driver, just in case. When they left the hotel today, he and Tina would start their campaign of flashing those pictures all over town along with Tina's business card and a cell phone number. Granada wasn't that big. Everyone said so. Someone must've seen them.

Unless they hadn't arrived yet.

***

Kai pulled hungrily at Tina's breast, drinking his breakfast. The humming of the air conditioner in the corner window drowned out the sounds of Granada waking up on this cloudy day. Outside their patio door, the sky was full of grey clouds, as the day lightened. Kai hummed as he drank, a sound that Tina wanted to remember always. Often bringing tears to her eyes, his tiny vocalizations were exquisitely dear to her. Even when this child was grown and had his own family, she wanted to always remember the sound of his hum as he swallowed and sucked. And the look of joy on his face as he stroked her small breast with his little fingers. Jamey said he looked like he was playing the violin while he breastfed.

Was her son's safety compromised in this third world country while they searched for Wyatt? If she believed that to be true, she wouldn't be here. Jamey would have had to try to find Wyatt without her. The trouble was, her psychic abilities were intertwined with Jamey's, connected in such a way that the ability worked much better if they were together. She had to be here. As long as her baby had a comfortable place to sleep when he was tired, food, diaper changes and attention and love from his parents, she believed it didn't matter where they were as long as they were safe. With the stroller/car seat they could take Kai almost anywhere in their search. And, Jamey was a master at co-diapering his son on the run, able to hold him in his strong arms, while Tina wiped, bundled up the dirty one and slapped a fresh diaper on Kai's round little bottom.

Only once had their son squirted into the air before the new diaper reached him and now Jamey aimed the baby away from Tina's face. Kai loved being dangled from Daddy's height.

She'd brought baby food and boxes of dried cereal powder from Puerto Vallarta, not sure if they'd have time to find jarred veggies and fruit. The one thing that tugged at Tina's guilt was that her plan had always been to make her son's food from organic produce. Fresh food blended in her food processor wasn't possible while they traveled this way. Tina reminded herself that Kai favored her breast milk to solids, even at seven months, and as long as she kept producing that, she was doing the best thing for him.

After a couple of good burps and some happy smiles, Tina made a fortress of pillows on the king-sized bed and propped her son in a sitting position with his favorite rattle in his hand while she dressed in her navy blue cotton cargo pants and a T-shirt that read "Tina's Dive Shop" with a sea turtle under the logo. She'd been wearing the same two outfits for ten days now. She'd be glad to get into different clothes once life was back to normal. Buying a new T-shirt seemed needless and almost selfish when they were frantically searching for little Wyatt before he got trampled by a horse. Their condo in Puerto Vallarta had had laundry facilities so at least they'd been able to wash their few clothes every couple days.

As she pulled a brush through her long brown hair and fastened it in a ponytail, the door to the room opened and Jamey walked in. "Hello, my little family," he said in a baby voice to Kai on the bed.

Tina searched her husband's face for a clue to his mood. "Any luck out there?" They no longer used conversational niceties, going straight to news of finding Wyatt instead.

Jamey reached for his son and lifted him into his arms. "I saw the accident again, on the street in front of the restaurant." His voice was monotone, an eerie contrast to his words to Kai. "Good morning, Kai Kai," he said, kissing the folds of his son's neck, then clutching him to his chest in a needy way.

When Jamey finished the hug, Kai shook his rattle and smiled, reaching for his Daddy's sunglasses hanging on a neoprene fastener around Jamey's neck. The baby dropped the rattle and tried to put the Maui Jims in his mouth. "Didn't Mommy feed you?" Jamey crossed the room to kiss Tina on the lips and smile at her. "Seeing the accident was good news, I guess."

Tina nodded. In a normal situation, she would make reference to the fantastic sex last night, but when she imagined saying something out loud, it seemed too crass in light of their mission. Especially when Jamey just said he saw the accident. "Is the town waking up? Should we eat something and head out?" she asked.

Jamey stood at the glass door leading to the balcony, looking out. "Yup. We're going to find Wyatt today if I have to search every house, hotel, and building in this town myself. And if we don't, I'm going to the police. I don't care what Carrie says. This has gone on long enough. Let's see if we can get the police involved in this third world country. Maybe they can scare up a child abductor.

The worst mistake Carrie has made so far might have been not calling in the police. Protecting that mother fucker."

After coffee, eggs, and toast at the hotel coffee shop, they took off to wander the town of Granada. If they hadn't had a dire mission, Tina would've loved to be a tourist in this town. It was charmingly picturesque with the old-world, colonial look. The yellow church, the pastel-colored buildings, stark white trim, and dark wood pillars. The square park in front of the hotel was filled with shade trees, hiding the craft vendor booths recently set up for the day.

Jamey pushed Kai's stroller through the park while Tina flashed photos of Wyatt and his abductors to everyone, giving out her business card with her cell phone number. Knowing that the Spanish culture adored children and valued family life with a fervor comparable to the catholic religion, she and Jamey had agreed to say that the child they were searching for had been abducted by the two adults in the picture. Call the number if they saw the threesome. If anyone wanted to converse in Spanish, Jamey had to do the talking, but the plan had been for Tina to not correct anyone who thought Tina was the boy's mother, as she spoke with sympathetic listeners. Jamey remained available, but a mother's grief garnered more help than a father's anger. They hoped to remain undercover if Kevin and Rose were nearby. Kevin had only seen Jamey running after his truck in Puerto Vallarta. Not Tina. He had no idea that Tina was with him or that they were traveling with a baby. If Kevin was looking for Jamey, which was highly unlikely, he wouldn't suspect that the couple wandering around town with a stroller was on his trail. Jamey wore a baggy T-shirt to hide his toned physique, along with sunglasses and a local straw hat. Although Kevin didn't know Tina except for a brief conversation with her at the wedding, she wore a loose dress and a hat like Jamey. Tina hoped they looked like Joe and Judy Tourist.

They travelled the planned hipica route down Xalteva around the park to Calzada, a street that was more like a wide promenade to Lake Nicaragua at the bottom of the route. This was the accident street. Taking turns, Jamey and Tina ducked into shops, restaurants, and businesses to ask if anyone had seen the couple in the picture. When Jamey showed her the accident site, she confirmed the look of the Hotel, juice bar, and the shops. "This is it." She took a deep breath hoping that the horse never fell on Sunday. "If we find Wyatt before then, we have to try to keep that horse from falling on the old lady," Tina said.

Jamey agreed.

By one p.m., Kai was cranky from being in the stroller too much and Tina headed back to the hotel with him in her arms, pushing the stroller. She'd let him sleep in the air-conditioned quiet of the hotel room. Jamey's plan was to finish the parade route, then branch off to the restaurants and hotels off the beaten path. He'd then catch a taxi to the grocery stores and gas stations.

When he arrived back at the hotel at four o'clock the look on his face said it all. He hadn't found a single soul in the town who'd seen Kevin, Rose, Wyatt, or the truck. "Maybe they haven't arrived, Jamey."

"Entirely possible. It's a four day drive, six if you stop to sleep." He carried two beers he'd probably bought downstairs. She wished she could have one, but it wasn't a good idea. Too early. They took Kai out to the balcony to watch the street. Jamey chugged the beer and then took Kai from Tina's arms. "Have you been out here watching?"

"The whole time, except for when I had to pee." She'd seen plenty and had even been called to by some American guys from Boston to come down and have a drink with them. Tina was sure they'd have never been interested if she'd had Kai in her arms. There'd been no sign of Kevin, Rose, or Wyatt. "If you want to stay with Kai, he's had his cereal and a good feed. I can go out and ask around for a few hours before dark."

Jamey drained the bottle and reached for the water on the little table between their chairs. "I probably needed to hydrate on this first, not the beer. Man that was good." He bounced a giggling Kai on his lap and smiled at his baby. "Okay, but don't stay out late, and be careful out there. I think this town is safe for an American tourist girl, but you know."

She did know. He worried. Especially now. Since the birth of their son, Jamey had taken on an almost manic protectiveness. Not just for the baby, but for her too, and she'd had many conversations with her husband about how capable she was and how she'd existed just fine before she'd met him. He'd told her it was something he couldn't seem to completely control. "Don't go into any seedy neighborhoods."

"I'll be careful," she said kissing both her boys. And while Jamey distracted Kai, Tina slipped quietly out the door of their hotel room. Daddy and Kai would have some quality time together while she wandered around to see if she could pick up on anything. If Kevin and Rose hadn't arrived in Granada yet, that would explain why they weren't getting any intuitive feelings and why no one in town seemed to have seen them.

Tina walked around the town for an hour without any hints of Kevin or Rose coming through, then took a taxi to the road that led to Managua, asked the driver to wait for her and got out. She stood staring at the traffic that drove in from the capital city, took a deep breath, and concentrated on the black truck and the threesome that would drive along this road to get to town. Nothing. After five minutes, she got back in the taxi and told the confused driver to take her to the grocery store.

Walking up and down the aisles of La Colonia, Tina tried to imagine what they might buy at the well-stocked store. Wyatt liked candy and chips like any other kid, but would they indulge him? She stood by the milk, then the cereal, even the beer, with no results.

It was getting dark. She had to be done for the night. Without the slightest hint of a clue, she had to believe that the truck hadn't pulled in to Granada yet. Climbing the steps to their hotel room floor, Tina hoped to God that they wouldn't just blow into town on Sunday. Two more days of this would be torture.

CHAPTER 10

Jamey's phone had been pinging all day while they traveled and Tina tried to not ask him who was texting. Probably Carrie. Or Chris. But while Jamey was showering, a text came in, and she glanced at the screen. "Leilani" it said, with a set of emoticon lips after the name. Tina had no idea who it was and thought nothing of it again until Jamey was out of the shower and another text came in and he grabbed the phone quickly.

He walked to the balcony and shut the door leading outside. Tina tried to not watch him but she had a strange feeling about his behavior and watched anyhow. Her husband stood leaning on the railing of the balcony with a sexy smirk on his face, reading the text.

After wondering what or who could make her husband smile that way, Tina took a deep breath and got ready for bed. Jamey was a flirt, something she'd admired in the past and hadn't worried about. Women loved him and he didn't seem to realize this. Many times when Jamey was single, he'd told her that he hadn't noticed when a woman was interested.

When Jamey came inside the hotel room, he looked to her in the bed and turned his phone volume down. "I closed the door because I didn't want to let out the air conditioning," he explained without looking her in the eyes.

***

In the dream, Jamey and Tina were at a restaurant on what looked like Lake Nicaragua. The wind blew off the lake making whitecaps on the open water. Tina sat with Kai at a table for four. A man ran up to Jamey, holding a piece of paper. The stranger looked Spanish. He had grayish curly hair, a bushy grey moustache, and a small, wiry physique. "I got directions." He pointed beyond the restaurant to a cluster of small islands; from this angle, it was impossible to tell what was mainland and what wasn't attached.

Jamey shot a look at Tina who gave him a thumbs up to indicate she was in the jump too. "Chocolate chip cookies," she said. He signaled back. The blurred edges of the horizon and the pale colors indicated this was a premonition.

The man held up the sheet of white paper. "The boat driver knows the house, but we have to go now. All the boats are booked in an hour for a tour group." He was probably about sixty years old, but looked to be in excellent shape. He wore a wedding ring.

"Good," Jamey said, not knowing exactly what was next in this scene. "Hey, can I ask you something obvious?"

The man nodded. "What?"

"What day is today?"

The man squinted. "You feel okay, or what? It's Friday."

Jamey smiled. "I just wanted to hear you say it. I've got until Sunday to find these guys."

"What happens on Sunday?"

Okay, so this guy didn't know anything much. "I want to go to church." It didn't really make sense, but Jamey hoped the stranger in front of him didn't care.

The man nodded and looked over at Tina. "Is she coming with us on the boat?" he asked.

"What do you recommend?" Jamey tried to be elusive, get a feel for what they were about to do.

"Well if there's a shit storm and it ends up with you grabbing the kid and taking off in the boat, you might not want the baby there."

This dude knew they were looking for a kid. "That's true." Jamey continued. "Hey, I think I've been saying your name wrong, man. How do you say it?"

The man looked over at Jamey like he didn't believe him. "Diego. You been saying it perfect, Jamey. Diego."

Diego. Where did he meet this guy? "I'll just tell Tina to wait here. How long do you think we'll be?" *Doing whatever it is we're going off to do.*

Diego looked out at the islands. "With any luck, half an hour."

"Let's do it." Jamey nodded and ran over to Tina at the table playing with her baby. "We're heading off on a boat to an island. The guy's name is Diego. Apparently, he knows us. It's Friday."

Tina's raised eyebrows showed she was impressed they'd met someone and told him that much of their story. "Should I wait for you guys here? Do you think you're going off to an island where they have Wyatt?"

Diego was now within earshot and spoke to her. "Tina, my friend will take care of you if you want to wait here. We shouldn't be too long." He pointed to a man standing by the bar talking to customers.

"Sounds good," Tina nodded. "Hey Diego. Where did you meet Jamey?" There was a fierce pull backwards and they were out of the dream and awake in their hotel room. Kai had cried out in his sleep and torn them from the premonition. Damn it. They'd been doing so well.

"Shit." Jamey whispered, and looked over at his wife. There was just enough illumination from the outside streetlights filtering through the cracks in the blackout curtains that he could see Tina nodding.

"Yeah, but tomorrow we meet someone named Diego who thinks Kevin and Rose are on an island. Am I right?"

Jamey threaded his hand through his hair and took a deep breath. "I think you're right." He let it out slowly. "Thank God."

***

Tina woke from a disturbing dream and looked over to see Jamey gone. Not in bed. Her watch said 7:32. On his pillow was a note.

Doing my early morning patrol of the streets. Call me when you two wake up. J

He had such lovely penmanship compared to her scrawl. This was another thing about her husband that was controlled. Jamey was the neat freak and Tina was a bit sloppy. He'd been up to feed at 3 a.m., and must be tired. But now, Kai had slept through his usual 7 a.m. feed and was still sleeping, his arms flayed out like he was flying in his dreams. *What could a baby possibly have to dream about with their limited life experiences?*

Lying back in the tangled white sheets, she remembered bits and pieces of her dream from before she woke. There was an older woman; they were talking at a patio table. The woman's long, grey hair was braided down one side; she had a kind smile. Had Tina been telling her about motherhood? When the woman began to cry, babies poured from her eyes, like tears. Tina had to leap up to try to catch them before they hit the floor. Then she woke feeling disturbed about not being able to keep up with the flow of babies.

Dreams of late had mostly been about Tina's insecurities with motherhood. Was she doing everything right? How could she possibly avoid all the mistakes? Just the other night, she'd dreamed that when Kai was born the doctor didn't give him a drug to make him grow and he was doomed to remain a baby. She'd woken furious with the doctor, angrier than she ever remembered being in her waking life. It took Jamey twenty minutes and a box of tissues to calm her from the emotion of that dream.

As far back as she remembered, Tina had been a vivid dreamer and at times, a lucid dreamer. Jamey theorized that her paternal grandmother had some dreaming capabilities beyond lucid dreaming, maybe even shared dreams. Her grandmother once said that little Tina could sleep over at her house and they'd have fun dreams together. Go on an adventure in their dreams. When Tina told her mother this, she was not allowed to visit her Gramma alone again. Looking back on that decision to keep a five-year-old from her grandmother because of a sleepover fantasy, Tina wondered if her mother knew anything about dream jumping, or if her mother was simply acting protectively because Gramma appeared to be losing her grasp on reality.

After her twin brother's death at the age of three, Tina surmised that maybe her mother wanted to keep her remaining child close. Or maybe keep Tina from the trauma of bad dreams. Now that she was a mother herself Tina could understand how horrific the death of a child would be. It was a mother's worst nightmare, losing one's baby, especially to an avoidable accident like drowning in the backyard pool. Having your preschooler die because of your own negligence would be like sticking a knife in a mother's heart and letting her bleed out one drop at a time.

Thinking of her dream of babies falling to the floor, Tina shuddered to think of what might happen if for some strange reason they couldn't find Wyatt on Sunday, or couldn't get to him fast enough. She and Jamey had to do everything possible to make sure they never had to find Kevin and Wyatt at the hipica. They needed to find them today.

When Kai was fed and dressed for the day, Tina packed up the diaper bag and they ventured downstairs to the café. She desperately wanted coffee now that Jamey was partaking again. Nicaraguan coffee was grown just up the volcano that loomed behind the town of Granada and he'd said it was as good as its reputation. Tina smiled at the young waiter and ordered a fruit plate with a pastry and peppermint tea. For the first time that day, but probably not the last time, she wished she'd paid more attention in Spanish class in high school. "Con leche," she added, hoping that she was asking for milk.

Kai sat upright in his stroller playing with a string of toys fixed to the stroller. Soon he'd be out of the baby seat and in the next size if he continued racing towards the twenty-pound mark. He hadn't been weighed in two weeks. Had he gained while they were on the road? Since he'd started eating solid food in mush form, his growth rate had been steadily climbing like the only thing holding him back from his true weight was real food. Jamey guessed he was going to be a big guy like him, and Tina had to agree. Kai's hands and feet were large and if that was any indication, like it was with a puppy, Kai would take after his Daddy.

Just as the waiter placed the fruit tray in front of her, Tina remembered she hadn't checked in with Jamey yet. She'd been waiting for his return. She looked at the fruit and tried a bit more Spanish. "Muy bonita," she said, hoping she just told the waiter that the breakfast looked very beautiful.

He smiled patronizingly. "Enjoy your breakfast."

A quick call to Jamey's number had him connected in two rings. "You guys up?" he asked.

"We're in the café. Where are you?"

"I'm waiting outside a real estate office across the park and a couple of streets over. Apparently, there's an agent named Diego who fits our description and he's expected in to work any minute.

"That's great." If they could identify the man from the dream last night, get to the islands and find Wyatt, this nightmare might be over today.

"I have a good feeling about this," Jamey said. "Several people told me that my description sounded like this guy."

"How much are you going to tell him?"

"As much as I need to. Probably a portion of the truth if he seems like a good guy. I'll see what my gut tells me."

"I love your guts." This had become their inside joke.

He laughed. "This could all be over soon." He exhaled loudly. "How's our baby?"

"Full of peaches and bananas and mommy milk. Just playing in his stroller, watching the ceiling fan above us go round and round in the cafe." It was a good thing for Kai and his parents they had ceiling fans everywhere in Granada. "I miss coffee."

"I'm sorry. I'll quit again."

"It's okay, I'm just whining."

"Gotta go." Jamey said hurriedly. "I see him walking down the street. Bingo. It *is* the same guy."

***

Jamey sat in the real estate office of Diego Ramirez, waiting for the man to finish a client call. From what he could hear, someone was buying a house on the side of the local volcano, Mombacho. He'd heard that they grew coffee up there as well as having tourist activities like zip lining and eco tours. This country was gorgeous. It was interesting enough to want to come back someday. As he listed off best-case scenarios in his mind, Jamey realized that Wyatt could be sleeping with them tonight in their hotel bed and Chris would be on his way to Nicaragua to collect his son. That would be a beautiful thing.

It had been a shame what Kevin tried to get away with, what he did to Carrie and her family. To everyone. Hell, even Pops had shed some tears about the possibility of never finding Wyatt when Jamey talked to him on the phone the other night. "That man and his worthless, crazy girlfriend should be locked up in a Nicaraguan prison," Pops said, with a catch in his voice.

"We're getting closer all the time, Pops," Jamey'd said, hoping it was true.

Diego hung up on his call and returned to the small cubicle in the real estate office, sitting across the desk from Jamey. "What can I do for you today, Sir?" He had an accent, just like in the dream. He also wore the clothes they'd seen in the dream. A good sign.

Jamey sat forward, leaning towards Diego. "I'm going to be honest with you. I'm sorry to say I'm not looking to buy real estate, but I have a problem you might be able to help me with."

Diego raised his bushy grey eyebrows and tented his fingers on the desk in front of him.

"I'm looking for a man who recently abducted a child in Seattle. He's the biological father, but it's against international law to take a child across the border, away from the other parent. My ex-wife is the other parent. I'm an ex-cop and an American soldier, so I offered to come looking. I have reason to believe you might have seen them." Jamey held up the well-worn photo of Kevin, Rose, and Wyatt, taken at his wedding.

Diego's gaze fell to the photo and then slid up again to Jamey. "How do I know you're telling the truth? How do I know you aren't the one trying to abduct the child from his parents?"

Jamey nodded and reached to his back pocket where he kept a photo of Wyatt, Carrie, Chris, and the other kids. "This is the boy's family. He unfolded some papers. "And this is a copy of Wyatt's Passport, his mother's passport with her photo and a notarized letter saying I'm acting on her behalf." He laid the papers on the desk and watched Diego Ramirez study the documents.

"This little guy has been taken against his will. I don't know what these two have told him, but we have reason to believe that they smuggled him across several borders to Nicaragua and are now in Granada. The man is a horse lover and they might be in town for the hipica," he added, hoping it sounded good.

"Why do you think I know something?" Diego looked deep into Jamey's face.

Jamey had already thought out his answer. "Because they were in this office recently and you were seen here at the same time." He hoped he was right.

"Have you called the police?"

"No. I'd like to find this guy without using a foreign police department, if possible. Because it's an international offense. As a former police officer in Seattle, I know how long it takes to get something approved."

Diego took a deep breath and looked out the window. "Probably a good idea. The paperwork alone..."

"Have you seen any of these people?" Jamey pushed the photo closer to the man.

Diego nodded. "Yes. And I know where they slept last night."

CHAPTER 11

Tina pushed Kai's stroller around the Parque Central admiring all the wares for sale under the trees. It was tempting to buy a few things while she waited for Jamey's call, but there might be time for that after they got Wyatt today. When the phone rang, she was busy with a sweet little boy Wyatt's age who was trying to get her to buy from his mother's jewelry table. "Excuse me, Señor." She moved on with the phone to her ear. "Yes, I'm in the park. I'll be right there."

Jamey had told her to stand out in front of the yellow and white cathedral off the square and he'd pick her up with Diego. Things must've gone well with the man from their dream, but it wasn't until she and Kai slipped into the back seat of the car with the stroller attachment that she realized how well.

"Tina, this is Diego Ramirez," Jamey said from the front seat. "He knows where Kevin's gone."

"First I'd like your wife to tell me why you need to find this boy," Diego said, cutting off Jamey.

How much had Jamey told him? "He's been abducted and we're trying to find him."

Diego looked in the rear view mirror to lock gazes with her. "And why bring a baby on the search? Why didn't you stay home with your child?"

Tina supposed it was a fair enough question. What had Jamey said? She got the impression he hadn't talked about this aspect, so she forged ahead. "We had to bring Kai and two sets of eyes are better than one. And we're newlyweds." Even if Jamey told this man they were the parents, she hadn't given anything away.

He nodded, Jamey nodded, and they took off down a dusty road.

They arrived at Lake Nicaragua. Tina had seen it on the map, but up close it looked like the ocean it was so big. She wasn't able to see across to the other side. Granada was practically built on the lake.

"Unlike America," Diego said, pointing to the lake, "the poor people live by this lake because of the mosquitoes. The rich people live inland." Diego turned right and followed the lake road through a cement gate to the marina resort area.

"They rented a house down here?" Jamey asked.

"Not exactly." Diego pulled the car into a restaurant parking lot. "They rented a house out there." He pointed to the water and beyond where tiny islands dotted the lake and the wind was blowing fiercely off the water. "Your missing family is renting a house on a private island. I'm waiting for the rental agent to tell me how to find this island because in the Islets there is one island for every day of the year and I doubt we'll be able to find the house without some directions." He turned to face both Jamey and Tina. "This is your lucky day." His smile stretched across his friendly face, widening his thick moustache. "I believe your story, and I'm going to help you get a boat and get this little boy back."

They got out of the car and headed for the open-air restaurant where the wind was blowing napkins off the tables and several waiters ran around grabbing them from the floor. Five tables were busy with large groups of customers, laughing and eating under the large palapa roof. The center of the restaurant was a bar area, and there was a kitchen off to the right in an enclosed cement building. They seated themselves at a table out of the wind, behind a large sign advertising rental boats while Diego went to speak with the owner.

"This is where I wait behind and you leave on the boat," Tina watched Jamey watch Diego.

"Yup. I think this guy is telling the truth. What do you think?" Jamey lifted Kai out of the stroller seat and set him on his lap, bouncing the baby.

"I agree. He has a pure motive for helping us." She ordered a mango juice from the waiter.

"No, gracias," Jamey said to the waiter's questioning face. "Looks like Diego is on that phone call. Hopefully the one that tells us how to find the island."

"What're you going to do if you get to the island and Kevin has a gun?"

"I'm counting on Kevin negotiating with me. I won't turn him in if he'll give me Wyatt."

Tina hadn't known this. All along she'd thought that once they had Wyatt, Jamey would do something to Kevin to make him pay. She'd assumed Jamey was filled with so much anger he wanted to deliver justice faster than you could say *you're guilty of smuggling and kidnapping.* "Good. I'm glad you've dropped the plan to maim Kevin."

"Oh I haven't. I'm just going to say that until Wyatt is safely back in the U. S." His face had *Revenge* written all over it.

Diego paced the tiled floor in front of the restaurant's restrooms, then stopped at a table to write something on a piece of paper. He hung up, spoke to the man at the bar, who called over another man in jeans and a T-shirt. They spoke briefly, then Diego ran across the restaurant, back to where Jamey was now waiting. Just like in the dream.

"I got it. Directions." Diego pointed to a cluster of small islands off shore. "The boat driver knows the house, but we have to go now. The boat is booked in an hour."

"Good," Jamey said, then remembered that's what he'd said in last night's dream. He changed the dialogue because he didn't need to know what day it was.

Diego looked at Tina and the baby. "Is she coming with us on the boat?" he asked.

"Tina said she'll wait for us."

"My friend will take care of you." He nodded at the man at the bar.

"Sounds good," Tina found herself saying, just like in the dream.

This was where they'd woken last night. She crossed her fingers in case it helped keep them from ending up back in their hotel room bed.

***

The boat they took to the island was called a panga and was built for slowly touring around the islands, but once they were out of the small docking area, the driver took off at the punt's top speed. "Shouldn't we look like a tour boat, not a James Bond stunt?" Jamey said over the noise of the motor. "I want to look as inconspicuous as possible, maybe even sneak up on them." He'd put his hat and sunglasses on, hoping that if Kevin was watching the water, he wouldn't notice that Jamey was closing in.

"It's an outer island, but we should be there in five minutes," Diego said. "That's when we'll slow down." Diego tapped his skull like he'd thought of everything.

Would Kevin feel smug about being in this Central American country, far from detection? Jamey wasn't getting any sort of a reading here in the island group. As they wound their way through the islands, Jamey was once again impressed with the beauty of the area. Some islands were no bigger than a swimming pool, and others were big enough to hold several houses. One had a restaurant with a string of pointy flags around a patio and another had a monstrosity of a house, docks, satellite dishes, and water toys.

"Six hundred thousand U.S. dollars," Diego pointed. "The island is 4,000 square meters. If you want to make an offer, let me know."

The driver spoke to Diego and slowed down to cruising speed. They rounded a small island with a blue shack. Once they were close, the boat operator cut the motor and they drifted until several tiny rock islands and another just big enough to hold a house came into view.

"See the red roof over there?" The wind was blowing harder out here where there was little protection from the weather coming across the lake's vast surface.

Jamey nodded. "That's it?"

Diego handed him the binoculars they'd brought from the office. "That's it."

They came up behind the house, and the driver paddled them to the cover of an overhanging tree. This was an excellent vantage spot where Jamey could watch the island without being seen. He had a perfect view of the front of the house and so far, saw no activity. "Can you swim in this water or are there crocodiles and sharks?" he asked, scanning the edge of the island.

"The locals swim. No crocodiles," Diego said. "But the lake has a type of fresh water shark. Probably not in here so close to shore."

Jamey looked over the edge of the panga boat into the brown water. He wasn't taking any chances. "Sharks love it murky." He wasn't going in. The island with the red-roofed house was small, barely big enough for the cottage-like structure. There was a stone wall built around the perimeter of the island. A crudely paved walkway led to the bright blue front door. *This was where Kevin and Rose planned to live with a child? There was nowhere for Wyatt to play, run around, be a kid. How would he have friends over, or go to school if they ended up living here?* Jamey had promised Tina he wouldn't pummel Kevin into unconsciousness, but seeing the home they'd moved into, made him want to change that promise.

The house was for sale, according to Diego. "They're renting with the option to buy."

The plan was to tie up to the dock, then Diego would go ashore, knock on the door and tell them he had a showing. He'd ask permission to peek inside the house with his client. Then Jamey would come around the corner. If Kevin had a gun, which was entirely possible, Diego had been instructed to get out of the way fast. The realtor seemed perfectly used to this sort of thing and he nodded when Jamey said the word gun, like it was an everyday occurrence, which maybe it was in this country.

Jamey ducked down as the tour boat made its way to the island's dock. Would Kevin recognize him if he was looking out the front window? He'd see a gringo wearing a baseball hat and sunglasses, bent over tying his shoe.

Diego hopped off the pointy bow onto the dock and called hello. "Anyone home? It's Granada Realty checking in," he called cheerily. The boat continued on to sneak along the wall, just out of sight until Jamey jumped onto the rock wall.

"Granada Realty," Diego said again.

Jamey caught up to Diego near the dirt path to the house.

"No one home, looks like," Diego said. The island was small enough that there weren't any hiding spots. Still, Jamey didn't trust Kevin. "You get back to the boat. I'll take it from here."

Jamey looked in the front window and didn't see any sign of people in the main room, or anyone ever having been there. There were no dishes in the little sink under the window, nothing on top of the table, and nothing disturbed enough to show that people were staying in the house. Diego had passed him the key before leaving and Jamey let himself in. After a check of the bathroom and bedroom, Jamey was convinced that Kevin, Rose, and Wyatt were not on the island and probably had never been here. Maybe they hadn't moved in yet. Or maybe Kevin was using this as another red herring and had continued south to Panama. No, he wasn't that clever, and besides, Kevin and Wyatt would be at that parade on Sunday. They were still in the area. Unless the future had already been changed by something Jamey'd done. Had Kevin seen them in town?

Jamey whistled for the boat and headed for the dock, then something caught his eye. He rocked back half a step in an effort to locate what he'd seen; looking down, he spotted the only clue on the island that anyone had been here recently. Lying between two wooden slats on the dock was a single piece of breakfast cereal, Wyatt's favorite. There was no mistaking that it was Wyatt who'd somehow dropped a pink marshmallow heart from a Lucky Charms box. Jamey picked it up, the confection still squishy and fresh. He smiled and jumped into the boat, handing Diego the key to the house. "No sign of them, but they were here. Recently." He held up the pink marshmallow for Diego to see. "Wyatt's favorite cereal. Always throws the hearts away, ever since his cousin teased him about them." Where would they go? "Did the house come with a boat?" he asked Diego as they took off for the panga docks.

"No, but it would be easy enough to rent one for the week." Diego shrugged. "Maybe they've gone grocery shopping in town."

Jamey had felt something in that house. Almost a sense of regret. From Kevin or from Rose? When he lay down on the bed to try to pick up a clue, he'd felt a surrender. Maybe Kevin realized this was a bad idea and they were going to arrange for Wyatt's release today. Maybe Tina had already caught a sight of them at the marina, but couldn't go after them with Kai. It wouldn't have been so long ago that Wyatt dropped the Lucky Charm. The three of them were probably on their way to the grocery store right now. But why did the house look completely abandoned? There was no sign whatsoever that anyone had been inside, aside from the feeling of regret.

***

On a hunch, Tina asked Diego if he knew anyone in the surfing town south of Granada.

"We have an office there," he said.

"Can you fax the photo over and ask them to keep a lookout? Maybe have them send the photo on to the surf shops in town?"

Jamey agreed it was a good idea and Diego headed back to the office after depositing them at the Hotel Plaza Colón to call San Juan del Sur. Although she didn't want to admit defeat, Tina was beginning to lose hope that Wyatt would be found today. It was already midafternoon and they'd been driving around for an hour in Diego's car in hopes of seeing someone. First the grocery store, La Colonia, then on Diego's recommendation, Jamey had paid a taxi driver to rush to the Managua airport with the promise of a big reward if he identified the threesome. The driver hadn't phoned yet. Did Kevin know Jamey was in town? He could have seen Jamey, skipped town with Rose and Wyatt, and been half way to South America. If they'd left town, Wyatt would escape his death on Sunday by not even going to the parade, and that was a good thing.

Once Kai was fed, burped, and diapered, they walked the few streets over to El Camello, a restaurant that Diego had recommended. "Best ribs this side of Kansas

City," he'd said. It would be a nice change from all the rice and beans.

Settling at a table overlooking the street, Jamey and Tina watched the traffic at the intersection outside until the waiter arrived. Jamey guessed he was the owner of the restaurant, a mid-thirties, tan, non-Spanish-looking man. "Hi Folks. How's your day so far?" He gave them menus. ""I'm Leroy. Can I get you drinks first?" His first language was obviously English.

"I'd love a really cold Diet Coke," Tina said.

"Tona for me," Jamey said. "And a glass of water, please."

"Sure thing." The man walked around behind the restaurant's bar.

"You've got to be kidding," Tina said. "Avocado fries with cream cheese dip. I have died and gone to heaven." Too late, she realized her words were inappropriate seeing they were trying to change the future so Wyatt wouldn't die on Sunday. She looked apologetically at Jamey.

Jamey reached over to move a wisp of hair from her face and smiled. "I feel like we're close again, but not close enough to grab Wyatt." he leaned over to pick up Kai's toy from the floor and wiped it with a napkin before handing it back to the baby in the stroller. "The floor looks clean," he said. They read the menu in silence for a minute. "I'm going to have the Kafta. What do you think we should do this evening?"

He sounded unsure.

"It's only Friday. Remember that. We have time." She closed her menu.

"True," Jamey said. "I'm changing to the green curry with fish. I feel like some spice." He snapped his menu shut.

"I thought you'd order that," she said. "And not because I'm psychic." This was one of their jokes lately. Adding those last few words to sentences.

Jamey laughed.

She smiled at Kai. He was such a sweet baby. So satisfied to go everywhere and see everything. "I think after we eat, we'll feel better and should walk the town again. If Kevin and Rose think they're safe here, someone has to see them eventually, right? Let's go to every restaurant, every grocery store. They have to eat something. And the truck is large enough that someone has to have seen it."

"If they're still driving that truck," Jamey added. "Knowing I have their plates, they might have sold the thing." When the waiter set the drinks on the table, Jamey grabbed the photo of the threesome. "Have you served these three in here recently?"

"Who are they?" He studied the picture.

Tina and Jamey were used to this question. People wouldn't give up information without knowing they weren't risking getting someone killed.

"See that little boy?" Jamey said. "He's my godson and these two have abducted him from his mother in Seattle."

The waiter didn't look surprised, but he shook his head. "Granada attracts some strange dudes. I wish I had, but no. They haven't been in here recently, and I've worked every day this week. I'm always here because I'm the owner." He looked at the picture again. "That's rough." His expression was genuine.

Jamey handed him the business card with his cell phone number. "If you do…"

Tina had to add something. "We have reason to think they just came in this morning from one of the islands."

"That's a good hiding spot, the islands. But they'll turn up," the waiter said. "This place isn't so big that someone could hide from the rest of us living down here. Except for tourists, I know pretty much every gringo in town. I'll ask my wife if anyone new registered at the English school recently. Can I take the picture to the kitchen?"

Tina handed over the photo and smiled her gratitude. "Thanks."

"Today is the day." Jamey swigged his beer and narrowed his gaze, looking out at the trucks and taxis. "Today is the day, Tina."

When the meal came, the proprietor had news. "Ana hasn't seen them at the school but says she maybe saw them yesterday, but the hair is different."

It would make sense they'd changed their looks since Mexico.

"Where?" Jamey asked.

A beautiful Nicaraguan woman came out of the kitchen, followed by a little girl about six years old.

"This is Ana, my wife," Leroy said.

The child was a gorgeous mix of both parents with her father's smile and her mother's big brown eyes.

"Ana said the woman has short black hair and the boy was dressed in a Star Wars costume and has really short hair. They were at a little bar near Cana Castilla on the road to Tepeyac, at about sunset yesterday," he said.

"What time?" Tina looked to Jamey to translate, but the woman nodded.

"Six, maybe." Ana shrugged.

The little girl was playing with Kai, shaking his rattle and making him laugh.

Tina looked at Jamey and back to the woman. "You sure it was them?"

Ana nodded and spoke in rapid Spanish to her husband.

Jamey translated. "She noticed the boy because he had a light up saber sword, just like in this photograph. He was playing in the bar's courtyard while the parents were at a table nearby."

Ana showed the photo to the dimple-faced little girl and she nodded. "Yes," she said, then added a few whispered words to her mother.

Leroy spoke, "They both saw them. Anaise said the sword was a blue light."

Tina smiled at the threesome. That was Wyatt all right. "Gracias."

Jamey spoke. "Do you think a taxi would be able to find this bar?"

Leroy watched a family enter the restaurant and seat themselves near the bar. "Definitely, just say the road to Tepeyac and have him stop at the little bar on the right with Christmas lights, off the main road."

"Thanks." Jamey nodded at Tina. "Let's eat and get going."

***

Diego called just as they were paying the bill to say he was finished work for the day and could drive them around. "Come get us at El Camello," Jamey said, leaving a thirty-dollar tip for a very inexpensive meal. Diego was there within five minutes in an old Chevy pickup truck. He waved to Leroy before they took off down the street.

Tina settled into the backseat with her baby strapped in beside her. "So what happened to the Honda from this morning," she asked.

"That's my town car." Diego said. "If we're going up Mombacho, we need this thing."

Tina was sure her husband missed his truck back on Maui. Men loved trucks and as it turned out, she did too.

Passing a large gated cemetery, Tina hoped that she'd get a feeling from this bar with the Christmas lights. She wanted to get a clue as to where they'd gone. Every breath she took was filled with hope. They'd sit at each table, touch every napkin holder, whatever it took. This was the best clue since the pink marshmallow. They were closing in.

As they dodged various obstacles on the road, like a donkey pulling a cart of sticks, various people crossing, and a broken-down bus, Diego told them that he lived up Mombacho. "The bar just opened for business. I pass it every night on my way home. Might not be open yet, tonight, but the owner lives on property and we'll be able to talk to him. Nica people are very family-oriented. We don't like this type of thing, stealing a child," he said passing a slow bus by crossing a solid yellow line.

Tina looked out the window and wondered which direction they were headed. Not north. That was Managua. The boat captain inside Tina liked to know where she was at all times. Next time she went in a store or gas station she'd buy a map of the area.

Just past a rugged cement school painted royal blue, with bars on the windows instead of glass or screens, Diego slowed down, preparing to turn off the main road. Groups of people stood at the junction, "waiting for a bus," he said. As they navigated the dirt road's potholes, she peered over the front seat to see why they were bumping around so much. It looked like parts of this road had been host to a small river's invasion not too long ago. Diego waved to a family walking along the side of the road with baskets on their heads. Everyone waved back, smiling.

"Are you from around here originally?" Jamey asked.

"I was born in Managua, educated in Los Angeles, and came back here to live when I was forty-five, after I met my wife."

"Is she from here too?" Tina asked.

"No, she's American, but she loves Nicaragua, Mombacho in particular."

They pulled off the road to park in front of a sunshine yellow and lime green cement structure with a sign that said. "Coke/Cerveza". Multi-colored Christmas lights were strung along the edge of the tin roof. The outside patio was encased by a three-foot high cement wall. Maybe the pigs and chickens she'd seen roaming the sides of the road had a tendency to wander into the bar. The small cement building that was the bar looked to be locked up for the day. How did anyone make a living with such a small place?

Jamey and Diego got out of the car and she waved them on while she unstrapped Kai. Soon, he'd need a feeding. She'd given him spinach and carrots at El Camello, but he'd want to breastfeed again soon. She kind of hoped she wouldn't have to feed him here, in the stifling heat of the afternoon in the truck. Sweat rolled down her back into her waistband as she carried Kai to the front door of the bar.

Diego returned from a hut next door with a rotund man who had huge white teeth and an uneven haircut. They said their hellos and when the man opened the door and let them in the building, Tina wondered what Jamey or Diego had said to gain access. Jamey couldn't just tell them he was a fricking psychic and needed to walk around and touch everything. "Hola," she said to the owner who looked over at Kai and smiled. "Was he on duty last night?" she asked Jamey.

"No, his brother was here, but he's gone to Managua for the day." Jamey sat at the first table. "Why would they come here? It's so far from the island house and out of the way." He seemed to be speaking to himself.

She answered anyhow. "You said that they didn't leave anything at the house. Maybe they moved near here."

"Then why would they sit in a bar on the road, like this? Waiting for something? The key to their new rental maybe."

"Or they were thirsty. Did the owner try to call the brother?"

"He's not answering." Jamey moved to the next table. "How would they even find this place?"

Diego handed them each a Toňa and drank half of his in one gulp. The owner readied the bar for business, turning on the Coke neon sign and setting out napkins. Howler monkeys called from off in the jungle and the fine hairs on Tina's arms stood on end to hear them.

Wow!

She looked at Kai's expression. He'd stopped fussing to listen. If she wasn't mistaken, her baby loved all this adventure. He heard the monkeys, but couldn't know how special and rare it was for an American to hear monkeys in the wild. Just then, the owner of the bar turned on the overhead fan inside the building and Kai's attention was captured. Tina walked around the little room with Kai in her arms desperately trying to watch the fan. She tried to pick up on something but couldn't pull anything in.

Someone's phone rang to the tune of the Mexican hat dance song.

Diego called over to Jamey. "He's talking to his brother who says he served the man a beer, and the woman and child cokes."

Jamey nodded like this verified something. "Ask if he talked to them, if he knows where they are staying. Were they driving a big black truck?"

Tina held her breath, waiting. The answer was given in rapid Spanish, but she had no idea what it was. When the call ended and Jamey approached her to take Kai from her arms, he translated. "He said they were rude, unfriendly, they called the boy Luke, and when they left in a taxi that was waiting for them, they headed towards Granada."

Why in hell would they end up here, up this obscure little road, so far from town? If they were in a taxi, it looked like they didn't have the truck anymore. Well, this was something. Not much, but something. Why couldn't she get a reading from anything here? She walked outside to the patio where the threesome had been for ten minutes and put her hands on the metal table. Breathing deeply, she concentrated on Wyatt. When Kai started crying from Jamey's arms, she'd had a faint idea that Wyatt was pretending to be Luke Skywalker, fighting Darth Vader. Then her concentration was broken by her baby's cries.

Jamey walked over, sweeping Kai around like an airplane to still the crying—a distraction that worked. "I'm going to wait here for a few hours, see if they show up again, talk to taxi drivers, ask around. They must've been here for a reason. No one would just stumble upon this joint. You and Kai might as well go back to town with Diego."

It would be dark in two hours. Then what? Another day without Wyatt, or Luke, if that's what they were calling him now. "I got the sense Wyatt was here, playing Star Wars. That was all."

Jamey nodded. "Me too. And that Kevin was at loose ends with what to do next."

Diego thanked the bar's owner, patting him on the back like a long-lost friend, slipped him some bills, and they all walked out through the wrought iron gate together. Diego turned and spoke to Jamey. "You sticking around here then? I can help you, Jamey."

"If you could take Tina back to town, it would help a lot. I appreciate you offering to stay with me but…"

Diego interrupted. "Hey Man, when I offer to help, you need to accept it." He nodded at Jamey. "Tell you what. I live just up the road a few miles. How about I take Tina and the baby to my house." He turned to speak to Tina. "My wife Annie is there. You and Kai can take a nap, or eat, or just stare out at the view. See some monkeys. We're on the monkey highway. Then Jamey and I can come back here, go up and down the road, find out if anyone knows anything. If not, we can go back to the island and check if they ended up there."

Diego was right. It was a good plan. Taking her back to town would waste time and this way, she'd be close. "As long as your wife doesn't mind the company," Tina said.

"I'm sure she won't mind. I'll call her now to tell her you're coming." He grinned at Tina. "Annie is a great cook. She'll make dinner and you'll thank me for introducing you."

A feeling of relief settled over Tina. Kai was fussing again. He needed to sleep and this detour sounded like a good plan. Again, she felt guilty for leaving Jamey to do the work, but Kai was her priority. "Are you sure, Jamey?"

"If I know you're safe, I'll be able to get more done," he said, reading something on his phone.

Tina knew this to be true. Jamey wouldn't be worrying about Kai and distracted by them. "Okay, take me to your house," she said. But before she hopped in the truck with Diego, Jamey got a text and stood by a palm tree reading. The same flirtatious look crossed his face as he read and Tina's heart squeezed for the second time in twenty-four hours. Jealousy was not a trait she wanted to embrace, especially if she was reading this expression all wrong. Something about that look did not say he was exchanging messages with his brothers or Carrie. Whoever it was had said something that amused him in a way that she once had.

Tina eased in to the back of the truck with Kai and took off up the rutted road. Glancing out the back window, she watched Jamey shut his phone and take off down the road for the bus stop, hoping to find someone, anyone who saw two gringo adults and a Star Wars clad kid yesterday having a drink on the road to Mombacho.

CHAPTER 12

Kai fell asleep on the way up the mountain in spite of all the bumping and jiggling. When they arrived at Diego and Annie's house, Tina set his car seat in the guest bedroom.

Eventually she settled on the deck overlooking the view below, picking a spot where she could see Kai through the glass door. There was a beautiful rectangular, sparkling pool and Tina longed to jump in. She hadn't gone swimming in weeks, which was a torturous first for her. Swimming seemed like a frivolous pastime when trying to save a child's life.

She and Annie had what her hostess called a "late afternoon how-do-you-do." Diego's wife had a thick gray bun at the nape of her neck, turquoise jewelry, and a friendly, lined face. Tina was immediately intrigued by the woman. She'd picked up on a deep underlying sadness, but seemed very cheerful that afternoon. Tina relaxed in a sling back chair beside the pool, sipping an iced tea and having the best conversation she'd had in weeks.

Annie was originally from the Los Angeles area, had moved with Diego to his homeland, Nicaragua, so she could paint and him sell real estate to Americans. "Nicaragua is more cost effective than Los Angeles," Annie smiled. Her colorful paintings of flora and fauna were hung all over their ranch-style house and Tina was already a big fan. Diego's wife was a wealth of information about the area and all the creatures and critters that lived on the volcano. Tina was fascinated.

They eventually talked about Wyatt and how the plan was to search the crowd of the hipica on Sunday. "The birthfather is a big horse fan and we're pretty sure they are in town for this parade. Otherwise they'd have moved on to surf," she said, finishing her second glass of ice tea. They talked about how Diego and friends had built this gorgeous house, and after an hour more of conversation, Tina had to remind herself that she was still on a mission to find Wyatt, not to make friends.

"Wait until the monkeys arrive," Annie said.

"What's the Monkey Highway?" she asked.

"It's a route that the monkeys follow through the tree system on the side of Mombacho." Annie's bracelets jingled as she reached to pour more tea. "But one of our stupid neighbors who bought the lot over there with no intention of building for years, cut down a crucial tree on the highway to make room to build his house and now the route is all screwed up. The monkeys have to backtrack and take a detour. That's why we end up with howlers in these trees at night." She pointed to the enormous deciduous trees above them. "It's the end of a cul de sac." They laughed.

"Called a Chilamate tree. They produce a fig that the monkeys love to eat."

"Do they come every night?"

"Not always, but lately. Around dusk." Annie smiled warmly. "It's a good life here on the side of Mombacho. Better than Los Angeles. Maybe in some ways similar to yours with your husband on Maui."

Tina nodded. "It's hot there in August, like here, but we don't have monkeys, or sloths. Maui is very built up now and getting more crowded with hotels every year."

"That's why we like Nicaragua. Don't tell anyone how beautiful it is here. We want to keep it this way."

Tina pretended to zip her lips shut and looked out over the canopy of trees below the deck, towards the town. Half of the view was taken up with the vast, blue lake beyond Granada. "Did you have to cut trees for the view?"

Annie shook her head. "No. We built the house at a natural opening." A large mixed-breed brown dog ran onto the terracotta patio and flopped down with an avocado in its mouth. "Chile, did you find a ball?" Annie laughed. "Our gardener took the dogs up to the water tank for a walk. Diego usually hikes with them at sunset."

Then another dog arrived, a small terrier mix with wiry gray hair, charging towards Tina and barking.

"And that's Frisco. He's all bark and no bite."

Tina held out her hand for the dog to sniff.

"He can't seem to shut up. Barks all day long. We tune it out, but I hope it doesn't wake your baby."

She looked to see that Kai's eyes were closed. "He sleeps through all kinds of noise."

"A wonderful trait in a baby," Annie said, standing up. "Come to the kitchen with me. I'll make dinner and we can open a bottle of wine. Do you like white or red?"

"Either," Tina said, and followed through the house with the dogs in tow. Just as the cork popped on a bottle of Sauvignon Blanc, Jamey phoned.

"Are you okay there for another few hours?" he asked.

"Yes, but I feel badly about having a good time."

"S'okay. Just take care of our son. Diego and I are going back to the island to see if they've shown up. We didn't get anything at the taxi stand."

"I feel like I should be out there with you." She wandered back to the patio where darkness was falling and Annie didn't have to overhear her side of the conversation.

"Me too, Darlin'. I know you want to be in on this, but I tell you, Diego is a Godsend. This guy knows everyone." He sounded distracted.

Tina watched Annie chopping food in the house. "You'd really like his wife too. I think I dreamed of her recently. The one where the woman was crying babies. Looks a bit like her," Tina said.

"We're here." Jamey was distracted. "Diego says to tell Annie to save him some dinner."

She could hear Diego's voice in the background. "I will. Be safe and I'll see you in a few hours." She ended the call and noticed Kai was awake. "Hi Sweetie." She walked through the patio door to see him fussing with his left ear, a cross look on his face. He'd been pulling on that same ear all day. She picked him up and snuggled him into her. Walking back to the kitchen, she spoke to Annie. "Looks like our men are going to the Islands to check out the house again."

Annie pointed to a glass of wine on the counter. "There's yours." She looked the baby up and down and then her brow wrinkled. What usually followed this thorough sizing up was a comment about how cute her baby was or at least how big he was, but Annie said nothing. Tina jiggled Kai on her hip to quell his fussy cry.

"Going out on the water? At this hour?" Annie turned around, a look of concern clouding her face.

Tina nodded apologetically. "That's what he said."

"Well, I guess if they're looking for a child, they have to try everything." Annie shook her head and went back to chopping vegetables. Just then a call that sounded like an amplified drainage pipe noise reverberated through the house. "Here they go." Annie said, like that horrible sound was an everyday occurrence, which it was.

This was the same sound they'd heard down at the bar by the bus stop, but much, much louder and closer.

Others chimed in. Kai went stiff in Tina's arms, his eyes wide. "It's okay. It's monkeys!" She tried to make light of the horrific noise in the trees above them, but Kai was scared. As much as Tina wanted to go outside to look at the monkeys, she wasn't sure it would help her son.

Then Kai started crying. Jiggling didn't help.

"Let's go see!" she said like it was going to be so much fun!

Stepping outside to the tiled deck, Tina was amazed to see the trees above the house filled with brown fuzzy creatures, moving from branch to branch, swinging and calling to each other. Most watched them below. She pointed to a mother with a baby on her back and then noticed that Kai had gone quiet. His gaze was fixed on the monkeys above them. Tina smiled to see him so engaged, his mouth a little O shape. She watched the babies get settled in the branches, mothers close by. The only ones making the guttural howling noises were the big ones without babies.

Annie arrived with both glasses of wine. "Your baby likes the howlers." She set the wine on the patio table. "Only the males howl that really low sound." She looked up into the trees.

"Are they gathering their group for the night?" Tina asked.

"They're telling other howlers out there where they are. It's a way to say this campsite over here is full."

Kai reached for Annie's dangling earrings and Tina pulled him back.

"Oh no you don't." Annie looked at the baby like she might warm up to him if she was given a month or two.

It was hard for Tina to be around Kai without touching him, but she understood that some people did not have the need to touch and kiss babies. Her best friend Pepper wasn't overly affectionate with babies.

"When Kai can walk around and talk, I'll be a better godmother," she'd said.

Tina just happened to be baby crazy. Always had been. And recently she'd told Jamey she wanted to have as many of them as they could before her eggs dried up.

"Then let's get going," he'd said pressing himself into her in their bed.

When the monkeys grew silent, and the only sound was a very loud frog near the pool, Tina sipped her wine. Dinner was in the oven and Annie had gone out to her art studio while the chicken cooked. Tina's thoughts drifted back to Hank and the baby they might have had. She wondered if he'd have been a good father. She'd banked on it when they were married, but all that she knew about her husband now, and his scheming and shadier side, leaked doubts. The funny thing was, he'd always loved kids, and they'd returned the affection. With an arsenal of kid jokes and games always on hand, he was a favorite with their friends who had children.

Noble was a different story. Like Annie, he seemed indifferent to children. She remembered when Noble suggested they have a baby after Hank died. That was a strange time in her life. She'd never fully understand either of those two men, but looking back, Noble was more of an enigma, seemingly so devoted to her. But as it turned out, he wasn't to be trusted.

A month ago, she'd had a dream about walking with Noble through a park with a picturesque lake. They'd talked, just like the old days before she knew he was using her for a con; back when she still thought of him as their best friend. In the dream, they'd laughed about something, then Noble looked her in the eyes and said, "I miss you," so intensely, she woke. Thinking about the dream all the next day, she'd wished things had been different with both Hank and Noble. For years, she'd admired their friendship. "Through thick and thin," Hank said. But it was a sham. She knew that now. They were brothers who had a bond that included a twisted hatred as well as brotherly love. Had she mentioned her feelings about the dream to Jamey, he'd have said what he always did. "Those relationships are behind you now." She'd used her husband as a sounding board long enough. Now, she had Doc Chan to interpret her dreams.

Tina and Annie set the patio table for four just in case the men arrived soon. She hoped that Jamey had Wyatt with him and they were on their way up Mombacho. He'd probably call the moment Wyatt was safe. Right after the call to Carrie.

The lights of Granada twinkled below the house, beyond the jungle top as Tina settled Kai in the car seat again to eat her dinner. Annie had prepared coq au vin, with wild rice and mangoes, and it smelled delicious, the aroma of the seasoned chicken and bacon wafting through the house for the last hour. Her fork was only half way to her mouth when Kai started fussing and pulling at his ear. Tina jammed a forkful of food into her mouth and moved to her son while she chewed. Kai was now crying, his face red and angry. "Excuse me, Annie, I'll take him in the other room. Maybe he'll go to sleep."

"Looks like his left ear is bothering him. Maybe he has some congestion and the altitude is making it worse."

Tina pulled Kai out of the seat and snuggled him in to her shoulder. "Are we up high enough for that?"

"If he's congested." Annie nodded. "The guest room's yours if he falls back asleep and you want to lay him on the bed."

"I might do that." Tina disappeared to the back of the house. Twenty minutes later, Kai was half asleep and she heard her cell phone ring in the living room.

"Hello?"

Tina heard a voice in the other room, presumably answering her phone.

"Just a minute, she's right here." Annie pushed the door open, handed Tina the phone and left the room.

"Hi," she whispered, hoping it was Jamey and not the dive shop on Maui.

"No luck," Jamey's voice was full of surrender and exhaustion. "Diego got a call that they vacated the island house because it was too small, but nobody knows where they went."

"Oh, I'm sorry. Kai just fell asleep." she explained her whispering.

"We're on our way. See you in twenty minutes, Diego says."

"We have time until the hipica, Jamey. We'll find him."

"I know, but I wanted to get him today, long before the parade. Just to know he's safe." He sighed. "Where the hell are they?" He didn't expect an answer.

"Nothing else we can do tonight. Let's see if we dream."

Tina didn't know much about baby ear infections but maybe the wind at the lake today did something. When she was young her nanny often put cotton in her ears when she had an ear ache. Kai was soon asleep and she set him on the bed, creating a bumper with pillows in case he rolled. "No luck, they'll be here in twenty," Tina said returning to the table.

"I'm sorry."

Tina finished her food, while Annie polished off the bottle of wine. "There is something about home cooking and of course, chicken in wine sauce," she smiled. "You are a great cook, like Diego said.

Annie smiled at her dinner companion. "I imagine you're hungry with a baby.

Tina nodded. "I normally eat a lot." She chuckled and held a forkful of creamy chicken and rice to her mouth. "I don't cook, but I'm always saying I'm going to learn. Jamey has two daughters who are twelve and when they come to visit, I try to make kid food." She chewed and thought about the twins. "Last summer, I was pregnant and everything repulsed me so I wasn't much help in the kitchen, but now I make baby food. I've extended my culinary repertoire to pureed peaches and bananas."

Annie laughed. "Kai isn't suffering. He's big for his age. Soon those arms of yours will be wishing he was crawling."

"Already. I wonder when babies crawl," she said as much to herself as anyone.

"Oh, eight to ten months," Annie said.

"Soon then. Do you and Diego have children?"

Annie shook her head. "Nope, but lots of friends had children and I remember a few things." She set her half-full glass on the table. "Your husband has children from a previous marriage?"

"Yes. Twin girls who I genuinely love. I know good manners shouldn't be a gage for likeability, but they have them and are such sweet children."

"They live on Maui?"

"No. They live in Jamey's hometown with his ex-wife, a small town near Seattle. Carnation is a pretty little place on a river. A lovely spot to bring up children. Jamey's family is a big, wonderful group of kids and adults who all get along and work stuff out if they don't."

Just then Annie caught her wine glass before it fell off the table and smashed, but not before wine spilled on her lap. "Oh gosh, what did I do?" She jumped up; her pants and top wet. "Excuse me a minute."

Tina sopped up the table spill with napkins, and just as she noticed one of the dogs lapping up the liquid on the deck, lights of a car illuminated the patio. The two dogs barked and took off for the driveway.

"That'll be Diego and your Jamey," Annie said. "I'll get their plates ready," she called from the house.

Tina walked to the truck that stopped in an open-ended garage and watched the two very different looking dogs wag their tails, waiting at the driver door. The frog continued croaking from the swimming pool and Tina imagined the dogs had woken up the barking frog.

It looked like a good life here on the side of the volcano. Granted, the drive to the house from the main road was challenging and bouncy, but Annie had said they bought their lot for a mere fraction of what it would cost in America.

Jamey exited the car first, gently closing the door behind him, looking exhausted. Tina approached him with open arms. "We have food for you." What else could she say? He was disappointed.

He kissed her forehead, lingering longer than he usually did.

Diego walked towards them flanked by his two dogs. "No luck. But we're closing in, I just know it."

She smiled at him. Good attitude. Hopefully he was right. "You guys must be hungry. Annie made some delicious chicken and rice."

Jamey put his arm around her shoulders and they followed Diego. "Has our son gone to sleep then?"

"He has. I think we might need to have his ear checked tomorrow. He was fussing."

Jamey nodded, his forehead wrinkled. "Poor 'lil Dude." He whistled at the view of Granada beyond the pool. "Gorgeous house, Diego."

They stood arm in arm looking at the lights of the city while Diego checked on Annie. "I've had such a nice afternoon and dinner," she said. "I feel badly that you've been navigating a boat around the islands in the dark. Were there many mosquitoes?" Tina kissed Jamey's arm, as high up as she could.

"Out in full force. I might be scratching tonight."

"We're spoiled on Maui." At home, they hardly had any mosquitoes.

"It's much cooler up here," Jamey added

"And no mosquitoes. But there's a huge family of howler monkeys sleeping above us right now." She pointed to the trees. "We saw them at sunset. They were amazing. At first, Kai was afraid because it was so loud, but then he noticed the monkeys and stopped fussing."

Jamey's smile contrasted his serious expression. "He did? I wish I'd seen his face."

"You'll see them in the morning, if we sleep here. Annie suggested we use the guest room. Kai's already in there, and the road is not very good in the dark."

Jamey looked out to the jungle below the deck. "Yeah, we almost hit a pig on the way up. Probably a good idea. And, I hate to ask Diego to drive us back to town."

"Ask Diego if we can leave first thing in the morning."

Jamey turned to her, his eyes full of concern. "If Wyatt is down there, somewhere, I feel like we need to get back to town. Back to the accident site. But there isn't much we can do tonight. I just hate waiting for this accident to happen."

"Me too." Tina understood his need to not stray far. "The likelihood of Kevin and Rose wandering around with Wyatt at this hour isn't good."

Diego arrived to tell them that Annie had gone to bed with a headache. "She said to give her apologies to everyone." He handed Jamey a plate of food and a beer. "I heard you're crashing in the guest room tonight. I'll run you down to town at the crack of dawn. Or I can take you down after dinner. But first, let's eat. I'm starving."

CHAPTER 13

Jamey sat upright in bed. Something woke him. Then he heard it again. A strange noise above the house that must be the Howler Monkeys starting up. It didn't sound like howling but he couldn't think of a better word. He looked over to see Tina smiling, her breast exposed to his son's hungry mouth.

"Monkeys," she whispered.

Others had joined in. It was more like a mechanical sound, like bass feedback, at a very high decibel level. "Wow," he mouthed. "Did you sleep?"

She nodded. "No dream jump though," she said.

"I had a normal," he said.

"Me too."

Kai looked over to his Daddy, reached for him and when Jamey offered him his thumb to hold, the baby went back to nursing happily. He'd had a strange dream, one he hadn't had in a very long time. It was a recurring dream that had bothered him as a kid. When he woke at two, he barely remembered the details. The gist of it was that his sister Jenny was a baby and was in danger. He had to keep her safe. Jenny was now in her mid-thirties so laying there in the dark, remembering how the dream haunted his childhood, Jamey guessed he'd done his job. All this worry about Wyatt had dredged up repressed feelings about protecting everyone. When the twins were babies, he'd almost driven himself crazy with worry. Carrie had to put up with a lot of his paranoia, and in those early years with their daughters he'd tried to distinguish dreams from just plain worry about being a good father. With Kai, he'd learned to calm down and not take his dreams so literally. According to Tina's parenting books it was normal to have these dreams.

He and Tina lay staring at each other in the pre-dawn light, listening to the monkeys in the trees above the house. As more woke, the noise gathered in volume. Kai ignored them as he sucked and swallowed.

"You should see the babies," Tina smiled.

Jamey smiled back. "As cute as our baby?"

They looked at Kai now lazily sucking his morning milk. "No. But fuzzy, with long arms and darling faces."

Jamey heard someone in the kitchen moving around, dishes clanging in the moments between howls. "When he's done with breakfast," he nodded to Kai, "we'll head to Granada, have our breakfast there."

Tina nodded then looked worried. "I wish we'd have a big ole' dream jump with Kevin, showing where Wyatt is."

"You and me both." He slipped out of bed, threw on his cargo shorts and the same T-shirt he'd been wearing for days. "I'll see if that's Diego out there."

The kitchen was mostly dark, but someone was making coffee wearing a headlamp. It didn't look like Diego. "Good morning," he said.

"Hi Jamey." The woman didn't turn around. "I'm just making the coffee. Sorry I didn't get a chance to meet you last night. I'm Annie." She half-turned and waved, then turned back. Her dark hair covered a good deal of the back of her pale robe, making her look like some mythical creature in the semi-darkness.

"I hope your headache is better," he said.

She set her hands on the counter as if to brace herself, and looked out the window. "I didn't have a headache," she said in a strange voice.

He got the impression she was about to admit to something else. Something bad. The skin on the back of Jamey's neck prickled and he had a flash of something. The dream about his sister Jenny, Wyatt at the hipica, keeping Kai safe. Then, Tina screamed from the bedroom and he was off. In several bounds, he was inside the room where Tina stood with Kai in her arms, three feet from the bed, staring at the pillows. "There's a huge spider in the bed." She hugged the crying baby to her. "Oh, my God, Jamey, it's enormous. Do they have tarantulas here?"

Jamey flipped on the overhead light. "I don't know." He took off his shoe, and holding it like a weapon he approached the bed.

Tina slipped into her sandals. "It was on your pillow going towards the wall." Her voice was higher than usual.

"I'll get it, Ti. You just calm Kai." This must've been what he foresaw in the kitchen just before Tina screamed.

Diego rushed into the room and they pulled back the pillows to reveal a black spider as big as Kai's hand scrambling up the bed to a space between that and the wall. "Banana Spider," Diego said.

They pulled the bed away from the wall and Jamey smacked it several times as the hairy thing tried to shuffle away to safety. "Venomous?"

"Can be. It's good you noticed it," Diego said, picking up the dead insect by a leg and carrying it out the patio door. "Some fancy guest room we offered you two," he called back.

Tina had turned on the overhead ceiling fan to calm Kai and as he lay in his mother's arms, watching the blades go around and around, the crying stopped. "I felt it before I saw it," she whispered to Jamey. "Thank God. Right now I'm so grateful for this intuition."

He agreed and kissed his son on the forehead.

"I think his ear is still bothering him."

She stood in only her underwear, more worried about Kai's ear than Diego's presence. *That's Tina.* Luckily, she had a healthy fear of spiders too. The bedside clock read 6:32. He hugged his wife from the side. "Let's take Kai to a doctor today." He shuddered to think what might have happened. There were some things he couldn't control and that was not an easy feeling. He liked to be in control. Responsible for his own fate. And sometimes for his loved ones' fate.

He just hoped he could control getting to Wyatt in time tomorrow before the horse got to him.

***

The doctor at the clinic prescribed antibiotics for Kai's ear infection and although Tina didn't want her child to take drugs at this age, her baby's screaming as they drove down the mountain was enough to make her want to try anything to relieve his pain.

Once they filled the prescription, Tina and Kai were dropped off at the hotel, while he and Jamey continued on to the real estate office. The men's plan was to see if the island house renters had been in touch about where they went. If not, Jamey said he might try one more trip out to the island. If the house still looked deserted, they'd visit other rental places in town to see if Kevin and Rose were there.

Tina laid down on the hotel bed to nurse Kai who seemed to want the boob more than ever now that he wasn't feeling well. She'd given him the antibiotic and was waiting for it to work its magic. When her cell phone rang, she hoped Jamey had good news.

"It's Annie. I'm sorry I didn't say goodbye to you three this morning. I know it seems strange, but I had an inspiration for a painting I'm working on and went out to my studio. When I came up for air, everyone was gone."

She sounded surprised she'd been deserted, but Diego had told them she was still sick and was lying down. "That's fine. We really appreciated dinner last night and your guest room."

"Spider and all?" Annie asked. "I'm horrified that thing got so close to you and your baby."

Tina shuddered to think how close Kai had come to being bit by a venomous spider. She would've crushed the thing in her bare hand if she'd seen it coming for her baby. Arachnophobia be damned. "Part of living in the tropics, I suppose. We have scorpions on Maui and centipedes."

"Yes, it's a risk. But then life is one big risk." She laughed nervously. "I enjoyed our visit yesterday. Diego seems very fond of your husband." She paused long enough for Tina to speak.

"He's quite lovable, especially when we aren't trying to find an abducted child." *Or save that child from being trampled by a horse.*

"Diego called him James, not Jamey. I can't remember what I called him when I saw him this morning. I hope it was the right name."

"He was born James, but goes by Jamey now.

"Did you take his last name when you married? I always wonder what the young newlyweds are doing nowadays." Annie seemed chatty. Tina didn't mind. Kai was nursing lazily.

"I did. I was pregnant when we married and we wanted to have a common family name, so I became Tina Dunn. Not so different from Tina Greene." She remembered back to the conversation she'd had with Jamey about his last name. He'd told her he didn't care if she took his name or not, but when she did, he was obviously pleased.

"The reason for my call is to ask if you two would like to join us for dinner tonight. If your plan allows for a night off."

Regardless of the search for Wyatt, Tina wasn't sure if going up the mountain again was the best thing for Kai's ear and said so. "I just gave him a dose of the antibiotic. I doubt it'll work that fast. But thank you for the offer, Annie. A lot depends on if Jamey makes any headway today in locating Wyatt. And if he sees Kevin and Rose. I'd have to say no."

They made plans to keep in touch. Kai had fallen asleep and slowly his slack mouth released her nipple so Tina positioned the pillow between him and the edge and settled beside him on the bed. But not before checking for spiders on the white linens.

The dream came right away. Like it had been waiting. Like something that blocked it was now clear. In her lucid state of mind she was excited to see the blurry edges. It was a premonition. Granada. She walked towards the hipica parade route, alone, floating almost, advancing faster than she would up top. The weekend festival was under way. Annie walked briskly up ahead, her face behind the brim of a big straw hat. The grey braid gave her away. The older woman half-ran through the crowd and Tina followed close behind. Turning the corner, she watched Annie duck in to a café that was bursting to the brim with revelers. The ceiling of the cafe was covered in piñatas, streamers, and colorful balloons. Should she go in, brave the crowd to look for Annie? Moments later, Annie exited another door on the far side of the restaurant, with Wyatt on the other end of her arm, struggling. Annie started off down the street, pulling the boy.

Kevin came out of the restaurant, momentarily blocked by a group of people singing. "Annie!" he yelled.

She whirled around. "So help me God, Kevin. I've got him now. You screwed up." She pointed her finger at him.

"You don't know the whole story."

"I don't care what your side is," she yelled back. "You ruined everything for me." She turned to Wyatt. "Come with me, child." Wyatt looked terrified as Annie pulled him through the crowd.

Then Tina was out. She opened her eyes in the hotel room, with Kai sleeping quietly beside her. What the hell was about to happen? Was Annie somehow tied up in this?

CHAPTER 14

According to the rental agent, Kevin and Rose found another house. "They told Manuel that they found something else, but didn't say where," Diego told Jamey. "He thinks they're settling in Granada for the time being. When Manuel found out that the dad is a surfer, he suggested San Juan del Sur, but the mom said no. She's waiting for her parents to join them in Granada." Jamey and Diego were having lunch at El Camello. Leroy had recommended the Lamb Stew, but Jamey was looking forward to the Ribs and Diego wanted Spaghetti. Jamey had just taken his first bite of the ribs when Tina called. He wiped the sauce from his fingers before answering the phone.

"I dreamed that Annie is in on this somehow," she whispered.

Kai must be asleep. "What?"

"In the dream, Annie entered a restaurant and came out with Wyatt. Kevin chased her and she told him that he'd screwed up, ruined everything. Wyatt was scared. Oh my God, Jamey. This is weird."

Jamey looked over at Diego who was eating a plate of Spaghetti Bolognese. "Precog?" he whispered.

"Yes. And Kevin knew Annie somehow. He used her name. Wyatt was frightened, but she hung on to him and ran off through the hipica crowd. Then I woke."

Shit. No wonder she couldn't look him in the eyes and kept disappearing. He nodded at Diego. Did he know? "I'm having lunch with Diego, then he has afternoon appointments so I'm on my own." If Diego was in on this, he didn't want to tip him off. Damn. Had his new best friend been leading him away from Wyatt all along? Was there a bigger picture with child trafficking involved? What in God's name was going on?

"I think you need to confront him," Tina added. "We don't have time to waste."

He took a swig of his beer and looked around the restaurant. He couldn't fully trust Diego now. Maybe Kevin and Rose hadn't even rented a house on the island. Maybe this real estate agent was leading him around on a wild-goose chase while Kevin hid Wyatt. "I'll come back to the hotel in twenty minutes. We'll make a plan." He hung up the phone, his mind whirling.

"She okay? Kai alright?" Diego picked up his Tona.

"Yep, baby's sleeping." *What do you care, you motherfucker, if you're just buying time while Kevin gets out of town.*

Jamey wished he had a gun right now. Not that he was going to shoot anyone, but he sure as hell felt like a gun would encourage this woman, Annie to talk. He recalled their strange conversation in the half dark this morning. He hadn't seen her face. Then when it was light, she was gone. Evil had a way of building up inside a person so that the eyes were full of it, but Tina hadn't noticed anything unusual.

He called Tina back to tell her that he was going to confront Annie first. Tina agreed that was the best plan. Her afternoon would be spent wandering around town in her straw hat with the stroller, hoping to see the restaurant from the dream.

Jamey drove along the highway out of town to the turnoff to Mombacho, the thoughts inside his head bouncing around like the bingo machine balls at the Carnation Bingo fest. Diego had lent him the truck thinking Jamey went back to the hotel. If Annie was in on this scheme somehow, then Diego would be too. Had Jamey been set up the day when he was told that Diego was talking to Kevin in the real estate office? No, Kevin probably was there, but Diego had left out the part about him knowing Kevin, and the important part about being on Kevin's side. No wonder Diego was so happy to help Jamey and walked right up to that rental house without the fear of being shot.

Jamey turned the truck on to the rutted dirt road, drove past the bar where Wyatt had allegedly been seen, and realized that Kevin and Rose were probably at that bar, waiting for Diego. Passing the turnoff to the convent, he wondered what he'd say to Annie —the woman who was friendly to his wife, and then suspiciously disappeared every time he got near. Tina had just recounted a strange fact-finding conversation she'd had with Annie hours earlier, asking them to dinner again. Of course, they wanted to monopolize Jamey and Tina's time.

If Annie was running some black-market child abduction ring, Jamey wasn't sure what his next move would be. The FBI would have to be called in. If this was that serious, he needed to play this next move smart, not rush in like a Navy Seal and risk never seeing Wyatt again.

When he pulled the truck onto the bumpy driveway and passed the turn at the enormous tree that looked like a colony of people could live inside, the house came into view. It sure was a pretty place with the terracotta tile roof and the veranda that stretched along all four sides. And the view. Man, what a setup. Had they funded this house somehow with child racketeering? The idea made Jamey mad. Two barking dogs ran to the driver side, tails wagging. The dogs probably expected Diego to get out. Would they bite him when they realized he wasn't their master?

"Hi there, doggies," he said in a high, baby voice, watching their ears for signs of attack. Turned out they weren't very good guard dogs. They escorted him up the path way to the house and as Jamey walked closer, he got a flash of the dream he'd had in the guest room about his sister, Jenny. Then, setting foot on the veranda tile, he had a powerful feeling that something was about to happen, like when he was in a fight and second-guessed his opponent's next move. He looked around but didn't see anything out of the ordinary. As a precaution, he dialed Tina's cell phone and told her to stay on the line, listening. "I'm going to put the phone in my pocket. I'm at the house and something feels weird."

"Be careful, Jamey."

He followed the dogs past the pool and turned to look inside the house. The doors were wide open like when they'd left this morning, and Jamey wondered if monkeys ever wandered inside the house. "Annie?" he called. Maybe she was in town grabbing Wyatt right now. No, her truck was in the open garage. Tina had said in the dream it looked like festival day, but the town was already filled with decorations, with more going up every hour.

Jamey walked in to the living room and headed for the master bedroom. Nothing. The doors were open to both bedrooms and the bathroom. "Where's Annie?" Jamey asked the dogs as he peeked in the guest bedroom. No one.

The kitchen had been cleaned, all dishes from last night done. Walking out the back door towards their garden, Jamey heard the swish of a broom around the far side of the house. He followed the sound, expecting to see Annie, but instead came upon a small Nicaraguan woman in a blue dress, surprised to see a stranger. "Hola," he smiled. It probably wasn't her fault her boss was a child trafficker. "Annie?" he asked.

The woman looked to a small cabin behind the garden and lifted her chin to indicate that her employer was in the studio. Last night, Jamey had heard that Annie spent copious amounts of time painting. That must be where. "My wife is a loner," Diego had said and continued eating his dinner. At the time, Jamey felt badly for Diego who seemed to be extremely outgoing, but they seemed to make it work after almost thirty years of marriage. Tina said Annie was sociable enough when Jamey asked her about the day, and even went so far as to say that she got a very strong feeling that they would be friends. Not very damn likely if Annie was selling children.

Jamey made his way along the stone path, past the thriving garden and a row of banana trees, which reminded him of the huge spider this morning. Music wafted from the studio window, Vivaldi, he guessed. He knocked on the wooden door to the palapa-roofed hut. "Annie? It's Jamey Dunn."

"Come in, Jamey." She didn't sound surprised.

He pushed the door open to see that the woman facing him from her stance at the easel was someone familiar to him. Very familiar.

***

Tina listened from the other end of the phone. She couldn't hear anything for a while and just as she heard Jamey call out Annie's name, Kai began to scream. He'd fallen over from his sitting position and couldn't get himself sitting up again. "Shhhh" She covered the mouthpiece and righted her son with one arm. Would Annie and Jamey hear this from Jamey's pocket? The plan to listen in was precautionary and she wasn't sure what she'd do if Jamey was ambushed. She'd have to get a taxi to take her and the baby up the mountain. The thought might have been amusing if it wasn't worrisome. When Kai was happily playing again with his toy, Tina crossed the room to hear better, away from Kai's verbalizing. As sweet as his little sounds were, she needed to hear what came next.

The phone was dead. Did Jamey hang up or did someone hang up for him. "Oh no," she said out loud. Now she wished Jamey had a gun. It would've made her feel better, especially because this was a potentially dangerous situation. They didn't know who this person, Annie was. She might have a gun in her house. She dialed Jamey's number and he picked up. "Are you okay?"

"I'm safe. Annie and I are going to have a little conversation and I'll call you after we talk." Jamey sounded furious. She could imagine what his face looked like. It was an expression she'd seen in dream jumps when their lives were at risk. He'd probably start with asking Annie how she knew Kevin. Or where Wyatt was. Tina hung up, took a deep breath, and packed the diaper bag in case she had to run out with Kai. But then the phone rang and Tina was surprised to hear Pops' voice on the other end.

"Hi Kid. How's my grandson?"

"He's good, Pops. How are you doing? Is everything okay? You sound like you have a cold."

He cleared his throat. "Everything is fine here, except we're all worried about Wyatt."

Tina interrupted him, knowing she needed to keep the line open for Jamey's call. "We have a lead on something and I can call you later this afternoon if it pans out, but right now I'm waiting for Jamey to call me back. He's talking to a woman we met here named Annie, who was in a jump with Wyatt. We think she might be in on this abduction."

"She isn't. I can guarantee you that much. But she might be able to lead you to Kevin."

How did Pops know any of this? "Did you talk to Jamey?"

"Nope, I talked to Annie." There was a pause and then Pops asked Tina to sit down.

She did.

"This gets weird, Kiddo." He took a deep breath, and then the words spilled from his mouth. "The woman you met named Annie, is Virginia, Jamey's mother."

The blood rushed to Tina's head, like she'd been in an accident and was going into shock. The mother who deserted her children when Jamey was five? Annie? "You've got to be kidding."

"'Fraid not. Ann is her middle name. It's a long story, as you can imagine, but Virginia called me this morning, after thirty-six years of silence, to tell me that she believed our son James was in Nicaragua, where she now lives. She asked if that could be true."

"Oh, my God." Jamey's mother was a child trafficker? "We think she kidnapped Wyatt or at least is in on the scheme," Tina said. "He's confronting her right now."

"I don't know the woman anymore, so I can't say, one way or another." Pops voice was full of sadness. "I better not keep the line tied up, but I tried to phone him and he's not picking up. I wanted to warn him."

"Oh Pops." This was a strange piece of information. "Did she say anything about Kevin?"

"No. Our conversation was very brief. She asked one question, I answered, and she hung up. But maybe Jamey will find out. Keep me posted, will ya?"

Tina felt like she had verification that the world was actually flat. "I'll call you as soon as I hear anything, Pops." She sat on the side of the bed, watching her son play with a pop up toy they'd bought at the toy store near the market yesterday. She wished that Jamey had left the phone line open so she could hear the conversation between Jamey and his mother—the woman who left the family and never looked back. Would he recognize her? This was a woman Jamey hated. Kevin was originally from Carnation. Rose too. What was the connection? They didn't have long before the festival and hipica started, and Wyatt would be trampled by a giant prancing horse.

They had to find him before that happened.

CHAPTER 15

Initially, all Jamey thought when Annie turned around was that there was something achingly familiar about the woman standing at the easel facing him. She looked guilty of something. Then it hit him like he'd run his truck into a tree. Although he hadn't seen her since he was a young boy, her smile was the same. Her voice too. His mother stood across the room, looking like someone had killed her puppy. He shook his head, looked down at the floor, and took a deep breath. "So it's you, after all these years."

Her eyes were filled with tears but Jamey was immune to her sadness. "After all you've put my family through, here you are. Hiding in Nicaragua."

"Yes. It's me, James." A sob escaped from her throat and she set her paintbrush on the easel. "I saw you last night and wondered if it could be you."

"That's why you pretended to have a headache?"

She nodded.

"I see you're still a coward." Jamey felt like he'd been punched in the gut. Repeatedly. He hated this woman for what she did to Pops. To the kids in his family. To him. He'd never forgive her for skipping out on a family of young children, leaving them motherless. Abandoning a husband to raise the four children she'd brought in to this world. What could he say to her? He reminded himself that he didn't have to say anything about deserting the family. His mission to find Wyatt was why he'd come here to talk.

"How do you know Wyatt?"

"The boy you're looking for? I don't know him." She looked confused.

Jamey's instinct told him she was telling the truth. What the hell?

"What makes you think I know the child?" Her eyes narrowed and she tipped her head to the side.

The sound of the two dogs playing outside cut through the afternoon quiet. Did she know about his premonitions? His ability? He used to tell her stuff that he dreamed, but as he recalled, she didn't think they were any more than silly dreams. She'd tell him that it wasn't real, just stories that his brain made up while he was sleeping. His real talents hadn't manifested until after she left. He'd play it safe. "I put two and two together and came up with you. Annie, the artist on Mombacho." He said the last part like it was an insult.

"I don't know what that means, James." The mother he used to know broke through and Jamey remembered being talked to in that scolding tone, decades ago. Did she not know Wyatt? Maybe she knew one of the others. "What about Kevin and Rose? Do you know them?" *Please give me something here, besides a deadbeat mother who's hiding spot has been found.* "Kevin Lenz and Rose Stevens or Stevenson?" Was that the connection?

Annie went over to a dresser by the window where she found what looked like a photo album. Flipping to the middle, searching for something, she then approached Jamey with the album. "Do you see Rose in this?"

The photo had been taken facing the sun, making it overexposed and less than perfect. But standing in a group of dinner party revelers on a patio was Rose, smiling into the camera. He pointed to her in the group. "That's Rose."

Annie pursed her lips and put the album down on the dresser. "Mary Rose. From Fall City. Her mother is the only person I still know from my former life."

She kept in touch with someone but left her children. "Lucky her." Sarcasm dripped from the words.

"I didn't mean to keep in touch with her. I saw her in Los Angeles years ago." She sank to the couch. "She stood outside this restaurant in Marina Del Rey. I almost ran, but she recognized me. She wasn't in touch with anyone in Carnation anymore. Moved home to Florida with Mary Rose. Kind of like me, she left." Annie looked apologetically at Jamey. "I convinced her to visit here when Diego and I moved. Two years ago, she bought a vacation house up the road. Mary Rose and Kevin were here then." Annie looked at Jamey. "If Rose is in town, I expect it's because her mother is arriving tomorrow."

Jamey interrupted. "Why didn't Diego recognize her?

"He's never met her." She held up the photo. "He was in L.A. when this photo was taken."

Where's the house?"

Annie nodded. "I'll take you. It's off the road off a trail." She looked at Jamey solemnly. "But you have to promise me that if you see her you won't hurt Mary Rose."

"Only if she won't give me Wyatt," he said.

The woman in the truck beside him was his mother, the person who, along with Pops, gave him life. As he recalled, she'd been a good mother up until the day she ran out. The loss was devastating; like someone pulled the floor out of the family home, and they all were left clinging to the sides of a pit that threatened to swallow them. When Jamey finally decided she wasn't worth ruining his life, what was left in him was a fierce anger. A chip, people said, without knowing why.

And now she was driving him up a volcano to find his godson. He had to play nice with this person until he knew she couldn't help him anymore, then he'd probably spew all the painful thoughts he'd pent up for decades and leave her in the dust. Not that she'd care, but he wanted to tell her the mess she'd left in her wake; he wanted to hurt her as much as she hurt all of them.

The truck turned at a fork and continued up another route that was framed in overhanging trees. At the top of the hill, Annie pulled the truck onto a flat dirt patch and killed the engine, pointing to a footpath ahead. "It's about a quarter mile down there. The only house up here." She sat back, lost in thought. "Jean isn't expected until tomorrow, but I suppose Mary Rose could be there. Even as a toddler, she was a strange little thing. Shy, but demanding."

Jamey wanted to tell her to shut up. She sounded so concerned about other people's children. He hopped out of the car and softly closed the door. Just because there wasn't another car in the pullout, didn't mean Kevin, Rose, and Wyatt weren't there. A brave taxi driver could have brought them up the hill. Or they might have hitched a ride with someone else. It happened all day long on the mountain, Diego had told him. Someone was driving up, and people jumped into the truck bed for a ride if they stopped. "You wait here," he said to Annie. "I don't want to be worrying about you if this turns bad."

Annie looked like she was going to speak, then closed her mouth. Just as well. He wasn't ready to face this woman and her misplaced concern now. "Keep the keys in the ignition, stay behind the wheel. If I run out with Wyatt, we need to take off quickly, you hear?

She nodded again, this time looking fearful.

He took off down the trail at a run. If they had Wyatt at this house, his plan was to distract them somehow, rush in to grab Wyatt, and take off to safety. He'd case out the joint first, see what the exits were. Kevin might have a gun. If he'd been able to sneak into several countries with a hidden child, he might have been stupid enough to pack heat. Jamey would have to be ready for anything.

The green stucco house came into view and Jamey got off the trail to come through the brush undercover. It wasn't dry enough here to have snapping twigs on the groundcover. Not much would give him away with the humidity of this country. Ahead, there was no movement, no sign of anyone, no noise. He crouched in the jungle growth watching for ten minutes. When he didn't see anything, or hear anything, he planned a route to the house. He'd use cover right up until the last little sprint where he'd be out in the open until he got under a window. He took off, ducking behind a thick bush, then an outbuilding, until he was up against the house, listening under a window.

Nothing.

The window was shut. You'd think in this heat, they'd use the screens. Were they asleep? He listened for another few minutes then inched up to sneak a peek. It was a crude house with an old rusty fridge and stove. There was a wooden table in the center with handmade benches. Very unlike Diego's and Annie's. Scooting along the side of the house, he ducked under the next window and listened. Nothing. On second thought, he should have just let Annie walk up the trail saying, asking if anyone was home. She offered but he didn't want to put anyone at risk. Even her.

Inside the one bedroom, was a queen-sized bed covered in a red sleeping bag. And on that red cover was a toy. It looked like the Star Wars character, Chewbacca. Verification set in. Wyatt *had* been here. His heart jumped. Noiselessly slipping along to the next window, he peeked in to the main room. No one. They could be hiding in the bathroom or outbuilding, or could be gone for the day. He tried the door. Locked. The kitchen screen came off easily and he slipped inside. The bathroom was empty. No one under the bed either, and after going through the place, he concluded that the place had been occupied by Kevin, Rose, and Wyatt. The fridge held milk, beer, water, and various snacks. Taking one last look at the house's configuration, Jamey went back out through the window, replacing the screen. The outbuilding was unlocked. Inside he found tools, chairs, a hammock leaning against the wall, gas cans. No people. No little boy wondering what the heck he was doing in this far off country without his family.

They'd be back. Of that Jamey was sure. And he'd be waiting when they got here.

First he had to tell Annie to go home. He didn't need her waiting on the road to give him away. When Kevin and Rose arrived, Jamey would be waiting to grab Wyatt, any way he had to. He'd deal with the abductors later, when he was sure the little guy was safe and unharmed. And if the boy had so much as a bruise, Jamey wanted to make sure Kevin and Rose were dealt with.

An eye for an eye and all that.

***

Tina tried calling Jamey, but his phone kept going to message. He had either turned his phone off or it died. She hoped the former. It had been an hour since she'd heard from Pops. Her thoughts included valid concern, imagining every terrible thing that could have happened to Jamey. Were he and Annie still talking? Was he yelling at her? Or was he figuring out why his mother was mixed up in the abduction of Wyatt? With all the pent up anger Jamey had about his mother's desertion, Tina imagined how heated the conversation might be. Maybe he'd stormed out and was on his way back now. She and Kai sat on the balcony of their hotel room, watching the horses down below. He'd just finished dinner of creamed carrots and rice cereal. Kai's chubby arms waved around as he watched the activity in the park. Her phone rang.

"Tina, it's Annie."

A jolt like electricity shot through Tina's nerves. Why wouldn't she call Jamey? "Hello."

"I'm delivering a message from Jamey. He turned off his phone, but wanted me to tell you what's going on." Annie sounded out of breath. Just because she was Jamey's birthmother, didn't clear her from the suspicion. "Turns out that your Rose person is someone I know. Her mother has a house on Mombacho. Jamey is checking out the house now and waiting in case they come back."

"How do you know Rose?" Tina didn't want to let down her guard just yet.

"I know her mother. That might be why they've brought the little boy here. Mary Rose has been here before."

"But why would they rent the house on the island?" Tina's mind was playing through all the possibilities, including Annie lying.

"I don't know. The mom is arriving tomorrow. Do they have a vehicle to make it up Mombacho?"

"They had a truck, but I don't know if they still have it. They were using a taxi the other night."

"Anyways, James asked that you stay put, stay safe, he said. He's waiting for them to return. He'll be in touch as soon as he gets Wyatt."

Annie called him James. A slip from her old days as Jamey's mother. It wasn't until he married Carrie that everyone started calling him Jamey. So, he was waiting for the threesome. Jamey was a soldier, trained for this sort of thing. "When you see him again, tell him that I love him and we need him to stay safe too." If Annie was a criminal and planning anything against Jamey, Tina needed her to know that he was loved, she was watching, and it wasn't like Jamey was on his own in this country. He answered to someone. She and Jamey were a team and with or without Kai, she was prepared to rescue Jamey if he needed her. "Tell him that."

There was a pause and Annie cleared her throat. "I will. How is that baby's ear? Any better?"

"Maybe a bit."

"What will you two be doing while you wait?"

She didn't want to give up any information in case Annie wasn't a friend. What should she say? "We'll go for a walk, I guess."

"I can have Diego come get you after his appointments, if you like."

If Tina trusted this woman, the invitation might've made sense. But she didn't. This whole situation was just weird. Something was off. "Thanks anyhow, but I think we'll stay in Granada. Have Jamey call me." That was twice now that Annie tried to get Tina to her house today. What was going on? If Tina had to rescue Jamey on Mombacho, the hotel had a babysitting service that was said to be very good. She couldn't imagine giving Kai to a stranger in this country. She'd sooner drive over to that restaurant, El Camello, and hand Kai to the owner's wife, Ana, who seemed very trustworthy.

Hanging up, she thought about the worst-case scenario, something Jamey had taught her to do. If Annie and Diego were somehow tied into this abduction, then she had to steer clear of them, hope that Jamey was safe. A bad mother like Annie might abandon her children, but she wouldn't kill one, would she?

Tina gathered the diaper bag, loaded Kai into the stroller, and headed out to the park. From there she could watch the hotel front door, just in case Diego went in looking for her. She didn't want to be a sitting duck in the hotel room if that happened. That lesson had been learned in Afghanistan when she waited for the military to come to her room and was taken by insurgents. Having learned a thing or two, she'd now rather play it safe. Wandering around the park for a few hours, maybe getting food from a cart in the square, while she avoided her hotel room, seemed like a prudent plan, at least until she suspected Diego was out of town.

Shortly after four p.m., Diego bounded up the steps to the hotel. Tina was sitting on a hidden park bench across the street, under the cover of a tree. She'd been right. He came looking for her. Was he upstairs knocking on her door hoping to convince her to get in his car? And what if she'd been there and said no? Would he try to force her to join her husband who was being held captive at Annie's house? Her imagination had had plenty of time to concoct stories and what ifs while she watched the hotel and she hoped she was wrong about all her theories.

When Diego came out of the hotel, he stopped to glance up and down the street before slipping into the car. Would Diego need Annie to come get him at the base of the mountain or could he make it up the mountain in the car? After circling the park twice, Diego drove down a side street near his office and disappeared. Just to be safe, Tina stayed hiding by the tree for another half hour, then wheeled Kai's stroller to a nearby restaurant. She wasn't sure what she'd do if she didn't hear from Jamey in the next few hours, but she had to eat something before she fainted from hunger. After ordering black beans, rice, tortillas, and fried plantain, Tina tried amusing Kai. His mood had improved from this morning. He'd get a good night's sleep tonight and be in better shape to go traipsing around the streets tomorrow looking for Wyatt. If Jamey found everyone tonight, they could leave town and avoid the madness tomorrow. Or could they?

What would be done with Kevin and Rose?

She hadn't thought that far in advance, only thinking about Wyatt's rescue and Chris's flight to Nicaragua. Yesterday, she'd spoken to Carrie briefly, before Jamey took the call. Carrie was understandably upset that her son hadn't been found yet, and Tina tried to calm her and say that they'd seen him at a parade on Sunday and that was their fallback plan. "We've both seen him standing with Kevin near a restaurant here in town, when a certain group of horses go by." Tina left out the part about Wyatt being killed by a horse, hoping that accident would never happen.

Tina was paying the restaurant bill when her phone rang. Seeing Jamey's number, she picked it up. "Are you okay?"

"I'm fine. How about you and Kai?" Their conversations started this way these days.

"His ear is better, I think. I've been worried about you."

"I'm watching a house that I'm pretty sure Kevin, Rose, and Wyatt are coming back to tonight. Rose's mother has this place up here and they have stuff in the fridge."

"Oh, thank God!" Annie's story was true. "I was worried that Annie and Diego had you tied up somewhere.

He chuckled. "No, but there's a long story about Annie, I'll have to tell you later. Didn't she call you to tell you where I was?"

"She did." Tina wouldn't reveal that she knew who Annie was. "So you're on a stakeout?"

"Yup, it's getting dark so I figured if they came up the road I'd either see the car lights, or a flashlight, or hear them. That's why I'm whispering. I gotta go, save the phone battery, but I'm planning on staying here as long as it takes. I'll call you when I have Wyatt tonight."

"Good luck. I love you."

"Me too. Kiss my son for me and tell him I'm bringing his cousin home tonight."

Tina hung up and realized she'd had her fingers crossed since the start of the call. She pushed the stroller out the restaurant door, feeling more confident that they'd soon have Wyatt in their hotel room. She'd contact the hotel's front desk and order an extra bed for tonight, or she'd sleep on the extra bed and let the little guy sleep with Jamey if he wanted. Walking with a spring in her step, Tina entered their hotel room and grabbed a chocolate bar from the mini fridge to celebrate. Then she'd order the extra bed, get Kai down for the night, and wait for Jamey's call to say that he had Wyatt in his arms.

When the call still hadn't come at midnight, Tina drifted off to sleep, waking shortly after to see someone standing at the foot of her bed. She gasped, then realized it must be Jamey. "Did you find him?" she asked sleepily.

"Not yet," her father's voice said. "But you will."

CHAPTER 16

The howler monkeys woke Jamey at dawn with their cacophony of rumbling vocals booming through the jungle canopy above. He'd fallen asleep, something he never usually did on a stakeout. He hadn't heard anything strange all night. Where the hell were Kevin and Rose? Looking around, he didn't see anything unusual. Didn't hear anything except the monkeys. Standing, Jamey realized that he'd probably slept two hours if it was almost six. The last time he'd checked his watch it was just after four and no one had turned up to sleep in the house.

Looking in the bedroom window he noticed the toy in the exact same position as yesterday. The threesome hadn't returned. Had they seen him in town and decided to not come back up Mombacho? Today was Hipica day and he'd failed Wyatt by not finding him before the accident. Now, everything had been left it to the last minute and Jamey would have to be at the dream site today to prevent Wyatt's death. If it even went down like the dream. Shit.

He walked out to the road and headed down the hill, listening to two different groups of Howler monkeys call out their dawn greetings. Crazy things. Placing a call to Tina he reported that he had no news and would be back at the hotel soon for a shower. Sounded like she'd had a terrible sleep too. Kai had slept through the night, which said a lot for the antibiotics he was taking, but Tina had been awake worrying all night. No dreaming, she said. "Just a quick normal about shooting heroin that was disturbing."

"It'll all be over today, Darlin'" he said. "And we can all have a good night's sleep tonight." How it would all play out, he wasn't sure. But he'd throw himself under that horse if he had to to save Wyatt today. He just hoped it didn't come to that.

The monkey's howling tapered off as he approached Diego and Annie's house. Should he wake them and say he'd take the truck down the mountain, wait for Diego to drive him, or start walking? The walk down would take him a good forty-five minutes to just get as far as the taxi stand at the highway. Then he heard something bang inside the house and both dogs ran outside barking at him.

"Hey doggies," he forgot their names. "It's me. Just me." Both dogs had wagging tails but continued to bark. The monkeys started howling again, joining the commotion.

Diego came around the side of the house looking like he'd slept in the bushes last night, himself. "Hey Jamey. Annie said you were up the road. Any luck?"

"Nope. Nothing. They didn't come back here."

Annie rounded the corner of the house, wearing a long robe, her hair loose, and carrying a cup of coffee. "Here, you must be exhausted and cold." She held out the coffee, her eyes not making contact.

As he took the mug from her, a flashback of his mother giving him hot cocoa when he was a child came and went. He'd fallen in the river out behind their house, it was cold outside, maybe autumn, and she'd reprimanded him for playing near the water, dragged him back to the house, took off his wet clothes, and after bundling him in two blankets, sat him down at the kitchen table for a cup of cocoa. "I have to get to town," Jamey said to Diego.

"I'll take you in a minute. Let me get dressed and finish my coffee." They walked back to the house, the dogs leading the way. Annie was silent but Jamey felt sadness and remorse from her. Had she been up all night thinking? Talking to Diego? Had her husband known about the other husband and family that was always waiting for her to show up some day in Carnation? He'd think about all that another day.

Today was the parade. Jamey had to get to the accident site and stand there all day if that's what it took. Right now, he had to ignore that his long lost, deadbeat mother had made him coffee in Nicaragua and was busy frying eggs and bacon at the kitchen stove for his breakfast. Diego got himself another cup of coffee and motioned for Jamey to follow him outside to the patio. They sat in two chairs by the pool and sipped their coffee. The morning air was chilly enough to warrant gratefulness for the hot drink.

"Annie and I were up all night talking." Diego's voice sounded as bad as he looked. "I didn't know that my wife had a family in Washington State."

Jamey didn't know what to say to this. Your wife is a deserter and a liar would be a start, but he was sitting in their chair, at their house, in a foreign country, relying on Diego's help.

"The fact that you are sitting here is God-damned amazing. I'm in shock, you can probably imagine." Diego's voice shook a little.

Jamey had to say something. "Me, too." He looked back at where Annie was plating breakfast. "I remember when she was my mother," he added, then thought better about opening up that wound.

"It must hurt. And here you are now. I'd say coincidence, but if you believe in six degrees of separation, the common denominator here is her friend, Jean. Mary Rose ended up here to find her mother, I suppose, and that's how you found us."

The town below was half illuminated by the morning sunshine rising in the sky behind the lake's edge. Even from here, you could see the glint off the cathedral in the city square. Tina would be awake now that he'd phoned her. Would he tell her who Annie was? Is? Probably. But today was too important to get distracted. He had to stay sharp.

"Food's ready if you boys are hungry," Annie said with two plates of bacon and eggs. She set the food on the table and disappeared inside the house, like a coward; like she wasn't his goddamned mother.

Diego reached for his fork, then stopped to speak. "I know you have a very important task to accomplish today and I'm going to help you, Jamey. But before we get going I want to tell you one thing." He looked inside the house. "My wife is a good person. I don't know what happened to make her leave four children and a husband, but knowing her as I do, it must've been something pretty powerful." He took a deep breath. "She isn't ready to tell me why. She did, however, tell me about your dreams and your visions.

So Annie did know.

"Must be hard to live with," Diego said.

Before he could censor his thoughts, the words slipped out. "Must've been too hard for your wife." Jamey set down his fork. "I'll wait for you by the car."

When Jamey arrived back at the hotel room, Tina didn't ask and Jamey didn't speak about Annie. She wanted to tell him she'd dreamed of her father at the end of the bed telling her that they would find Wyatt, but Jamey was distracted and headed straight for the shower. He needed to wash off the grime from hiding in the bushes all night. His legs were covered in bug bites, but nothing serious. His arms had fared better. Seeing her husband come out of the shower all muscular, wet, and naked, Tina's breath caught in her throat. He was a beautiful man. She hated to break the moment, but had to ask about Annie. It would be the elephant in the room until something was said. "So, Diego and Annie aren't child traffickers. That's good."

Jamey stepped into the same cargo shorts he'd been wearing for two weeks. "Nope. They probably aren't."

Tina stepped forward, put her head on her husband's shoulder, and wrapped her arms around his waist. He was damp and smelled like sandalwood soap. She loved this man so much it hurt sometimes. "Pops phoned yesterday to say that Annie phoned him to ask if you were here."

She waited for a response. All he said was, "Pops okay?'

"Surprised but okay."

"Good. Today, I have to find Wyatt," he said and walked away.

Tina followed, telling him about the dream, saying she thought she was awake but might not have been.

"Did you fully wake up?" he asked, stopping to put his watch on.

"No. That's why I think it was a dream. The memory was very faint this morning. But I think it actually was my father. Not a normal."

Jamey didn't know any more than she did but said it was possible.

Within ten minutes they met Diego and were combing the streets looking for the restaurant in Tina's dream with Annie. But she hadn't seen the place clearly and couldn't remember much except for Annie going in and coming out another door with Wyatt. Good thing Jamey had told Diego about the dream premonition or looking for a specific restaurant would be hard to explain.

It was getting difficult to maneuver the traffic and soon it was near impossible to drive around Granada. With bumper-to-bumper cars and trucks, it was faster to walk. Many roads had been closed off for the celebration. Diego said that the center of town would be like a rat's nest and he was right. A rat's nest with a party atmosphere.

Within an hour, Granada was buzzing with preparations for the day. Stages were being set up, banners hung, garlands of flags being strung between shops, trees, across narrow streets. Apparently, the road from Managua was jammed too, everyone arriving for Granada's big day of honoring its patron saint. If it was hard to find someone in this town before, Tina imagined it was going to be almost impossible once all the out of town people arrived and started clogging up the streets. At ten o'clock, the traffic was ridiculous, and the noise was building to match the energy of the town.

At a street corner, Jamey helped lift Kai's stroller off the curb and Tina realized how much she was slowing Jamey and Diego's search. "Am I helping or hindering you guys?" She looked at Jamey as his keen eyes scanned the crowd ahead.

"Probably hindering now," he said.

The frantic feeling of the celebration escalated with every hour and as a new mother, Tina was genuinely frightened for the safety of her baby. "Maybe I should go back to the hotel." The stage beside them played extremely loud taped trumpet music and it was hard to hear. Kai started crying, startled by the music.

"That might be a good idea," Jamey said.

"I can watch from the balcony, phone you if I see them," she added.

Diego laid his hand on Tina's arm and leaned in to them. "Do these dreams always come true?"

Jamey had told him about Annie taking Wyatt out of the café.

She shrugged.

"Because the dream where you saw Annie doesn't sound right. My wife wouldn't come to town on hipica day for anything. She rarely comes off Mombacho anyhow. Hates it down here. Believe me, she won't be looking for Wyatt in a restaurant today." He looked at Tina sympathetically. "Why don't you take the baby to my house and stay with Annie. We'll come up with the boy later."

"That's a better idea. Get out of town, avoid all this." Jamey added.

She knew this was what he wanted. "That might be best." Her baby continued to cry in her arms. She tried jiggling him.

"I'll run her up to the house." Diego told Jamey. He signaled to Tina to follow him to the truck that he'd strategically parked on the outskirts of the congestion, pointed towards Mombacho.

Diego grabbed the stroller and led the way while she carried Kai. Once in the truck they drove out of the core of town and broke free of the traffic. Near the cemetery, the traffic thinned out on their side, the lane leaving town. "How will you ever get back here?" Tina asked.

"Oh I have a secret route. Don't worry about me. These people," he pointed to the cars lined up to enter Granada, "are coming from other towns, but I'll make a wide circle and come in along the lake." He pointed to his brain and nodded.

At the Mombacho house, Tina settled in to a chair by the pool to nurse Kai. Diego had only dropped her off and turned around again. Tina had forgotten the stroller and car seat in her hurry to let Diego get back to town. Annie hadn't shown her face yet, but soft music played from inside the house and her truck was in the garage. As soon as Kai got comfortable, he fell asleep. She pulled him off the boob and lowered her T-shirt. Staring at the town of Granada below, Tina hoped that Jamey would find Wyatt today, or if not, at least be able to stop the accident from happening somehow. The town was the size of her hand when she spread her fingers and she wondered if a telescope would afford her any view of the parade. She hadn't seen one. She still believed that Annie would take Wyatt by the hand from a restaurant in Granada, but it might be any day if the restaurant kept their decorations. She'd assumed the scene took place on hipica day, but maybe it happened tomorrow. Or maybe Jamey would change the future by intercepting the horse today and it would never happen.

When Annie came through the house and found Tina on the patio, she looked older than two days ago. With what was going on, Tina doubted Annie had had a good night's sleep. What mother could live with the knowledge that she'd walked out on her children? Jamey had said that Annie and Diego were up talking most of the night.

As a mother, Tina had to think that seeing Jamey this week had been horribly traumatic for Annie. And telling her husband that she'd been living a lie with him. That she had a husband and four children who didn't have a clue what happened to their mother. Anyone who did that had problems.

"Here I am again. With my baby," Tina said. Then she realized that her baby was Annie's biological grandchild. Had the woman thought of that? But Annie's hesitance two days earlier to hold the baby or even look at him, hadn't been because she worried he was her grandchild. This was before she'd seen Jamey, phoned Pops, knew their last name, wasn't it? Maybe she did not like children. Why then would she give birth to four of them if she wasn't cut out for motherhood?

Tina smiled tentatively as Annie plopped down in the other chair.

"I'm glad to see you again," Annie said. Her smile today was different, almost embarrassed.

"Me too. I heard the news about you and Jamey." Tina wanted so much to give her a chance to talk, but only if she wanted.

Annie looked at her lap. "It was quite a shock after all this time."

"I can't imagine." Tina wasn't sure what to say in case they left here tomorrow, never to be seen by this woman again. "I hope you and Jamey get a chance to talk after all this."

Tears fell to Annie's lap. "Me too. I can see how he hates me and I don't blame him. They must all hate me. Well, the boys anyhow. Jenny was too little to remember me, at least." Annie wiped her face with her shirtsleeve. "I'm sorry Tina. I like you, but I can't invest anything in you or Jamey, in case he never forgives me."

Tina understood. She nodded. "Can I put Kai in the guest room again? I think this will be a big nap."

"Of course, you can." Her head tilted as she studied the baby in Tina's arms. "I used to like children, you know. But it's too painful." Annie got out of the chair and disappeared inside the house. If she'd been good with babies, Tina might have considered leaving Kai with the woman and going with Diego back to town to search, but Annie wasn't trustworthy and showed no grandmotherly tendencies. Besides, Kai still needed her breast milk.

Staying out of this new situation was going to be difficult. If Jamey ever wanted the story, if there was one, it was for him to ask. She took Kai to the guest room and laid him between the pillows that she braced under the sheets to keep them from shifting. Away from the wall, even though she'd seen the dead spider. Annie was nowhere to be seen when Tina came out of the guest room. She was probably back in her studio, painting. The dogs were gone too. She settled with a magazine in the chair by the pool and alternated between reading an article on nutrition and glancing at the town below the volcano. From here, she couldn't tell that Granada was jumping with activity, music, horses, and celebration. It looked exactly as it had two days ago, like a fairytale town on a huge lake with pointy volcanoes in the distance. It was noon, Tina was hungry. She didn't want to go digging around in some woman's cupboards after Annie's remark about not wanting to invest anything in the relationship if Jamey decided against forgiving her. Now she felt unwelcome. An intrusion.

It was a bad idea to even come here. She should have stayed in town.

***

When Jamey found a quiet spot amongst the madness, he opened his phone to call Pops. When his father picked up, Jamey didn't know exactly what to say. "Tina told me you know she's here."

"She called."

"You okay?"

"Surprised, but doing fine. How about you, Son?"

"I'm angry, but I can't really deal with Mom today. I'm looking for Wyatt." It felt strange to call anyone Mom.

"That's right. You find that little boy."

"Pops, did you know a Jean person who was Mom's friend?"

"Briefly. But she's long gone. She left the area when you were probably ten or eleven. Is she there?"

"She's Rose's mother."

"You don't say. Well, at the time of your mother's disappearance, she seemed as surprised as me." He sighed. "That was so long ago, Son. But I'll call around, see if I can turn up anything." Pops was at Carrie's house, waiting. Everyone was there, hoping, waiting for the phone call from Jamey to say he'd found Wyatt.

"If you can. I asked Annie to see if she could get in touch with Jean, but apparently she's travelling today."

"How's she look?" Pops asked.

"Sad." Jamey didn't need to ask who. "And sorry."

Pops fell silent.

Jamey added. "I'm counting on her coming through today, finding Jean, but it's hard to trust her."

"I'm sure, but I don't think she's in on taking Wyatt, if that's what you mean."

They hung up and Jamey stood leaning against the brick building. It was still a possibility that Annie was tied to this somehow. At the very least, Jamey knew that she didn't want her friend Jean implicated, or even involved. Before he'd left that morning to come down the mountain, he'd told her flat out that she owed him this. "Find Jean. Get a phone number for Mary Rose. Get Jean to convince Rose to give herself up, or when I find them, it won't be nice." His words probably scared Annie, but he didn't care. It was the truth.

When Diego returned to town he helped Jamey get a bunch of disposable phones, buy minutes and recruit teenage boys to be on the lookout for Kevin, Rose, and Wyatt. There would be a nice reward for anyone who led him to the threesome. The parade wasn't scheduled to begin for hours. He had time to find them before the accident, but with the crowds and congestion, the search was slow. He could've used Tina's sharp eyes out here, but that wasn't going to happen. He and Diego split up and after an hour, when Jamey's phone rang, his first thought was that he didn't recognize the number. It was local.

"Hello?'

The boy spoke in rapid Spanish and Jamey had to tell him to slow down. Soon, it became clear that the boy had just seen the family in front of the Mombacho Cigar Shop, heading towards the cathedral.

"Follow them." Jamey asked the boy what they were wearing, got a fairly good description, and said he was on his way.

Racing through the crowd, he stuck to the center of the road where it was possible to move. Only four blocks from the Cathedral, it was slow going. If he was lucky, his arrival at the Cathedral steps would coincide with Kevin's arrival. According to the boy, Kevin wore a dark cap, Rose had black hair like they'd been told, and wore a blue dress and sun hat. The little boy was in shorts and a white T-shirt. Jamey could see the top of the cathedral now. Yellow with white trim, a bell on top of the spire. He wound his way through the park, which looked like a clearer path than the streets.

This was it.

He could feel it.

Was it just hope or was it intuition? Wyatt was close. Not seeing them on the park side of the cathedral, he ran around the block to the backside of the church, the direction they'd supposedly come from. A stage had been set up and a group of teen girls in traditional Nicaraguan costumes were dancing to the music on stage.

Jamey ran up the cathedral steps and scanned the crowd, swallowing a desire to yell out Wyatt's name. "Where are you, Kevin?" he whispered. First, he inventoried the edges of the scene, people disappearing around corners, then visually moved in. People were everywhere. It was hard to see an individual. Watching for less than a minute, he frantically searched for what looked like a mom, dad, and a seven-year-old. Mariachi-style music played in the background and a dog barked near him. He didn't see the threesome. Or even a twosome. Next, he was off the steps, running around the crowd, trying to pick out a black cap, a Caucasian child and a woman in a blue dress. Was the teen still following? Would he call again? Where the hell were they? Possibly in a store. They might still be wandering their way towards the cathedral. Jamey ran back up the steps and scanned the sea of people in front of him. After another minute, he wondered if they'd turned around, headed back towards the lake. His heart beat wildly against his ribs. No longer was there a definite feeling that Wyatt was close. He hoped he was wrong.

He'd call the kid.

Then someone grabbed his shirt and Jamey looked to see a local kid about thirteen, motioning for him to follow. "Where?" he asked as he ran.

The boy pointed and continued running through the crowd and down an alleyway. Six streets over and out of the hub of the festival, they ended up at a café, much like the one from Tina's dream. Jamey had hope. "Wait here," he motioned.

In the café, the festivities were in full force. People were drinking beer, singing, eating. Every table and inch of floor space was filled with revelers, like a London pub on a Friday. Music blared from speakers in the room's corner. He didn't see Kevin. Luckily, he was tall enough to see over most people. He walked to the next room which was an open courtyard with tables around the edges. Jamey quickly walked the square, searching for any combination of the three. The center of the room was filled with trees and plants. "Is there a back door," he asked a passing waiter.

The man shook his head. "Only through the kitchen," he said, pointing behind him.

Jamey watched another waiter duck into the kitchen, and through the open door noticed a hub of activity in a steamy room. He followed. Cooks grilled in one corner, two women chopped on a huge cutting board and several others lined up plates at a counter. The door at the back of the room led outside and Jamey ran through the kitchen, sliding out the door before anyone could tell him to leave. The alleyway was deserted except for two dogs who looked like they were waiting for a handout. He chose to go right and sprinted down the alley to the end. He ended up back near the doorway where the boy still waited for him, hands in pockets. Seeing Jamey run around the corner, he looked confused. "Nada?" he asked.

Jamey shook his head, looked around, and then ran down the alley the other way. Coming out on a quiet street, he searched the area, walking around looking inside doorways, then when he concluded this was the wrong direction, ran back to the teen waiting at the door to the restaurant. One look from Jamey and the boy shrugged. "I saw them go in here," he said in Spanish.

Jamey wasn't sure if the boy was telling the truth, but it fit Tina's description of the restaurant. He couldn't afford to ignore this one clue. His only clue today. He told the kid he'd be right back and did another look inside, including the one bathroom for customers. They were nowhere to be found. He waited for almost five minutes before he went outside to ask the kid if they came out while he was inside. No. Reaching inside his pocket, Jamey pulled out some cordobas and paid the boy, but asked him to stay. If he saw the people, he was to call again and he'd make double the money if he led Jamey to them. The boy nodded and seated himself on a cement slab near the doorway.

If this was the restaurant where Annie found Wyatt in the dream, the kid might still call. Trouble was that the hipica would start in two hours and he didn't want to take any chances by not being at the accident site. His plan had always been to stake out the area and wait there for hours. God damn it. He could be close, but he had to get to the other side of town.

***

Tina waited for Jamey to call. Annie was gone. Shut up in her studio, Tina guessed. Kai woke only an hour after he fell asleep which was too soon. He seemed happy enough when she took him out to the couch. He wanted to nurse again so Tina fed him and then after a good burp that sounded more like a belch, they played peek-a-boo. Hearing the studio door close, Tina picked him up to walk around the side of the house, see what Annie was doing. With his chubby warmth in her arms, they searched for monkeys in the trees above them, but it was too early. Not sunset.

Annie came around the corner with a broom in her hands. "Help yourself to anything to eat or drink, Tina. I'm just working in my studio."

"We're fine. Thanks. I might grab a snack." She didn't want Annie to feel she had to entertain Tina and Kai, even if they were her daughter-in-law and grandson. The woman did not want to talk. Had she wanted conversation, she'd have shared the afternoon with Tina. As it was, she was obviously avoiding them. By now, Tina's tummy was growling loud enough to compete with the howler monkeys in another few hours.

"There's fresh banana bread in the fridge." Annie paused, as if contemplating whether to say more, then turned and went down the path to her studio. When Tina heard the studio door close, she went to the kitchen to find food. With a baby in her arms, she was only able to grab a slice of the bread and a chunk of cheese. She wouldn't set Kai on the floor. Not after seeing how fast that Banana Spider could go. There was nothing but beer, sprite, and water to drink that wouldn't necessitate two arms to pour, so she grabbed a bottle of water and stuck it in her cargo pants pocket and walked into the living room.

According to Jamey, the hipica started around six. Tina was hoping they'd have Wyatt safe by eight pm. What would they do if Wyatt never showed up at the site? Would Jamey stand there all night, waiting? He'd call, at least, to let her know what was going on. The wait was torturous but she imagined Jamey was in a worse state in Granada if he hadn't seen Wyatt yet. If her husband was able to prevent the accident today and grab Wyatt, what would happen to Kevin and Rose? Jamey wouldn't let them get away with this. He was a straight up guy, former police officer who believed in justice and incarceration for people who didn't follow the rules. It wouldn't be unlike Jamey to get Wyatt on the plane home and then take off after the other two. And he'd catch them, but then what? They were in a foreign country. Jamey couldn't slap handcuffs on Kevin and Rose to take them back to America.

And what did Carrie want? Jamey had kept Carrie and Chris informed with phone calls every day, sometimes twice a day. They'd be frantic with this waiting. Tina could only imagine the tension at Carrie and Chris's house today, even without knowing that Wyatt was at risk of losing his life under a giant horse.

CHAPTER 17

Jamey's headache was screaming against his skull. He'd gladly take some meds to cut the pain, but didn't want to go back to the hotel or stop at a store. The sun was dropping in the sky and the hipica would begin soon. After hours of scanning the crowds, his eyes were almost crossed. Now he was planted at the accident site, waiting. Watching. He'd tried to report in to Tina, just now, but he couldn't get a line out. Then he'd phoned Diego who was at his office charging his phone.

"The cell service isn't good now with so many people in town using their phones," Diego warned. "As soon as I get my phone charged, I'll come to you. I'll be there before the parade starts."

Diego was a good guy. Thoughts that this was his mother's new husband, maybe the person she left them for, decades ago, crept into Jamey's head, but he ignored them. He didn't even want to consider how Pops had been crushed when his wife left him. Jamey would only deal with that when Wyatt was safe.

With time before the parade began, he took a moment to buy food from a street vendor. It smelled good, and even though he wasn't sure what he was buying, he handed over the money. He was handed something wrapped in a banana leaf—pork, he guessed, and some boiled vegetable in a sauce that was actually very tasty. He bought seconds and a bottle of water.

As he stood eating his food, Jamey looked up at the volcano looming in the distance and wondered what Tina was doing. He hoped, for her sake, Annie was good company and Kai's ear was doing better. He couldn't wait for this ordeal to be over for Wyatt's sake, and so he could get back to normal life with his wife and son.

From the moment he'd laid eyes on Kai, maybe even before his son's debut in that Maui Memorial Hospital delivery room, Jamey loved his child with a fierceness he didn't know he'd had. Or didn't remember he'd had. Kai was his third child, but his daughters were approaching their teen years, and he'd had time to forget the intensity of what he'd felt when they were born. He did recall protectiveness consumed him for the first years. Almost to the point of obsession. Carrie had felt it too, but he had to think that a father was built with this ingrained need to keep the monsters from the door. The mother was the nurturer. Or was supposed to be. For some reason Annie had lost that. Strange thing was, he clearly remembered sitting on her lap, being read to, burying his face in her neck, and being hugged back. He'd clung to those memories when she left. And for years after her departure, Jamey believed that she'd loved him and his siblings. He'd gone into her closet that first week and took a soft sweater that smelled like her perfume. He'd slept with it until Gavin took it away and said James better get used to life without a mother. The idea that his mother had planned a departure and walked away from him was almost too much for Jamey to admit in those days, instead preferring to think that she was taken from him. Or that she died and couldn't come back to her children. And here she was, his beloved mother, who had gone off to marry another man and be a painter in the cloud forest of Mombacho Volcano while her children continued to ask themselves why their mother didn't love them enough to stay. *God damned selfish woman.*

When this was over, he was getting as far away from Nicaragua as possible. He'd have to tell his siblings he found her. They had a right to know. Then he'd try to forget her.

Just then, the crowd noise intensified and Jamey realized the hipica was about to begin. It was over two hours late, something Diego said was common, but now he could see horses down the street, coming his way. He stood firm, knowing the next hour was crucial.

***

By the time Tina finished walking down the driveway and back with Kai, her arms were tired. She set him in the corner of the couch and alternated between playing with her baby and staring at her phone, willing it to ring. The sun was low in the sky and down the mountain, the hipica would be underway. Diego said it went on for hours. When Kai's mood turned sour and his little face scrunched up in a wail, she changed his wet diaper and took him outside again.

Monkeys were arriving in the trees above the house. So far, only a few, but they helped to distract him. Surely it wasn't time to eat again. She'd brought a few jars of baby food, but he'd gobbled them up earlier. The antibiotics were making him hungry. All she had now was breast milk. And mashed bananas. When the monkeys lost their attraction, Kai resumed crying. At least he wasn't tugging on his ear anymore. He arched his back and screamed. She felt his diaper but it was still dry so she sat in a patio chair and positioned him for nursing. He latched on fiercely and Tina stroked his little head as he hummed.

By the time the monkeys were settled in the trees and the calling began, Kai was fast asleep on Tina's second breast and making some noises himself. The howling was almost deafening, and when Tina watched a big plop of monkey poop fall next to her chair, she took her baby in to the guest room. She closed the doors and windows until the howling stopped, just to make sure he fell off into a deep sleep. Jamey often said Kai slept like the dead, an expression she wasn't fond of as a new mother.

Once she had Kai snuggled into the bed, she pulled the guest room door closed, and sat on the couch, making a mental note to check on him in another ten minutes. He was off schedule, but obviously tired, probably still affected by the antibiotics. She kept her phone close in case Jamey called. The sound of a truck starting up outside had Tina wondering if Annie was going somewhere. She wandered around the side of the house just in time to see Annie's Chevy truck disappear down the driveway. The dogs stood watching until there was no sign of the vehicle, then turned and wandered back to the house, obviously used to being left. Had Annie gone somewhere? Tina walked to the studio, knocked on the door and when no one answered, she went inside. "Annie?" The small cottage was empty of people, but there on the easel was a shockingly beautiful portrait of Jamey's face. Still wet.

Tina stared at the painting of her husband. This is what Annie had been doing all day. Painting a portrait from memory of her youngest son. The way he looked now, as a forty-year-old man. The expression she'd caught on canvas was a determined one, his mouth set in a grim line, but his eyes were soft and kind, as always. Probably the exact way he looked at Annie. Tina took a deep breath and hoped that this discovery between mother and son didn't end badly for either. The room smelled of paint. The two dogs drank from a bowl sitting in the corner on a matt that said "Good Dog". The rendition of Jamey's face was lovely. It really was, and Tina imagined that Annie wanted to get the visage on paper before he left and she forgot what her grown son looked like. Annie obviously cared or wouldn't have spent the day in the studio painting. Tina pulled the door closed behind her and walked along the lighted stone path, back to the house, distracted by thoughts of a mother and her son.

It got dark quickly here. The monkeys were all but finished their nightly noise and Tina marveled at what a good sleeper Kai was. He'd been trained well on Maui with the noisy birds next door and the downshifting sugar cane trucks on the highway behind the house.

She listened at the guest room door but heard nothing. Still asleep. In the kitchen Tina grabbed another water bottle from the fridge, and then made herself a plate of food with potato salad, pickles and chicken salad that Annie had offered earlier. Standing at the refrigerator, eating, and reading the notices for poetry readings and art exhibits, Tina wondered about Diego and Annie's life on the mountain. It certainly was a remote place to hide if privacy was what you wanted. After she finished eating, she checked to make sure her phone had a charge and put it back in her pocket. Then, she remembered that the guest room doors and windows were shut. The room might be warm.

As she approached the door, a feeling of dread hit her like a wet towel across her face. Something was wrong. She entered the dark room and crept over to the bed. Leaning over the pillow barricade, she looked down to see Kai's sleeping area empty. Feeling around she found only pillows. She frantically flicked on the light.

Kai was gone.

Her heart flew to her mouth. The floor was clear, the room empty of anyone besides her. The attached bathroom was empty but then she noticed the low window was wide open. A whimper escaped her mouth. She looked out the bathroom window to see a wooden chair with a caned back perched just underneath. It would be easy for someone to step in through the window and land on the bathroom floor. And back out again.

"Who's there?" she shouted. She flew out the bathroom window and rounded the house, adrenaline pumping through her body. "Bring back my baby!" she yelled. Then she remembered the truck leaving. "Annie!" It had to be Annie. That woman was sick in the head. First she left a family of four children, then she stole a baby. Had she driven off with Kai? Tina ran the length of the house. "Annie, bring back my baby!" she said running. What the hell was Annie's cell phone number? Calling Diego's number proved fruitless. The lines were busy.

With nothing else to do, Tina stood at the top of the driveway and screamed, "Bring him back, Annie or I'll kill your dogs and set your house on fire!"

CHAPTER 18

The hipica had begun. Horses dressed in elaborate finery and ribbons pranced along the route, stopping to high step at every corner. Music blared and fireworks shot off every minute.

Jamey intently watched the horses advance, on high alert for the speckled giant that would fall in front of the juice bar. But his attention was also focused on the crowd. Namely, looking for Kevin and a small child holding his hand.

Groups of horses advanced until finally Jamey located the grey-speckled horse down the line. From what he could see, the beast with the long mane and tail did not have a bloodied hoof. Yet. That happened closer to the juice bar. Jamey scanned the crowd again, looking for Kevin's black cap. He had to be here, somewhere. Or coming this way. Unless the future had been changed.

There were plenty of kids lining the parade route but none were Wyatt. Then his gaze locked on the old lady who'd go down with Wyatt. A young man was helping her to walk to the curb to view the horses.

The horses were getting closer, the speckled horse only thirty feet away. His hoof was still unblemished, but when Jamey looked away to check if Wyatt and Kevin had arrived, and then looked back, the hoof was bloody. Where was Kevin? By now they should be moving in to watch. Kevin would soon turn away to buy a beer. The beer cart was where he'd seen it, behind him by the juice bar, but there was no sign of the two in the crowd. At this point in the dream, Jamey was sure they were already at the curb.

His phone rang. He was going to ignore it but it could be one of the boys with a phone, having spotted them somewhere else along the route. A quick glance at the phone told him it was Tina. She wouldn't call unless it was important. "I can't talk."

"Kai's gone. He's missing," she shouted. "I think Annie might have him. I put Kai down for a nap, and when I checked on him, he was gone. I watched Annie drive off earlier." Her voice came out like ragged sobs.

Jamey's heart jumped in his chest. "Did you check the property? Her studio?"

"Yes, yes. Her truck drove off and she's not here. Or Kai. You need to find her. Or get up here." Tina's cries filled the phone line.

The horse was ten feet away. The old woman beside him was smiling and clapping. Still no sign of Wyatt, or Kevin. Soon the horse would fall. "I'll be right there. Annie won't hurt him. If she even has him." He didn't know why she'd take the baby. "Can monkeys pick up sixteen pounds?" Maybe it was possible.

There were only seconds remaining before the horse went down. "Hang on." He stuck the phone in his pocket, still connected, and ran over to the horse. When the firework went off on the other side of the street and the black horse lurched sideways, he had a hold of the bridle. The rider jumped off his horse, yelling at Jamey.

"Your horse is bleeding," Jamey said in Spanish to the man. "Blood!" Jamey yelled, pulling the horse farther to the center of the road, away from the old woman, before he let go. The horse now stood still with his leg bent, blood dripping to the pavement.

Two drunk men rushed in ripe for a fight, their fists up, yelling at Jamey to leave the horse alone. Jamey backed up and took off through the crowd, hoping no one was following him. A block later, he brought the phone to his ear. "Stay on the line" he said, then fumbled, and the phone fell to the road and fell apart. Shit. Couldn't stop. He had to keep going. Get up the mountain to Tina.

He dodged people, zigzagging through the crowd, thoughts firing in his brain as he ran. Why would Annie take the baby? Did she think Tina had gone somewhere? Where the hell would she take him?

If something sinister was going on, Jamey needed to put everything he had into finding Kai. The horse hadn't fallen on Wyatt and for now, the abducted boy was safe.

***

"Jamey?!" Her husband hadn't responded. Tina hung up and looked around Diego and Annie's property, searching for anything that might lead to finding Kai. Whoever took her baby would know it was wrong to kidnap a child so calling out to bring him back was probably fruitless.

Jamey had suggested a monkey might have Kai, and as unlikely as that seemed, she had to look. She turned on all the lights, including the ones for the outside patio and raced out to scan the trees. These monkeys weren't big enough to carry a large baby, were they? The thought was ridiculous, but still concerning. If they had him in the tree and dropped him... She called into the trees. "Kai?" knowing no one would answer.

She'd seen a wicker basket full of headlamps in the kitchen. Annie had said that the power went out regularly on Mombacho. Tina rushed into the kitchen, put on a headlamp, grabbed the rest and ran out to the trees. Nothing except monkeys stared back at her. Kai would be crying if the monkeys had him, wouldn't he? Unless he couldn't cry. She shone the flashlights around the jungle floor under the trees, looking for a body, praying she would find nothing unusual.

Someone put a chair at the window to make it easier to get in without being detected. Not monkeys. And, if Annie didn't take him, like Jamey said, then who? Then she remembered two things. The housekeeper the other day had held Kai lovingly. Was it possible she came to get him? And, the second thing was, where the heck were the dogs? She hadn't heard or seen them in twenty minutes. She ran up the path to the studio and found both Cisco and Chile sleeping on the couch. Shit! She'd left the watch dogs shut inside while someone roamed the property. Maybe Rose took him. She wanted a baby but was in town. In the premonition, only Wyatt and Kevin attended the hipica.

Anyone who thought it was perfectly allowable to kidnap a seven-year-old, wouldn't blink at the thought of stealing someone else's baby. The verification came to her immediately, like her instincts received a confirmation telegram. Rose had him, and he was not safe. Did Rose intend to hurt the baby? Tina sprinted back to the kitchen for a butcher knife. If she was going running around on the mountain looking for Rose, she wanted a weapon.

***

Jamey burst through the door of Granada Realty to see a receptionist seated at the front desk. "Where's Diego?" he asked breathlessly.

The woman shrugged. "He left for the day."

"Can I use your phone?" Jamey picked up the telephone and dialed Diego's number, which he'd memorized by now. He hoped that Diego wasn't in on this if Annie took the baby.

"Granada Realty, Diego Ramirez."

"Diego, where's Annie? Someone took Kai from the house. Tina thinks it was her."

"Annie is with me. No baby. Oh Dios. Where are you?"

"At your office. Where are you?'

"In the truck. Wyatt's with us."

Oh, thank God.

"Run three blocks along the street, away from the park. That's the closest we can get. We'll meet you there."

Jamey hung up, shot out the door, and started running. Three blocks down, Annie's truck pulled around the corner. The vehicle stopped abruptly and Jamey hopped in the passenger seat beside Annie. In the backseat Wyatt grinned, his eyes big, his smile bigger. Diego sat beside the boy.

"Jamey!" he said trying to get out of his seat belt.

"Stay in the belt, Slugger." Jamey turned to Annie. "How fast can you get out of town and up that mountain?"

"Just watch me," she said, pulling a U turn and speeding down the street away from the hipica.

Jamey turned to Diego and Wyatt. "Long time, no see, Slugger. How's life?"

"Oh, my name is Luke now," the little boy rolled his eyes. "Kevin said so."

"Cool name." Jamey glanced at Diego. "Where did you find him?" Jamey reached for Annie's phone. "Mind?"

Diego nodded towards Annie. "Granada Café."

"Kevin was mad she took me." Wyatt pointed at Annie. "Kevin will be worried so you need to call him."

"Okay, I will." Jamey dialed Tina's number.

Wyatt tapped his shoulder. "Where's Mama and Daddy?"

"They're coming, soon. For now, you're with me." Jamey smiled at Wyatt and ruffled his shaved head. So, Annie had marched into that restaurant and found Wyatt, just like in Tina's dream. Tina's phone rang and rang. "How did you know where to find Wyatt?" he asked Annie.

Annie pulled onto the main road out of town. "Jean called. Said Mary Rose and Kevin had taken an apartment behind the Café. Mary Rose didn't like Mombacho. Jean made a few calls and found out that Kevin and Wyatt were having lunch at the café. I tried to call you two but no luck, so I came down."

Jamey kept hanging up and dialing Tina's number. "Diego, can you call Wyatt's Mama?" He dictated the number and then Diego put the phone on speaker.

Carrie picked up on the first ring. "Hello?"

"I'm looking at your son right now." Jamey said. "He's fine." *Shit. Where was Tina?*

"Oh God. Put him on the phone." Carrie sounded like she'd been holding her breath for weeks. "Jamey has Wyatt," she said, probably to a crowd of people beside her.

Diego took the phone off speaker and handed it to the little guy.

"Do you think Rose is on Mombacho?" Jamey looked between Diego and Annie.

"She is. Jean told me." Annie nodded her head.

Wyatt spoke happily from the backseat to his mother. "When are you and Daddy coming for the big birthday party? Kevin promised," he said.

Finally, Tina picked up. "Who is this?" her voice sounded haunted.

"It's me, Honey. Are you okay?"

"I think Rose took him."

"We're on our way."

"I got a feeling."

"She won't hurt him. Remember, she wants a baby. If she took Kai, she'll be careful with him. Keep that in mind."

"I think she's going for payback. I feel it."

Shit. "Don't do anything. We're close. Rose wouldn't hurt a baby."

"I think she would."

"We just passed the cemetery," he said. "I'm watching the road for them."

"I'm going to get my child." Tina's voice was shaky like she was running.

"Wait for me. Don't go running around the mountain. She might have a gun."

The line went dead.

***

Diego and Annie seemed like the type of people who'd have a gun and lucky for her, they did. Tina checked the handgun's safety and left to find the woman who'd stolen her baby. As she raced up the road, she remembered what Mr. Takeshimi, her Lahaina neighbor, used to say. 'Fall seven times, Get up eight.'

Fucking eh.

She'd not only get up, but deal with the psycho who pushed her down. Retribution was in order but only when she knew Kai was safe. That was the first priority.

Navigating the folds of the road, she let the dogs lead the way. Hopefully they knew the house and had accompanied Annie this way enough to think they were going again. How stealthy could she be with dogs? It didn't matter. If Rose was there, she'd march in and take back her baby. She wasn't afraid to use the gun as long as Kai wasn't harmed. If Rose had a gun, at least Tina had the advantage of surprise. If she had to shoot that bitch through the heart to get Kai, she would.

The dogs ran off the path after something in the brush, and when Tina came to a fork in the road, she chose to go left and soon came across a short driveway leading to a dark house. It was steep going and her breath was ragged as she approached. The house was shut up tight, no residents, and wasn't the rustic cottage Jamey had described on the phone. Annie's dogs were nowhere in sight. She returned to the road and took the other fork, listening for any hint of a baby crying. The stillness on Mombacho was chilling until the dogs crashed through the underbrush, panting and happy. Passing two turnoffs, she followed the dogs to a pullout off the main road. A footpath led in to the jungle and far off, she saw a faint light, like a lantern. This was it! Her legs burned, but she didn't slow down. Had Rose walked all this way with Kai in her arms?

With her phone and headlamp turned off, Tina stole along the trail quietly, using only the faint light from the moon to see the edges of the path. Jamey had described the house as a rugged structure without electricity, and a porch framing three sides. This was it.

She heard the crack of a door closing up ahead. Then Kai cried into the night. *Oh, thank God. He's alive!* Until that moment, she'd worried that the reason she hadn't heard his cry was her most horrible nightmare. Her instinct was to sink to the path in relief. Instead she continued on, spurred by revenge. These next few moments were crucial. If Kai was safe, she had to play this smart and choose her moment. She crept along the path, and once closer to the house, noticed that the place was partially illuminated by lanterns. There was a light perched on the veranda railing and another in what looked like the main room. She moved up behind the house, behind an out building. Kai cried softly like he hadn't fully woken, and Tina heard Rose speak. "There, there, my little boy. Mommy's here."

Her instincts told her to rush at the house, find Rose, and scream at her that she was not the mother. Instead, she watched. After a minute, when it looked like no one was moving inside, she left the shed and crossed to the back of the house. Someone sang softly inside the back room and Tina crept to the window and peeked in.

Rose lay on the queen-sized bed on her side, her back to the window. From what Tina could see, it looked like Kai was sleeping in Rose's arms. The dogs barked down the path and Rose disengaged from the baby, sat up, and cocked her head to listen. "What was that?" she whispered. Turning back, she carefully gathered Kai in her arms, blanket and all, pulled him in to her chest and left the room.

Tina fingered the gun in her pocket and considered getting it out and ready. She inched along the far side of the house and peeked around the corner. Rose stood on the far edge of the porch, staring off into the jungle. Maybe waiting for dogs to appear. Wearing a tank top and dark shorts, Rose now had cropped, dark hair. From the back, she looked like any new mother-- holding her child, swaying, cooing to the baby. She looked surprisingly normal for someone who'd just abducted a baby. But if you knew Rose, you'd also know how much she loved her long, blonde tresses. Her hair now looked like the monkeys had hacked it off. This new ragged haircut was indication enough that something was terribly wrong with this woman.

Satisfied that nothing was amiss, Rose settled into a deck chair and spoke to the sleeping baby and Tina strained to hear the words. "Daddy is going to give Luke back. That's okay. Luke talks too much about his other family."

From her vantage spot, Tina couldn't see Kai in that bundle, but it sure looked like Rose held a baby. Tina listened. Some words were unintelligible.

"I can't believe I heard you cry. I was just walking up the road." She gazed down at the baby with such love that Tina almost shot her right then and there. "I won't ever hurt you," Rose said, softly. Then her voice changed, like she'd flipped a switch. "He can't make me kill you," she whispered defiantly. "Not when I've waited so long." She chuckled. "Oh no."

Kill? From her crouch, Tina had a good view of Rose's face and her new expression was disturbingly vacant.

Rose stared out into the darkness. "He can't control me."

Who the hell was Rose talking about? Kevin? Did Kevin want her to kill a baby? Or maybe Rose had voices in her head.

Rose looked down at the bundle and when she kissed his head, Tina caught sight of Kai when the blanket slipped. "I thought I lost you, sweet Christian."

After hearing the word kill, Tina was ready to storm the place, even though Rose didn't seem to have a weapon. Trouble was that Rose was near the deck's edge where it dropped off, and if there was any chance she might throw the child over, Tina had to wait. She held her breath watching, hoping Kai was safe, for now.

Rose got up from the chair, headed back to the bedroom, and Tina followed along the outside of the house to the bedroom window at the back. Rose laid the baby on the bed, kissed him and went to the kitchen to retrieve her phone. Kai needed pillows to keep from rolling on to the floor. Stupid bitch. Then Rose came back and laid down with Kai, stroking his head and kissing him. But when Rose's phone rang, Tina used the noise to slink along the side of the house and got ready to storm the bedroom.

"No, Kev. It's okay," Rose said. "Let her have him. My mother probably told her to take Luke. But it's okay because I have our baby. I heard him crying and knew." There was a pause. "He was at Annie's house, which is strange. Anyways, I'm at Mom's. Come get us. Hurry. We need to leave soon, just in case anyone comes looking." Rose sounded almost sane, but Tina knew differently.

While Rose was distractedly arguing her case of newfound motherhood with Kevin, Tina decided that when the conversation ended, and Rose hung up, she'd make her move. She fingered the gun in her pocket.

"Then don't," Rose sat up in bed and directed her whispered words away from the sleeping baby. "If you are not on board with this, go home."

Silence. Tina heard the creaky bedsprings and then Rose began to sing to Kai, using her own words. "Daddy's coming," she sang. "We'll leave here, yes, leave here and then we'll be a family."

It couldn't have been stranger if it was a horror movie. Silently drawing the gun, Tina walked to the doorway. Taking off the safety, she held the gun in front of her and moved forward into the bedroom.

When Rose caught sight of someone blocking the light, she gasped.

Tina spoke. "Get off the bed, motherfucker. Now. Easy. Don't touch the baby or so help me, I'd love to shoot you."

Rose looked to Kai.

Tina advanced, her gun pointed at Rose's torso. "Stand up, Mary-Rose, nice and slowly."

"Who are you? Where did you come from?" Rose didn't recognize Tina from the wedding a year ago. She looked to the baby and reached for him. "My baby." Tears filled her eyes.

"Don't touch the baby. Stand up and back away from the bed and maybe I won't hurt you." Tina glanced to see Kai still sleeping and hoped to God he wasn't drugged. "Make one wrong move and I'll put a bullet in you and throw your sorry body off the deck for the fire ants."

Rose stood, tears filling her eyes. "My baby," she moaned.

"Wrong. <u>My</u> baby. And I have the stretch marks to prove it."

Rose looked confused.

"Doesn't matter. Move over to the window by the chair." Tina saw a man's belt in a pair of jeans. "Take the belt out of those jeans, slowly."

Rose glanced at the baby, then did as she was told. "Did he send you to kill my baby? Because it's wrong to take the life of a child."

"You crazy woman. I'm taking back my baby."

Rose moved towards Kai quickly and Tina fired into the floor. The sound was thunderous and Kai startled. Rose dropped to her knees, covering her ears.

"Get up or the next one will go into your gut. Move over to the window."

Rose did as she was asked and Tina was able to slide Kai to the edge by pulling the blanket with one hand while still holding the gun on Rose. She scooped him up and backed against the wall, motioning for Rose to leave the room. "Take the belt. Let's go outside, shall we?" All she needed was enough time to get down the path. "Hands on your head Rose."

Rose did as she was told, which made Tina almost heady with the power of pointing a gun at someone. "Now walk to the shed."

Once there, she ordered Rose to put the belt on the door handle and go inside the shed. "Sit down with your hands on your head." The shed wasn't big but it would take Rose a few seconds to get to the door once it was closed. Enough time to quickly pull the belt around the latch and secure the door closed and locked.

Part way down the path, Tina heard Rose cry out. "My baby!" Then the kicking started and Tina knew it wasn't long before a crazed woman kicked down that thin, wooden door.

Tina got almost to the road when she heard Rose coming. Turning, she readied herself, slipping the gun out of her pocket again. When Rose was within thirty feet, Tina switched on her headlamp and pointed it at Rose's face. "Yeah, that's what it feels like when someone takes your child."

Rose looked unhinged. Her eyes darted to Kai and off the path in to the darkness.

Anger shot through Tina. "*You* took *my* baby, and now I'm taking him back," she said.

Rose covered a sob with her hand.

"You took Wyatt. Then you came into Annie's house tonight and took Kai. Now, turn your sorry ass around and head back to your mother's house. And hope that I won't shoot you right here on the path." Tina didn't want to fire the gun, but if it came to that… She held Kai against her chest and shoulder using her left arm, as far away from her right hand as possible, just in case.

Rose backed up slowly. "You won't get away with this. The police will come for you," Rose said this like she was on the side of the law.

"Back to the house. Now!" Tina said. Kai stirred in her arms, and she hugged him to her trembling body. Soon she'd need that second arm.

The dogs ran down the path from the house barking at Rose, passing her and continuing on to Tina. Rose turned and started walking. Half way up the path she turned. "I'll come for my baby, you know."

The laugh that escaped Tina's mouth was unfamiliar to even her. "Okay, Looney Tunes. I'll be ready," When she heard the house door close, Tina put the safety back on the gun and tucked it back in her pocket, then navigated down the path carefully, listening for footsteps, turning around every twenty feet. Kai stirred in her arms and even opened his eyes, but didn't fully waken. At the pullout, she didn't see anyone following.

Starting down the main road towards Annie and Diego's house, she saw car lights coming up the road from far away. At first, the headlights were small. They disappeared, then reappeared closer, larger. She continued down the road. Could be Jamey.

Or Kevin. She kept to the shadows, out of the headlights.

When the lights got close and the vehicle turned at the driveway up ahead, Tina recognized Annie at the wheel of her truck. Tina aimed her headlamp at the vehicle, hoping that someone in the truck would see the light. The dogs had run ahead and were on the driveway excited to see the truck. Annie stopped for them and Jamey flew out of the vehicle. He saw her and Kai.

"He's okay. He's safe," she called. When Jamey reached her, she nodded to her pocket. "Gun's in my pocket. Safety is on."

He reached in, his face grave. "The gun is hot. Tina, did you kill Rose?"

CHAPTER 19

He wouldn't put murder past Tina, knowing how much she loved Kai.

Tina nodded up the mountain. "I left Rose up there at her house. Alive but she's coming for her baby, she said." Tina shook her head. "She's gone off the deep end, Jamey."

He tucked the gun in his waistband. "I'll take care of Rose. Let's get you two back to the house." Jamey gently hugged his family. "Thank goodness, you're both safe." He took the sleeping baby from his wife and they started walking. An overwhelming feeling of relief swept over him and he had to keep from letting tears take over. His family was safe.

Tina held on to the sleeve of his T-shirt like she didn't want to get swept away.

"Wyatt is here," he said.

"Oh, thank God. Rose said something, but I wasn't sure." Tina stayed close to his side. "How?"

"Like the dream. Annie found Kevin and Wyatt in town."

She nodded. "Is he okay? Not hurt?"

"He seems fine." The house was in sight, the truck now parked.

"Rose is delusional." Tina whispered against his arm. "She just talked to Kevin, told him to come get her and their new baby."

Jamey nodded. "It'll take him a few more minutes to get out of town. It's crazy down there." He wanted to get his family back to the house, then he'd go after Rose.

Tina sprinted forward to greet Wyatt who was waiting for them at the top of the driveway. "Hi Wyatt." She crouched and hugged him and Jamey almost smiled to see the little guy angle away to avoid the hug. Same old Wyatt.

"You got your hair cut," Tina said, rubbing his bristly head.

"Kevin said it makes me look older." Wyatt shrugged.

"I believe he could be right," Tina said. "Let's go inside. I'll show you Diego's sword collection."

Jamey listened for a car on the road but heard nothing. Not yet. He kissed his son and breathed in Kai's sleeping baby scent, then headed to the house.

"Look at that one, Tina," Wyatt said, pointing at Diego's sword on the wall, like he hadn't been kidnapped and dragged through Mexico and Central America.

Diego looked worriedly at Jamey. "What's next?"

He needed to take care of Rose. He handed Kai to Tina. "I need to have a talk with Rose, and wait for Kevin."

"Don't hurt her. Please." Annie stood in the kitchen area, her expression one of pain.

"I won't be the first to try anything." Jamey looked over to Wyatt. "Hey Slugger, I'll be right back. You stay with Tina."

"Don't hurt Rose," he said. "She's been through a lot, Kevin says, and we don't want to make her sad." Wyatt took a glass of juice from Annie and sat down at the table to eat his snack.

"I'll be nice," Jamey said in a soothing voice. Yup, she'd been through a lot. Looney Tunes had finally snapped and he was going to see that she didn't kidnap any more children.

"Want company?" Diego looked ready to deliver some justice.

"Just make sure nothing happens down here." At the bottom of the driveway, Jamey heard Diego yell for the dogs to stay and then he turned to go up the mountain, flashlight in hand. Thoughts sped through his mind. Would Rose still be at the house? Did she even know that the baby she'd taken was his? She might not have recognized Tina. Kevin would probably be in town, trying to find a taxi.

Once on the trail, Jamey followed the sounds of a woman crying. Sobbing. It didn't make him feel sorry for Looney Tunes. Could be a trap. As he crept closer, he realized Rose was slouched in a chair on the veranda, her head in her hands. Jamey looked around. He watched from the shadows for a full five minutes.

Rose finally stood, wiped her face with her hands, and went into the house. A minute later, she emerged with a duffel bag on her shoulder. She pulled the door closed, extinguished the lanterns and set off down the trail with a flashlight aimed towards his hiding spot. Luckily, she didn't catch him backing into the bushes, and it wasn't until she passed him that he slipped back on to the trail to follow her.

Was she walking down to the main road or coming to get the baby? Jamey watched Rose turn at Diego and Annie's driveway and head towards the house. He let her walk almost to the top of the road. She snuck into the bushes, like him, and stood behind the cover of a huge tree to case out the house. He crept up behind her. "What are you looking at, Rose?" He shone the light on the back of her head. Her hands were visible at her sides. No weapons.

"I'm going to get my baby." She didn't sound surprised to hear someone calling her name from the darkness of the forest. "I couldn't do it. I couldn't kill him, like you said. Turned out he's my baby, not hers. I want to keep him." She turned and squinted into the beam of the flashlight.

Jamey dropped the beam to her feet.

Her expression changed. "Jamey? What are you doing here?" She looked embarrassed. "I thought you were someone else."

Kill the baby? "Are you planning on killing a baby?"

She looked horrified. "Oh no." She said, shaking her head. "No. I love my baby."

"Rose. Put your hands up, over your head, and start walking towards the house." He motioned with the flashlight.

"Listen, Jamey," she said. "This is none of your business. This deal with Wyatt is between Carrie and Kevin."

"You made it my business when you took my son."

Rose looked genuinely surprised. Her voice emerged as a faint whisper. "Wyatt is your child?"

"Nope."

"What then? The baby?"

"Start moving Rose, hands up. I don't want to have to get mean here, but your cooperation will help decide what I do with you."

She looked at him reproachfully. "You're not going to kill me. I know that. And without me, you have no hope of..." Her voice trailed off like she was confused. "Wait. Who took Wyatt?"

"I have Wyatt, the baby, and Kevin. Now get moving." The bluff had her thinking. And walking, which was good. He really didn't want to have to use more persuasive techniques to get her to the house. They rounded the last corner to see Wyatt standing on the patio with Annie. The boy ran to Rose and hugged her hips. *Shit, the kid liked her.*

"Hi Rose!" Wyatt put his hands in the air, imitating her. "Are we playing a game?" He smiled at the woman.

Rose smiled sadly at him. "Yes. Jamey and I are playing cops and robbers." She flashed a look Jamey's way.

Wyatt danced around with his hands on his head. It was at that moment, Jamey realized that Wyatt had changed since he'd last seen him in Carnation. Physically, he'd changed. He had tan skin, had grown at least an inch or two and his curly hair was gone, but also Wyatt seemed different. More outgoing. Happier somehow. And he had a genuine fondness for Looney Tunes. But that didn't absolve Rose from kidnapping both Wyatt and Kai.

Tina stood by the house, her arms folded across her chest, looking madder than he'd ever seen her. Don't be deceived by this woman, her expression told him.

"Tina? Can you show Wyatt where the monkeys are sleeping while I find Rose a nice place to relax?"

Wyatt's eyes lit up. "Come see, Rose." He dropped his arms.

Jamey interrupted. "Nope, Slugger. I gotta show Rose something else. You go." He nodded towards Tina and then noticed that Annie stood behind Tina with a sleeping Kai in her arms. Her grandchild. Wow. That was going to take some getting used to.

"Come on, Wyatt." Tina held out her hand for Wyatt. She led him around the house to the pool deck where the monkey trees canopied the far side of the patio. Annie followed.

Rose sat down in the closest patio chair and looked at the tile. "I heard a baby crying and came to see. It was my baby."

"Not your baby, Rose," Jamey said.

She shook her head like it might clear her thoughts and looked at Diego. "How do you know these guys?"

Diego stared at the woman. "They are friends, Mary Rose. Good friends." His voice couldn't have been more of a contrast to Jamey's harshness.

"I need rope or line to tie her up until morning. I'm going to put her in the studio for now."

"Will you turn her in?" Diego asked.

"Something like that." Jamey shrugged.

For the first time that night, Rose looked like she knew what was going on. "Where's Kevin? I want to talk to my husband." Tears pooled in her eyes as she looked from Jamey to Diego.

"You can talk to him tomorrow." Jamey needed to get rid of Rose, get her out of the way. Kevin would come looking for his wife soon, and Jamey would be waiting.

When Jamey pushed Rose into the studio and flicked on the light, the first thing he noticed was the painting on the easel. It was a portrait of him. Annie had painted his face, his hair, his neck, shoulders. He tried to ignore it, but damn, it looked a lot like him. He even had that five o'clock shadow thing going on. When did she paint this? "Sit down over there." He pointed Rose towards the couch.

Diego handed Jamey the ropes and they tied Rose's feet together, then her hands. After that, they tied her to the couch. Even if she managed to stand up there was no way she could walk while dragging that big, heavy thing.

"Is this necessary? Come on Jamey," she said.

"Shut up, Rose, or I'll shut you up."

Once satisfied that Rose was secure for the night, he closed the studio door and Diego locked it. They walked back to the house, musing on when Kevin would show up. Wyatt was chattering in the living room about seeing the monkeys and other topics relevant to a small child.

"Wyatt is excited about the big birthday party," Tina said, her eyes big like Jamey needed to play along. "When Mama, Chris and all the kids and Pops come."

Jamey nodded. "Hey, Slugger, we might have to do that big party back in Carnation. Mama needs you to come home. She can't come here because of baby Harley."

Wyatt looked confused. "But Kevin said they were already here. We're going to have a big birthday party for the whole family with presents and a horse and the real Luke Skywalker is coming too."

"Everyone wants to do the party at home because they say it's too hot here for Harley."

Wyatt seemed to buy that idea and asked when he'd go home. "Sooner the better, I guess." He shrugged his little bony shoulders.

"Daddy is coming on the plane tomorrow."

"Wow! I'm that far away?" Wyatt looked surprised. "No wonder we were driving so much."

"It'll be faster to take a plane, Slugger. But tonight, you have to get a good sleep. Tomorrow will be a fun day."

Tina broke through. "Can you sleep in the big bed with us? Me and Jamey?"

"Count me out," Jamey said. "Just you, cousin Kai, and Aunt Tina. I'm going to wait up for Kevin." He looked over to the couch where Annie and Diego were watching this exchange, silently.

Annie spoke. "I'll wait up with James. Keep him company."

Rose's phone rang and the call display indicated it was Kevin. "Here we go." Jamey handed the phone to Wyatt. "Just say hi to Kevin, but let's not tell him you're with me. It'll be a surprise."

"Hi Kev." Wyatt said with a twinkle in his eyes.

Jamey winked at the boy and listened in.

"Oh, my God, Wyatt," Kevin said. "You're with Rose? That woman who took you was Rose's friend, Annie. Are you okay?"

"Yes, I'm okay but…" Wyatt got that little look of mischief in his eyes that usually showed just before he put a frog in his sisters' sink.

Jamey took the phone. "Hi, Kevin," he said, then let the message sink in.

Silence.

"We're having a party at Annie's house. You're invited. Rose is having a pretty good time, aren't you, Rose? Well, she's busy dancing but come on up."

Silence.

"Rose, would you like Kevin to join us?" Jamey said, much to Wyatt's confusion. The boy opened his mouth to speak and Jamey put a finger on his lips to indicate quiet.

Finally, Kevin spoke. "I guess we're done now, Jamey. You have Wyatt."

"Yes, you're done. I have Wyatt. And I have your wife."

"Don't hurt Rose. She isn't capable of determining wrong from right. Something has happened to her." Kevin sounded desperate, his voice full of fear. "Please don't hurt her."

"Come to the party, Kevin."

"I'm in a taxi. Tell Rose I'm coming. Please be nice to her."

Jamey considered all the things he could say to this man. "Wait until you hear how close she got to my child."

Kevin didn't say anything.

"And, do you have any idea what's been going on in Carnation while you had a nice little vacation down here? Wyatt's family has been waiting for him."

"I'm Wyatt's family too."

"Not anymore." Jamey replied. "You didn't play by the rules, Kevin, and you're out of the game." He winked at Wyatt and smiled. "Come to the party." He hung up the phone knowing that was enough to lure Kevin up Mombacho.

CHAPTER 20

Tina was exhausted, and very soon got prone on the bed with Wyatt on one side and Kai on the other side. Jamey listened to her tell Wyatt a story about a little boy, like Wyatt, who loved Luke Skywalker. When the story concluded with the boy joining the Jedi Knights, Jamey shut the door on the way out. Such sweet real life existed in that room and such insanity in the studio. Annie and Diego sat in the living room with glasses of wine, their conversation ending abruptly when Jamey joined them.

"Thanks so much for everything today." He meant his words for both but looked at Annie. All his life, Jamey thought if he ever saw his mother again, he'd probably spit in her face, rage at her. So far, he hadn't done either. Sinking into the deep chair across from them, he estimated how long before Kevin showed up.

"We wait?" Diego asked.

Jamey nodded. "Are the dogs outside?"

"They'll bark when anyone comes up the road. They always do."

"They can't usually be bribed, either," Annie added. "I don't know how Rose got past them this afternoon."

"Tina said they were in the studio," Diego said. "I'm going to check on Mary Rose. I'll be right back."

Only Annie and Jamey remained in the room. To be alone with the woman he'd despised for the last thirty-six years was unsettling. Annie looked like she felt the tension too. Her gaze went to the door where Diego disappeared through. "I'm glad Wyatt is safe."

Jamey nodded. "Thanks for that. I appreciate you making that call and going to Granada. I didn't think you went to town on hipica day."

She shrugged.

"In the dream you looked badass with Kevin."

She smiled to herself.

"And, I didn't think you liked kids, but tonight I saw you holding Kai." He took a risk. Indecision invaded the space between them.

She wondered whether to say anything. "I usually avoid them."

You avoided us for thirty-six years. He almost said it, but held off. There was a long silence filled with the knowledge that Annie wanted Jamey to reach out, to say anything, only she didn't think she had the right to expect anything from him.

"I liked your painting." He wasn't exactly spitting in her face.

Annie looked away. "I wanted to remember you when you left."

He had a flash of his mother reading a bedtime story to him. He'd been sick and she'd rubbed some menthol stuff on his congested chest. Same woman, different mother. He leaned over to the coffee table and took a handful of cashews from a dish.

He popped a few in his mouth and had a clear feeling that Kevin was close. "He's here." Jamey stood. The feeling got stronger. "You might want to go to your bedroom. Keep safe." He motioned down the hall and disappeared out the kitchen doorway to the back of the house. The dogs started barking and Jamey almost smiled to think that his intuition was stronger than the dogs' noses.

Making his way through the darkness to the studio, he found Diego on his way out, and motioned for silence. "Kevin." He opened the door to the studio and called in. "Need anything Rose?"

"I need to be untied. What do you think you're doing? I haven't done anything wrong." She sounded delusional and Jamey surmised that her voice yelling into the night would be enough to tip off Kevin of his wife's whereabouts.

Jamey signaled for Diego to patrol the house. The dogs now barked from inside Annie's bedroom. Kevin wasn't an expert at this sort of thing and would probably head straight for Rose. But, just to be safe, Jamey planted himself half way between the studio and the house where he could watch the door to both, as well as most windows. He'd ducked behind one of those huge trees. If Kevin was smart, he'd realize that they'd just checked on Rose and he'd need to wait to bust her out.

Jamey settled down behind the tree and waited for a sign that Kevin would make the first move. He didn't have long to wait before he heard a yell from Tina's bedroom. A man's scream, like he'd fallen into a trap. By the time he got there, the light was on and Diego had Kevin in a choke hold on the floor. Tina sat up in bed, her eyes wide, holding a can of insecticide in her hands. The baby and Wyatt were still asleep and Kevin was yelling about his eyes and writhing on the floor.

"Kids okay?" Jamey asked as he helped Diego shove Kevin face down on the tile and tie his hands behind his back. The room smelled like bug spray.

"I heard the door open." Tina said. "When he got close I kicked him and sprayed his face. I need to get the children out of here."

Annie hurried in, sniffed and scooped up the baby. "It's not safe in here for little noses. They can sleep in my room, honey," she called back. "Diego, bring Wyatt."

Diego lifted the half-asleep boy, and Tina followed them out of the room.

And then there was only Jamey and Kevin. The gun was still stuck in the back of Jamey's jeans. It would be easy to shoot Kevin and be done with this. He'd seen soldiers kill for less in Afghanistan. But Jamey wasn't a killer. He only killed people in dreams and even then, they weren't real people. Even shooting Kevin in the foot now seemed unnecessary. Sure, this guy masterminded a plan to take Wyatt, but that wasn't Jamey's business. Retribution belonged to Carrie and Chris on that one. "This is the end, Kevin. Might as well stop struggling."

"At least wash out my eyes. I'll go blind." His voice was girlie high.

"You are a piece of work, you piece of shit." Jamey reminded himself of the moment when Kevin sped away from him in Puerto Vallarta. And then the time he didn't show up to hand off Wyatt when Chris flew to Mazatlán. And Jamey thought about what could have happened at the hipica when Kevin turned away from Wyatt. That would've been an accident. "I think I'll let you squirm and hurt for a bit," Jamey said.

"Come on, Man."

Kevin was part of the Carnation contingent, was nice to Jamey's daughters, and for that reason Jamey put the man in a different category than a stranger abduction. They'd had dinners together at Carrie's house, went on a picnic once with all the kids in Duvall, they'd had conversations about being fathers. Kevin had come to the wedding last year. Yes, Kevin had abducted his son and run to another country, but Wyatt had been treated well as far as Jamey knew. The kid seemed perfectly happy. Carrie and Chris had been through hell, wondering, so there would be a price to pay. Jamey sat on the side of the bed staring at Kevin when Tina walked back in, followed by Diego.

"Wyatt and Kai slept through it," she said, shaking her head. "Amazing." Tina sat beside Jamey and put her arm around his shoulders. Then she addressed the man on the floor who was blinking furiously. "Hello Kevin. Fancy seeing you in Nicaragua. What were you trying to do in this bedroom?"

"I thought I heard Rose in here."

"Nope. Just me with a can of bug spray." She turned to Jamey. "What's next?"

Kevin turned his head to watch them.

"Well, let's see. Rose abducted our child and said she was told to kill him. Luckily, she didn't. Kevin took Wyatt from his home in Washington State, crossed several borders with a child hidden in his truck, a child he didn't have legal permission to take, making the mother of the child frantic. But did we once call the police. Hmm?" Jamey paused. "No, we didn't. I'd like to stop Kevin and Rose from ever doing this again. I might shoot both of them," he said. "Leave their bodies out there for the ants to pick at."

"Well, before you do, I'm going to wash out his eyes." Tina got up and went to the bathroom, making Jamey wonder why he even tried to play the mean guy with his softhearted wife around.

***

Once they made a tentative plan on what to do with the abductors until morning, Tina left Jamey and his mother sitting on the couch talking. With Kevin in the guest room on the floor and Diego watching him from the bed, she joined Kai and Wyatt in the master bed. Jamey's phone was on the nightstand and when the texting ping sounded, she looked over to see Leilani on the screen. After all she'd been through in the last twenty-four hours, she didn't give a flying fig if Jamey didn't like her reading his messages. She picked up the phone and retrieved the text.

Lahaina is boring. Doug is driving me crazy. I need you. Get back here, Muscles.

Tina's heart jumped into her throat. Someone in Lahaina was calling her husband Muscles. Someone named Leilani. Tina scrolled through the history of their messages to see that this woman always said the same thing.

"Front Street has a cold front with you gone, Big Guy." "GI James—when you gonna teach me to dive? I want to go deep." "Obi came to see me today. Said he misses you too." "Call me, if you want the latest on how and what I'm doing without you, Manly Man."

She found nothing to suggest that Jamey had written her back. Who the hell was Leilani and what was she doing sending a married man these texts? Over the last week, Leilani had made her husband smile in a very disturbing way.

Tina got out of bed, opened the door, and when she locked eyes with her husband sitting on the couch, she held up the cell phone. "Leilani is trying to tell you how boring Lahaina is without you, Muscles." She threw the phone and he caught the careening missile just before it sailed over his head. Getting back into bed, Tina felt better. Now he knew that she knew.

Kai stirred with the first calls from the monkeys at dawn. He opened his eyes, and smiled at his mother who was staring at him. He murmured, then said something that sounded like "bugaw," which woke Wyatt.

"Monkeys!" Wyatt said, his eyes getting wider with the noise. After sitting up, he looked over to the baby on the other side of Tina. "And baby Kai!" He talked to Kai in a high baby voice, which made the baby kick his legs and squeal with delight. Wyatt attempted to imitate the monkey noises and got Kai belly laughing, which made Tina jump up to grab her phone to film them. Kai was fascinated that a child had appeared overnight and kept trying to grab at Wyatt's face. When Wyatt asked what time Daddy would be here, Tina reassured him that Chris would be landing at the airport after lunch. "He flew all night," she told him. She got the feeling that Wyatt had had a wonderful adventure with Kevin and Rose. He didn't seem traumatized in the least and mostly wanted to get out of bed to see the monkeys. She changed a diaper first and then told Wyatt they could quietly go outside.

Although the sky was barely light, everyone was awake and roaming around the house when they opened the bedroom door. Jamey and Annie were still on the couch looking like they had spent the night talking. They both looked exhausted, physically and mentally. Tina smiled at them sympathetically. When Jamey kissed his wife good morning and took Wyatt and Kai out to see the monkeys, Tina helped Annie make coffee. The plan was for Wyatt to go to the airport that afternoon where he and Chris would board the next flight back to the States. Chris had said that he wanted to return with Wyatt as soon as possible, not stay to visit or even see Kevin. He'd call between planes from Houston and they could make a plan on what to do with the man he was now calling "the criminal."

By the time the monkeys stopped howling and Kai was fed, Wyatt was bouncing around the house like they were all on a big vacation. He was not to know that Kevin was tied up in the guest room, and so far, Kevin had been quiet. Thanks to that sock and duct tape.

Tina scrambled eggs at the stove and watched the green jungle come alive with the arrival of the morning sun outside the kitchen window. She sprinkled a handful of cheese onto the eggs and then salted them. When the bacon had just crossed the line from floppy to crispy, she lifted each piece out of the cast iron frying pan. On the other side of the kitchen, Diego made toast, buttering each slice as it popped up from the toaster. If there hadn't been two prisoners tied up on the property awaiting sentencing, it would have been a lovely morning on Mombacho.

"Think our spouses will need extra sleep today?" Diego asked her, putting a stack of plates on the breakfast tray.

"Jamey is pretty good at going for days without sleep. What about Annie?"

"She'll pass out as soon as we finish breakfast."

They sat outside at the big table, as far away from the guest room as possible, and ate their breakfast, the monkeys having moved on by now. After Wyatt finished his last piece of bacon, Jamey asked if he wanted to swim in the pool. They'd take turns distracting Wyatt until it was time to leave for the airport.

Tina sat with Annie and Diego at the table, feeding Kai some mushed bananas. Annie looked exhausted, but there was a sense of relief in her eyes that Tina hadn't seen before. And there was a feeling emanating from her that something had been resolved. All Tina had heard so far about Annie's talk with Jamey was that their conversation was involved and not yet finished.

Before breakfast, Jamey and Tina had discussed the particulars of what to do with Kevin and Rose. He eluded to maybe letting them go on the stipulation they never entered the U.S. again. To do that and make sure it was enforced, he'd need to get a warrant out for their arrest so they couldn't cross the border. "I want to wait and see what Chris says," he'd said, reminding Tina that the outcome was also up to Carrie and Chris. Pepper knew a Federal Marshal back in Seattle if they needed one.

Birds called from the jungle below and the sun peeked from behind a cloud on the horizon. Already Tina's armpits were drenched. It was going to be a humid day, even on Mombacho. She thought of another time when she'd sweated through her clothes like this; she'd been in Afghanistan, a prisoner of a group of volatile insurgents. That was a time in her life she preferred to think of as a bad dream. Kevin was lying on the guest room floor. It was a far cry from when she lay in the dark room in Kandahar thinking they might rape or kill her.

Jamey's phone rang and Tina picked it up. "Hey Carrie." She listened and fed Kai another spoonful of banana. "He's swimming in the pool with Jamey."

"Does he look okay, no bruises? Was he dirty or hungry?" Carrie asked.

"He looks perfectly fine. His hair is short. No curls anymore. He had a great sleep, like nothing ever happened. He thought the whole thing was an adventure."

"I'm actually in Houston switching planes right now. With Chris. We both flew."

"Oh! You'll see your son soon."

When Tina hung up she looked at Jamey. "Carrie wants to see Kevin," she whispered. "She wants to be the one to decide what to do with him. Rose's fate is ours to decide."

***

When Wyatt left with Diego for the airport, Jamey checked on Kevin who was still lying on the cold tile floor of the guestroom with a sock taped to his mouth. He'd shuffled around enough to get to a sitting position against the far wall, but was unable to do much more. Annie followed Jamey into the room with some breakfast.

"Hungry?" she asked, pulling the sock from Kevin's mouth while Jamey watched.

"Is Rose okay?" he asked. "She's sick, Jamey. I brought her here because her mom knows a psychiatrist in Granada. An American doctor. Then I was going to fly home with Wyatt. I have a fake passport for him in my pocket. You can check." Words burst out of his mouth like they'd been waiting to be freed.

"Rose is fine," Jamey said, if you think delusional is fine." Jamey sat on the bed and stared at Kevin. "I agree your wife has serious mental problems. And you are a close second for abducting Wyatt."

Kevin ate some eggs from the spoon that Annie held to his mouth. "I have plane tickets in my back pocket for me and Wyatt to fly to Seattle tomorrow. Swear to God. Take a look." He took another bite. "I bought them two days ago. I've been waiting for Jean, Rose's mom, to arrive." He looked at Jamey with desperation.

Jamey knew this to be true.

Kevin continued. "Carrie is fucking nuts. You know that. You divorced her for a reason."

Jamey shot Kevin a look to tell him this turn in the conversation wasn't appreciated.

"She told me that I'd never see my son again. Told me to square up my taxes and shit before she'd let me have a formal custody agreement. She was threatening me. With Chris on the birth certificate, I don't have any rights to Wyatt unless I sue Carrie and I haven't got the money, plus I have to get my taxes in order. She's been driving me crazy, Jamey." He gulped.

Jamey was well aware of Carrie's temper and how fiercely protective she was. Their marriage hadn't been without fierce disagreements. "Carrie will be here this afternoon, so you can ask her for forgiveness then."

Kevin's eyes widened and he sat up straight. "She'll tell you to throw me into a crocodile pit."

Jamey didn't want to miss this opportunity to make Kevin sweat it out. "If that's the case." He shrugged like he couldn't care less.

Annie had finished feeding the prisoner and headed to the doorway, listening. She shot Jamey a reproachful look as she passed. "Mary Rose's mother is on her way from Managua right now. She should be here in thirty minutes."

Jamey nodded. Hopefully Jean wouldn't arrive with a lawyer, seeing as how they were doing this off the books.

Kevin continued. "If you want, I'll take Rose to Costa Rica. She can get help there." He tried to catch Jamey's eyes. "I need to get Rose help. She hasn't been the same since her last miscarriage. Have a heart, Man."

"Have a heart? Where was your heart when you took Wyatt to Los Angeles? And where was your heart when you crossed the border to Mexico. And why didn't *you* have a heart when Chris flew to Mazatlán to get Wyatt and you just never showed up?" Jamey pulled Kevin to a standing position to search his pocket for the tickets and passports. "I'll take these into consideration," he said, waving the tickets and pushing Kevin back to the floor.

Outside, on the patio, Jamey threw the passport and tickets on the table and lifted Kai from his stroller. Looking at Tina, he whispered, "I need to explain something to you," and motioned towards his cell phone. Tina found the texts from Leilani. Of course, Tina found them. At least with all that was going on, he had time to get his story together.

She nodded.

He and Kai strolled over to the patio edge to where the dogs were playing with an avocado. "Dogs have a ball," he said to Kai. "Ball."

Annie whispered to Tina. "I have to admit, I'll be glad when Kevin and Mary Rose are gone. It's unsettling, all this." She fingered the crystal around her neck. "I don't know why Kevin can't see Rose. He's obviously concerned about his wife."

"Kevin is dramatic, Annie." Jamey called back. "And even if you don't buy it, I don't want Kevin and Rose to speak to each other and change their stories. It's an interrogation tactic."

Tina looked at Annie. "Your son knows all about this stuff."

"And you should be glad I do," Jamey said, returning with Kai to the shade of the fig trees. "Otherwise, those two might be gathering up children all over Granada." He stared at Annie for a bit, then spoke to Tina. "Up until last night I wasn't sure if she knew that I dream jumped as a kid."

Tina looked over to where Jamey's mother was fiddling with the hem of her colorful shirt. "As a mother, didn't you worry that he had this ability?"

"Yes. But I knew his uncle had it. And Don promised to guide James through this strange ability and the life that came with it." She looked at her son with concern. "I didn't know that Don had died after a jump."

Did his mother feel badly having left him on the assumption that Don would help Pops guide him? "Annie and I talked about how it was for us kids to find out our mother was gone." His voice hitched on the last part. "She still hasn't told me why."

Annie finished her glass of orange juice. She set the glass on the table and circled the rim with her finger. "I needed to think about how to tell you my side of the story," she said. "Decide if the truth would make things better or worse; nothing will be the same after you know."

"I want the truth," he said. He sensed the truth like lava bubbling inside the pit of a volcano, building and rising closer to the open top. Something so horribly sad had happened that his mother had no choice but to leave the family. And then, it came to him. Jamey knew what it was.

Annie spoke. "Your father was better at handling your dream jumping than I was. He'd grown up with a brother who did the same thing. It frightened me. I was horrified to think that my sweet child had this strangeness. I didn't want you to know how much it frightened me. I wanted you to think it was perfectly normal. That *you* were perfectly normal. Your father and I tried to make it seem that way." She took a deep breath.

The air felt heavy and charged with possibilities. Somewhere in the deepest part of Jamey lived the knowledge of why his mother left. He'd been lying to himself all these years, telling himself that he didn't understand her departure. But he did. And now he needed her to verify his buried nightmare.

Tina took Kai from Jamey. "Maybe I should leave you two."

"No," Annie shook her head. "You should hear this."

Tina settled the baby into a nursing position and hoped he was amenable. He latched on immediately and started sucking.

Annie gazed at Granada down below. She took a deep breath and let it out slowly. "I left because I wanted to save lives. Save the family. Not ruin it." Her eyes filled with tears. "You had a dream, James. A dream that changed everything."

The volcano was about to erupt. "My dream," he said.

Fat tears dropped from Annie's cheeks to her chest. "You had a recurring dream that we'd skid on ice driving to Fall City." She caught her breath and continued. "We'd go off the Tolt River Bridge into the icy water. Everyone would die but you and me."

CHAPTER 21

Tina looked to her husband who remained perfectly still. Was he remembering the dream? His eyes were wide, his face frozen in shock, and rightfully so. His mother had just revealed that the reason she'd deserted her children was because of him. Because of a recurring dream he'd had. Maybe a premonition.

Annie took a tissue from her pocket and wiped her eyes. "I believed you could foresee the future in these dreams. I really did. So did your father, and so did Don. And by the time you saw this same dream for the third time, I was convinced. The future involved me driving that old car full of my precious children off a bridge into an icy river. Three would die in the water, but not you. And not me. We'd be injured, but alive."

Finally, Jamey spoke softly. "I remember telling you about the dream."

Annie dabbed at her eyes with a tissue. "I tried to avoid the bridge whenever we went out, but then I worried it would just happen another way." She took her wedding ring off, put it on again, did that over and over.

Jamey's face had turned a chalky grey. "We'd go off the bridge and end up in the river." He closed his eyes and then put his head in his hands. "I had the dream so many times, it seemed like a memory. The water was so cold when it leaked in the windows and filled up the car. I lost my breath. It happened so fast."

Tina held her breath to hear his words.

"I tried to get Jenny out of her seat belt but my fingers wouldn't work. My one arm didn't work. Gavin was floating around, his eyes shut, blood leaking from his head. The water was murky and I couldn't see you or Robert in the front seat. I had to get to the surface for a breath. Then I wanted to go back down to get the others, but when I got out the window and up to the air, you yanked me to the edge of the river, told me to get up on the bank. You went back in, but you couldn't find the car."

"I wasn't a strong swimmer." Annie's face was crumpled.

Jamey looked up, his voice devoid of emotion. "The water was so cold. People arrived, then the fire department, but when they found the car, Gavin, Robert and Jenny were dead inside." He turned to look at Annie. "When I had the dream the first time I woke up crying and told you it was going to happen. You told me all dreams feel like that."

Annie watched her son. "Then you had the dream again. And again."

"It was a fuzzy dream. I know the look of those now." He took a deep breath. "I remember thinking as we fell into the river that Jenny couldn't swim. She was only two." A sob escaped Jamey and his hand flew to his mouth.

Tina had never seen her husband like this and she wanted to go to him, but held off. He needed to face this realization. His mother had left the family to avoid killing her children in a car accident he'd seen in a premonition.

Annie took a steadying breath and spoke. "The year before the dream, you predicted that I'd break my wrist falling down the stairs to the basement carrying a laundry basket. Do you remember that? Sleeping in our bed one night, you woke up and told me not to go down those stairs. And, two months later, I fell."

Jamey nodded. "You had a cast. We all wrote on it. All but Jenny."

"And then you predicted that Gavin would lose his Dad's transistor radio at the school picnic. And he did." She leaned in to Jamey. "When you told me about going off the bridge, I didn't know what to do. Winter was coming. I was crazy with fear. I didn't tell your father because…" She took a deep breath. "Because I didn't see any way out of this except to leave and I didn't want to."

She sobbed and Kai looked over, then resumed his sucking.

"Had he known, your father would've tried everything to make me stay, but I couldn't risk my children's lives like that. I believed, and I still believe, that what you have is very exact. You'd never been wrong before and I couldn't take the chance that I wouldn't cause the death of my sweet children. Once my paranoia took over, all I could think about was getting out of your lives to insure you kids would live. By the time I left, I wasn't fit to be anyone's mother."

Emotion took over and hot tears filled Tina's eyes and dripped on to Kai's shoulders. What mother wouldn't have made that choice for her children? She lifted the baby for a burp and wished she could console her husband, but this moment belonged to Jamey and his mother.

Annie sobbed into her hands and Jamey moved to kneel beside her chair.

"I knew." He held on to her chair's armrest like a lifeline. "I knew it was the dream. I didn't tell anyone, but I knew. But all these years, I guess I buried it. I could've told Pops but I remember thinking it was my fault and I didn't want him to blame me. But, I knew it was me."

"It was better I leave than kill the other children. That was my choice, James. You warned me. You must never think that it was your fault. I had to leave. You might well have saved your siblings' lives."

This felt too private. Tina stood with Kai and left them. Strolling down the driveway, she hugged her baby's little body and continued patting his back. She couldn't imagine leaving a child. Even for the child's own good. How would a mother walk away from four children she'd loved every day of their lives without being tragically marked forever? All these years that Jamey had hated his mother for leaving them, and she was two states away, and then here in Nicaragua, mourning the loss of her life as a mother and her loss of the children who'd given her life purpose. She'd actually saved the lives of his siblings by unselfishly leaving them and hadn't wanted him to know it was this ability he'd been cursed or blessed with that caused her departure. Still thinking unselfishly. And deep down, he'd known it was him. His dream.

Walking down the long driveway with Kai, pointing out butterflies and birds, Tina only hoped Jamey didn't blame himself for any part of this. If he'd foreseen an accident, he had to believe it was going to happen unless the future was changed. And neither Jamey, nor Tina knew the intricacies of dream jumping and foretelling the future enough to know if Annie might have killed those children some other way. All three kids were still alive thirty-six years later. Annie's departure must've put an end to the pre-ordained accident off the Tolt River Bridge. Tina shuddered to imagine a car with four children plunging to the icy water of a glacial river.

***

Rose was brought into the house before her mother and stepfather arrived. Her wrists were untied. She looked oblivious to what was going on, defiant almost. Kevin came out from the bedroom, rubbing his wrists theatrically. *Such an idiot.* He sat beside Rose and hugged her.

With just Tina, Annie, and the kidnappers in the room, Jamey took the lead. "We're waiting for Carrie and Chris to arrive to decide what to do with you two. I'm pretty sure that wherever you're going, it's not together, so enjoy sitting there."

Kevin shot him a look as if to tell Jamey to soften up.

"And where you're going, Kevin, is probably prison, so enjoy being around a woman—for now," Jamey shot back.

When Rose's parents arrived a few minutes later, Jean rushed to her daughter. "Oh, Rosey. They cut your hair?" she asked.

Kevin spoke. "She cut it and dyed it and doesn't it look pretty?" His patronizing tone hinted that the mother should agree.

Annie hugged Jean, gave her a meaningful look and asked everyone to sit down while she explained the situation as she knew it from all sides. Earlier, Jamey had said he'd be the talker but the plan changed when he threatened to shoot Kevin in the foot if he didn't shut up about his wife being sick. "We all know she's a mental case, Kevin, but if you don't stop begging, I'm gonna take a toe off." He wasn't the best choice as a mediator, Annie had said.

After Annie gave an impartial account of the events as she knew them, detailing Wyatt's disappearance, being seen in Mexico, then turning up here, she explained how

Rose took the baby out of this house, and called Kai her own.

Tina glanced at Rose who was listening like she was one of the observers, not the abductor.

Annie finished. "Rose, let's hear your side."

Rose moved to sit at the dining room table with her mother, while her stepfather stood with arms crossed near the kitchen. Rose glanced around the room, her gaze settling on Tina. "My spiritual advisor told me that Kevin belonged with Wyatt. That day on the beach in California, the first day I met him, he told me to convince Kevin that we could give Wyatt a better life than Carrie could. So I told Kevin. Wyatt was better with us." She smiled, remembering something. "Wyatt has more fun. He's happier away from the kids who bully him at school." She looked perfectly sane saying this next part. "We decided that Wyatt thrived with us. Kevin thought Mexico was a good idea, then in Puerto Vallarta, we realized that Jamey was following us. We couldn't figure out how he knew we were there. Kevin said the best plan was to come to Granada to wait for Mom and Bob. Make a life here."

"What about last night?" Jamey asked, his face stoic. "What led you to creep in here through the window, and take our baby, then walk up the mountain to your parent's house and put him to bed? You renamed him. You called him yours."

Her eyes filled with tears, then narrowed in confusion. "I heard a baby cry when I was walking up the road from the taxi stand. At first I thought it was a monkey.

In my dream my baby cries for me." She pulled at the hair on either side of her head, her eyes now tightly closed. "The cries won't go away. Even during the day, I hear him. It's like he needs me." She sobbed into her hands then looked up at her mother whose face had wrinkled in a mask of pain.

Tina held her breath. It was painful to watch this woman in her swirl of grief and insanity.

Rose took a moment to smooth her hair, wipe her face, and continued. "Something must've happened last night when I heard the baby crying. He sounded so scared. Just like in my dream. I thought it was Christian, my baby. The next thing I knew, I was at Mom's house with him. It felt like part of the dream."

"Oh Rosey," Kevin whispered.

"It felt like Christian wasn't dead. My baby had been born to someone else. He even looked like me." She sounded so happy that Tina bit her tongue to not speak. "I brought him back to the house and tried to reach Kevin to come get us." She looked Kevin. "You know how my dreams keep telling me that my baby was reborn?"

Kevin nodded, his face full of sadness.

"This was him. The baby Noble told me to kill."

Noble? Had Tina heard correctly? Did Rose say *Noble*?

Jamey's head whipped around to look at Tina, a look of absolute horror on his face. "Who's Noble, Rose?" he asked.

There was silence in the room until Kevin broke through. "Rose has a..." he made air quotes, "spiritual advisor, who visits her in dreams. He guides her," Kevin said patronizingly.

"He comes to me when I sleep," she told the others, "and he told me that Wyatt needed us. You were there, Tina." She pointed. "You were on the beach, near the water. Noble told me to kill you, but I wouldn't. I just wanted to go to Mexico with Wyatt. Not stick around California like Noble said. Then, when we got to Mexico, he was angry that we left and said if I ever saw a baby with you, I should kill the child." Rose looked at her mother. "But I couldn't because he looks so much like me, Mom. Wait until you see him. If we can do a DNA test, I know you'll all be convinced."

"It was Rose's dream Tina jumped, not Kevin's. Jamey spoke. "When was the last time you talked to this Noble?"

"Last night when he told me to kill Tina."

Jamey stood. "You dreamed in the studio?"

Tina moved to her husband, realizing that there were people in the room who mustn't know about Noble. People who must continue to think that Rose was troubled, not haunted by the ghost of a man she and Jamey thought was dead and gone forever. She touched her husband's sleeve and hastened to interrupt him. "It might be helpful to speak with a counselor about your advisor, Rose. Tell them what he says, even what he looks like."

Rose looked out the window. "He's a very large, dark-skinned man, with long black hair. Almost kingly." She seemed proud of her advisor's stature.

Jamey broke through. "What else did he say last night in your dream?"

Rose's mother looked to Annie, her expression asking if this was necessary, but Jamey persisted.

"Was Noble happy that you took the baby yesterday?"

Rose's eyebrows knit together, her mouth turned down. "He was very displeased with me. Quite angry. He said I was to kill Tina. Someone had to do it." She looked up, her gaze fixed on Tina. "I could have the baby, he said, if I killed the mother. The only way to make sure I could have the baby was to take a knife from the kitchen and stab you in your sleep." She shook her head at Tina. "But I'm not a killer; I told him that before."

Tina interrupted. "Why kill me?"

"To break the bond between you and the baby." She seemed to remember something troubling. "He's waiting for you on the other side. He said he and his brother are waiting."

Kevin moved in and embraced Rose as if to quiet her.

Tina took that opportunity to look at Jamey whose face still wore a look of horror. Of course, Kevin and Rose didn't know that Noble was a man who blew his brains out in her backyard, then haunted her in her own house. She needed to talk to Jamey. In private. About Noble. "Jamey?"

"I need a few words with my wife." Jamey motioned to the guest room.

Once in the quiet bedroom, Jamey whispered. "Is it possible she's being haunted by Noble?"

Tina ran her hands through her hair and blew out a worried breath. "How else would she know about him?" She looked over to her sleeping child. So innocent in of all this. "I thought Noble was gone."

Jamey rested his hands on her shoulders and stared into her face. "Noble told Rose that Wyatt belonged with them, then told her to kill you. Then he told her to kill Kai." His forehead was wrinkled, his eyebrows angled down. "He and his brother are waiting for you? Do you think Rose could be making this up? Could she know our story, somehow?"

"How? I seriously doubt that she'd have been able to dig up the information that Noble and Hank live in the afterlife and want me there too."

"Sounds like he found Rose through the dream on that beach, then tried to get to you." He dropped his hands from her shoulders, walked to the window and back. "Now I'm wondering if that's how Noble committed suicide. Maybe Hank invaded *his* dreams. Got Noble to kill himself.

Hank can't get to your dreams, not after we found his body, and now he wants Noble to kill you. You'd think if Noble could get to Rose's dreams, he could get to yours."

"You think this all comes down to Hank?"

Jamey nodded. "I'm sorry Darlin' but he's a bad mother fucker. Or *was* a bad mother fucker."

Tina felt like she was in a recurring nightmare. "Do you think, if Rose killed me, I'd have ended up with Hank in the afterlife?"

Jamey shook his head. "I don't know. But I think it's obvious that Noble can't get into your dreams, or he would've by now. After this is over, today, we have to figure out how to finish him off."

Was this the right time to tell Jamey that Noble *had* been entering her dreams? It didn't change what they'd do with Rose. No, she'd wait. "Let's figure out Kevin and Rose, then deal with Noble."

"Agreed" Jamey said. "But in the meantime, Rose is a victim here. Do you agree?"

She did. "This changes everything."

When they emerged from the bedroom, Carrie and Chris had arrived. Wyatt was as happy as Tina had ever seen him, jumping up and down excitedly. Most of his favorite people were in one room.

Wyatt chattered noisily. "This is like the party, Kev. Except no other kids, or Pops." He counted off his favorite family members on his fingers.

"Yeah," Kevin said, reaching for him. "Come here, Luke Skywalker. I want to tell you something."

They listened while Kevin told Wyatt that he and Rose were going to stay here with Jean because they loved the monkeys so much. "But, you're going home soon to see everyone and have that party in Carnation." Kevin's eyes were full of regret. "We've kind of had one big fun party all this time anyhow, right Luke."

Wyatt sat on Kevin's knee. "I wanted to see the real Luke Skywalker."

"Dude," Kevin hugged Wyatt. "*You* are the real Luke Skywalker. So brave, and kind, and smart. He lives inside you, and I love you."

Wyatt pulled out of the hug. "You're crying because you're proud of me," he said and then patted Kevin's shoulder. "Mama, do you want to go swimming?"

"Daddy will take you," Carrie looked at Chris apologetically but Chris stood up and took Wyatt's hand.

"Sure, I will."

Jamey watched them walk off to the pool and touched Carrie's sleeve. "Before we start talking here, can you and I have a word in private?" Carrie nodded, and as she walked by Kevin, her eyes threw daggers at him.

Tina followed them to the far side of the patio where Jamey told Carrie about Rose's dreams and that Rose's spiritual advisor was the same man who killed Tina's husband, Hank. "It's Noble in Rose's dreams. She described him to a T. And Noble told her to take Kai and kill Tina."

Carrie looked confused. "Isn't Noble dead?"

"He is." Jamey looked like if Noble wasn't dead, he'd be the one to make that happen. "Tina and I are sure Noble's ghost has been in Rose's dreams. It's a long story how he gained access, which we don't fully understand, but Noble has been in this since Malibu."

Carrie let out a long breath and pulled her hair back into a ponytail, fastening it with a tie from her wrist. "Why kill Tina?" Her eyes widened, looking at Tina.

"We can only guess. Maybe Hank wants her in the afterlife." Jamey's voice was filled with quiet rage.

"This sounds pretty farfetched, Jamey. Like some paranormal TV show." Carrie shook her head and looked out at the view of Granada. "Are you telling me that all this was to get to Tina?"

"Not all," Tina added. "Kevin and Rose took off with Wyatt, but were influenced by Noble to keep him, we think. We don't know why."

Jamey added, "I think Noble locked on to Rose in that beach dream and manipulated her. Maybe to get me to follow them. Not sure." He looked apologetically at Carrie. "I don't want anyone but you and Chris to know this, understand? Not Pops, not Gavin, or anyone else. Just us. I plan to figure this out and put a stop to Noble, but in the meantime, I wanted you to know that some of Rose's crazy came from Noble."

Carrie took a deep breath and shook her head. "See Jamey? This is why we couldn't stay married. You come with all this." She gestured grandly. "It drives me crazy." She walked back in the house, leaving Tina and Jamey looking at each other.

"I like all this," Tina said to her husband, and took his hand. "Well, most of it. And the parts I don't like, are mine anyhow," she whispered.

"Good thing," Jamey said, squeezing her hand.

Back in the house, Diego asked Kevin to speak first. "Then we can hear from everyone who wants to say their piece."

Kevin jumped in like he'd been waiting. "I know I shouldn't have taken Wyatt. I know that now, but at first I was just going to take off with him to California, with Rose. My birthday week. Then Rose got to thinking we could make a life for ourselves in Mexico. When we got a fake passport made for Wyatt, it seemed too easy." He looked at Carrie pleadingly. "We got to Mexico and I knew it was wrong. I felt like a criminal. I always planned to bring him home to you eventually. I was trying to help get Rose over this loss." He looked at his wife. "Then, when I saw Jamey in Mexico, I was going to give him over that day, but Rose had a fit to think Wyatt was leaving." He glanced at Rose who stared at the table. "We agreed that we'd give him to Chris."

"You agreed," Rose said.

"Where were you that day?" Carrie interrupted. "Chris flew for four hours to get him. He waited all day. You never showed!" The background noise of Chris and Wyatt splashing in the pool contrasted to Carrie's words.

Kevin looked at Carrie. "I'm sorry. We started over that way, but Rose had a really bad day and I was worried about her."

Rose ignored Kevin's words, instead whispering to her mother.

Kevin continued, "Rose said if she lost Wyatt, there'd be no reason to continue. So I made a plan to come to Nicaragua. I didn't know if there was a warrant out for my arrest and didn't want to risk getting arrested if Chris had a bounty hunter with him. I needed to get Rose to her mother before I got caught." He looked over to Jean, who obviously loved Kevin and gave him a smile that told him that.

"My turn." Carrie sat down in a chair across from Kevin and took a deep breath. "I hate both of you for doing this to our family." She looked at Rose. "I hate you, Rose. Do you understand that?" She said the last part patronizingly. "I'd like to have you both arrested and sit in jail in orange jumpsuits while they evaluate how crazy you actually are. Both of you. But I think you have bigger problems, and I'm not going to have you arrested. What happens to Rose is up to Jamey and Tina. And what happens to you, Kevin, Chris and I have already decided. We never want to see you again in Carnation. When Wyatt is eighteen, he may choose to get in touch with you, but I never want your presence, or your cuckoo wife's presence, to tarnish my doorstep, or telephone or contact my family. You understand? No coming near any of us."

The lines in Kevin's face had deepened in the last few weeks. He looked sad, but thankful. "I do."

Carrie stood and went outside to the pool, looking like she'd had enough.

Tina glanced at Jean and Bob, then spoke. "As far as Rose goes, she needs treatment. I'm sure you know that. Maybe in a home where they can watch her." Tina asked for a promise that Rose would get professional treatment. "I don't want to send her to jail. I just want her to get over this devastating loss and get back to normal."

Jean let out a deep breath. "Thank you. And I'm so sorry that Mary Rose caused any of this," she said through tears. "I apologize. Thank you for letting both of them go. Mary Rose will get help. I'll see to it." Her expression of worry was that of a mother in crisis. "Bob's trying to get in touch with Brenda now to see if we can get an emergency appointment," she nodded at Annie and her husband who was on the phone. "Then, when I take her home to Florida, we'll get her into a facility. I won't forget this, and I won't let her down."

Kevin sat forward. "I want to go with Rose."

Bob finished his phone call and spoke. "She can take us in two hours." He nodded to his wife. "We'll stay in a hotel in Granada tonight."

There was nothing more to say. It was over. Rose would get help and Kevin would go with them. Tina heard

Kevin outside telling Wyatt he'd see him soon, even though he knew he wouldn't.

"See *you* soon, raccoon," Wyatt added.

Jamey followed the procession outside intending to take Kevin aside before he left the property to threaten him within an inch of his life. The baby monitor indicated that Kai was waking and instead of waiting, like at home, Tina went into the guest room to be the first thing her sweet child saw when he looked around.

When Jamey joined the others on the patio, he looked Tina's way and made a nipple twisting motion with his hand. She shook her head and tried to not smile at her husband. Apparently, Kevin had been warned.

Diego brought four beers outside and set them on the table. "Let's talk for a minute," he said.

Tina handed Jamey a beer, but didn't take one for herself. A feeding was coming up. Besides, keeping a clear head seemed like a good idea right now. Rose was crazy, Kevin was desperate, Carrie and Chris had been through hell, and Noble was trying to kill her. Kai's cheerful smile between his chubby cheeks reminded her that she had something good and pure in her life, something indeed to be thankful for.

Annie approached the patio, the dogs trailing her, and took a beer. "Wyatt and his folks are down the road singing to the monkeys. That kid looks so happy." She sat in a lounge chair beside her husband. "This has been a very unusual weekend."

Tina agreed. "It'll take a while to decompress from everything." She looked at her husband who had to be overloaded with emotions and information. "We are going to sleep for a week when we get home."

"I'm not happy letting those two go," Jamey added, shaking his head.

Diego nodded. "This therapist in Granada specializes in loss and grief." He looked to his wife to continue.

"Brenda's good and she'll recommend the best treatment when Rose leaves here. I've been going to her for years." Annie looked at Jamey and Tina. "I promise, I will monitor her."

"We'd really appreciate that." Tina said. "I need to know that her spiritual advisor isn't still telling her to kill babies."

CHAPTER 22

After the taxi pulled away from the stand outside the Granada cemetery with Carrie, Chris and Wyatt, Jamey reached for his wife. "Alone at last." He smirked, something she credited to his ability to bounce back from strange situations. Looking her in the eyes, he spoke. "Leilani is an activity consultant on Front Street around the corner from the shop."

Somewhere across the street a dog barked several times. "And someone you text?" Tina went ridged, her head tilted as she looked into her husband's eyes.

Jamey laughed and blew out through his teeth. "If you looked on my phone, Darlin', you probably saw that she texts me. I don't text her."

Tina stood back, crossed her arms, and waited.

"Does it make you feel any better to hear that Leilani is just coming out of the closet as a transgender? It's true that we've developed a friendship and on her part maybe she feels something more. But she knows I'm married to the woman of my dreams."

"I saw your expression. You smirk when she texts." Tina waited.

"I do. She's funny. And, I can't believe that after a decade of no one liking me in that way, I suddenly have attracted the attention of a woman trapped in a man's body." He took her shoulders in his arms. "You might be flattered too, Tina. I happen to think it's kind of sweet." He stared at her. "I smile at the texts because Leilani was raised Justin from Wailuku and because she's funny." His smile changed to a serious expression. "I watched her change from Justin the activity sales person to Leilani and we flirt because she doesn't deserve to be shot down. She's had a very hard life." He looked at her tenderly. "I'll tell her to stop when we get home, if she hasn't already. Personally, I think she's just practicing on me because she knows I'm safe."

Tina knew this was the truth. The words were solid and held a validity that was pure Jamey. How had she thought otherwise? "You're a good man, Jamey." She looked in the backseat of the truck's cab where Kai was asleep. "It's amazing what our son sleeps through," she smiled.

"Come on, Mrs. Dunn. Let's put that to the test."

On their way to the hotel, Tina noticed how tired her husband looked. His eyes were sunken. She felt badly that she had one last bomb to drop before they went to sleep but she had to tell him now. Especially because they were hoping to encounter Noble in a dream that night.

She timed the conversation, so they'd only have a minute or two before they reached the hotel. Taking a deep breath, she imagined herself jumping off a dock into cold water. "Since Kai was born, I've dreamed of Noble. A lot." She took a breath. "I thought it was my hindbrain dreams working through guilt I felt for his suicide. Now I'm not sure."

Jamey looked over. "Why didn't you tell me?" His face took on that pulled look of concern and anger.

"I told Doc Chan."

"So back on Maui? What were the dreams?" His jaw looked tight enough to snap.

"In the first ones, he told me he missed me, Hank missed me. We were the three amigos. He said it was lonely being gone. Without me. For both of them." She looked out the passenger window of Diego's car. "I thought I was making it up. That it was just a dream. Doctor Chan said to take charge next time, tell him that he made bad choices that almost ruined my life. That type of thing." Tina didn't want to upset Jamey, but if they were going to go looking for Noble later, he needed to know this. "So, I did, but it didn't work. He was persistent. I wondered if I was just torturing myself with thoughts of him. Then I started jumping out of dreams where he was waiting for me. Once you almost ran into him in a dream, but he disappeared before you saw him."

"Tina." Jamey sounded disappointed.

"And once I dreamed of him walking in to his childhood home in Compton. It was a remembrance. His mother lay in a lump on the couch, the TV was loud, and she was high on something. Probably heroin. Hank told me once his mother was a junkie and now that I know Noble was his brother… Anyways, Noble walked in and went over to the couch. He picked up a blanket to cover her and told her he loved her. He looked so genuine. Then he picked up the syringe and pushed the contents into her arm." Tina shivered.

Jamey pulled into the parking lot behind the hotel and parked the truck. "What happened then?"

"I think he killed his mother." Bile rose in her throat.

"What a life." Jamey took a deep breath. "He's been getting into your dreams for a reason. Do you see that now?"

She nodded.

"He's fricking dangerous, Tina. I want you to call me into the dream next time you see that God damned killer. You get me in there, regardless. Agreed?"

"Agreed."

Jamey closed the truck door and came around to her side. "And I want you to remember that even though I don't initiate jumps anymore, I'm the expert at this. Can we agree on that?"

She'd never doubted that. "Absolutely. You *are* the expert."

He unstrapped Kai from the car seat and put the sleeping baby against his shoulder. "We're going in tonight to put an end to this bullshit."

***

On their way from the parking lot, Jamey crossed to the park to grab some vigoron for their dinner. He'd said this local food was delicious and wanted Tina to try it. A kiosk at the corner of the park sold the town's best local fare and along with cobs of corn, it sounded perfect for tonight. Once back in the room, Tina spread a towel on the King bed in preparation. Her stomach felt like an empty pit.

When Jamey arrived, they ate the pork, salad, and cassava wrapped in plantain leaves, washing everything down with beer for him and a diet coke for her. Kai was wide awake, sitting in his stroller. Between bites, Tina finished feeding him his cereal and veggies. The evening was still young and they had time to talk about everything that had happened in the last twenty-four hours. It had been a crazy time and they both admitted their exhaustion. Soon enough, they developed a plan for dreaming that night.

When the last bite was gone, Tina gathered up the empty food wrappers while Jamey took Kai out to the balcony to see the horses. Stepping into the pristine white bathroom, she showered off the remnants of the sweat and dust from the last day. She stood for a few minutes to let the hot water pelt her aching shoulders.

Coming out of the steamy bathroom, she went to the balcony doorway. Kai was still with his Daddy, watching the horses and flapping his arms. Jamey had a big grin on his face, taking such delight in his son. "If we dream tonight, and Noble appears, I will be screaming at you to join me," she said, walking up to her husband and putting her arms around his waist. Her cheek rested on his warm back.

"Get me in there, and I'll take care of the rest," Jamey said. She felt him take a deep breath. "I'm going to try to kill him, so if you have a problem with that, you can step aside. Or you can remember that he tried to kill you, and he tried to get Rose to kill our child."

"I understand." She wasn't worried at all that Jamey might kill Noble. She was worried that it might go the other way. "I'll help, if I can."

"Just don't leave me there, Darlin'. Keep close, but not close to Noble or he'll use you against me in a hostage situation. Don't get close enough for him to grab you when things start going down."

Jamey sounded like such a badass. She took a deep breath of his sweaty shirt and man smell, realizing how much she loved that scent.

Later, when Kai fell into a deep sleep, Jamey and Tina stood at the sink brushing their teeth, their eyes locked in the mirror. She didn't know if she'd have this dream jumping ability if she'd never met Jamey, but she was glad to have him as her guide through all this craziness. Without him, she might still be having dreams of Hank swimming off Molokai, with nothing resolved. Slowly going crazy by herself. Certainly, she wouldn't have moved on from that horrible year after Hank went missing, and there would never be Kai.

She wiped the remainder of the toothpaste from her mouth and laid her cheek against Jamey's muscular shoulder. "I love you, Jamey Dunn," she whispered. "I love you so much it kind of hurts sometimes."

"I'm here, Darlin'."

"I'm kind of scared about dreaming tonight."

He reached up to touch her face, then leaned over and spit into the sink. "Trust me," he mumbled.

They slipped between the crisp, white, hotel sheets and turned to each other. Without words or a plan, they kissed. First just a friendly kiss goodnight, then another. Deeper. Then Jamey's hands found their way up under her sleepshirt to her breasts and she sighed against his mouth. Knowing what was ahead in their dreams, they prolonged the inevitable for another hour. A delicious hour of making love, reassuring each other with their bodies that they put each other first. Jamey was in no hurry and that was fine with Tina. She hadn't felt the freedom to love her husband like this in months, maybe longer. The absence of worry was freeing, and a long time after that first kiss, they lay together catching their breath.

"We need to do exactly this, more often," Jamey said pulling out of her and settling on the bed.

"I agree," she curled into his side and threw her top leg over his thigh. "Nicely done, Soldier Boy."

They lay listening to the noises in the street below their balcony, the whir of the room's air-conditioning and each other's heart beats. Soon after, Tina fell into a dream in which she was buying a house at a ski resort, touring the home with her real estate agent. When Noble walked into the room, the agent disappeared.

"Noble." She tried to sound calm, but hadn't expected to see him so soon, or in this dream. Jamey hadn't even arrived. It was like Noble had been waiting for her. The idea sent a chill through her dream.

"Together again. Finally." He walked slowly towards her.

"I'm buying this house. Do you like it?" Was her shaking voice noticeable?

"I like it if you like it." This Noble was cagey, scary. He had a smirk on his face she didn't like.

Looking into the snowy backyard, she willed Jamey into the dream, tried to call to him silently. They'd gone to sleep holding hands, vowing to jump together. He said he'd stay awake to watch her and he'd know when she was falling in to a dream. Why wasn't he here?

Noble came up behind Tina and massaged her shoulders. "You're tense."

"Buying a house is stressful." His fingers on her skin had made her muscles lock up in fear. Could he stab her?

"We both know you're not buying a house." He chuckled and stopped rubbing her shoulders, using his grip to turn her around to face him.

She reminded herself that she needed to take charge. If Jamey wasn't coming, she had to control her own dream. Taking two steps back she folded her arms across her chest and stared at the man who'd wanted her dead. "What do you mean by *finally*?"

"I couldn't get in for a while. Almost like you were trying to avoid me. But now here we are." Noble had a rakishly handsome smile.

"I'm not coming with you, Noble."

"I think you are."

Next, they were in a dark room, sitting behind a table with various weapons laid out. "See the control I have over you?" He turned his chair so their legs were touching. "This is actually pretty cool. As a dead guy, I can enter your dreams and make up shit, go places, take you with me."

She hoped that wasn't exactly true but didn't want to try to block him again in case Jamey was lurking. "Noble. This is a mistake." *Where the hell was Jamey?* She screamed his name in her head, tried to summon him. It occurred to her that she might not be safe with Noble and tried to leave the dream. She couldn't.

Noble looked around the room and back to the table of weapons. He seemed pleased. "I've been waiting to bring you here."

She stood and backed away from the table, remembering what Jamey said about not getting close to Noble. "You need to move on, be with Hank, or whatever you want to do. I'm not coming with you." She walked around the table. "Tell Hank I'm very disappointed in him. And I'm very disappointed in you, Noble. For someone who professed to love me, someone I loved, I now find you detestable."

Noble tented his hands on the table and smiled.

By now she stood on the other side of the table, at least ten feet away. "How many times do you and Hank have to ruin my life? Wasn't it enough what you did to me when you were alive? You have to kill me too? Look at me, you coward!"

He did and an emotion flickered briefly across his face. Loathing. He hated her. Up until now, she thought he might love her.

"If Hank is the one who is controlling you, Nolan," she made a decision to use his real name, the one his mother used, "you need to get a backbone and walk away from this."

"It's because of my backbone that I'm in this." Noble picked up a gun and aimed it at her. "It was my idea. Don't you get it by now? I call all the shots. Not Hank. I've always been in charge. Hank only married you because I told him to. He was always under my thumb. And you. Without knowing, you've been under my thumb, too. Poor Ti." He looked at her with pity. "Life has been hard for you, Tina. First you lose a twin, then Hank." He twirled the gun around then put it on the table and picked up a sharp knife. "Then your father dies unexpectedly." Noble sliced his finger on the blade's edge, drawing blood, then licked it. "Then your baby dies."

"My baby didn't die." She looked at him hard. "You are one nasty mother-fucker, but my baby didn't die."

He smirked. "He will." He set the knife down and grabbed a hammer. "Could you hammer your head so hard, you kill yourself?" He smiled. "Or what about these?" He picked up a vial of pills. "This would be a nice death." He shook the vial. "I killed Hank, I killed myself, then your father, and now I'm going to kill you." He spread the pills on the table and set a glass of water in front of her. "This is best, Ti. Just take the pills. Then we'll be together."

"You didn't kill my father. His heart gave out."

"Oh, and why did that happen? He was doing so well."

Noble's gaze pierced her heart. She wouldn't give him the reaction he wanted. *Her father died of a heart attack.* She had to believe that Noble had no connection to her father. "And I don't believe you've always called the shots."

Noble looked over a little too quickly, his eyes revealing emotion.

"I think this is exactly what Hank did to you. Drove you crazy with guilt until you killed yourself."

"You're wrong. I wanted to join him."

Tina realized the lie and dove in for more information. "Oh, no you didn't. Hank remained in your dreams, probably used this very table of weapons, didn't he? Then when you couldn't handle it anymore, you blew your brains out." She laughed. "You are the weak brother."

A twitch of his jaw muscle showed how disturbed he was by her comment. "I can kill your baby. I *will* kill your baby. See how you like that."

Tina tried to ignore his horrific words. He couldn't kill Kai himself or he'd have tried before now. "Let me guess what's going on. You are stuck here. And, by here, I mean my dreams or my subconscious. And you're bored. You can't move into the afterlife until your big brother lets you or something like that. Are you amusing yourself with this game, Noble? I have to admit, I was very shocked when Rose said your name. How were you able to get to Rose?" She hoped he'd take the bait.

The look on his face told her that Noble couldn't resist bragging. This was what she was waiting for. "You entered Rose's dreams three times," he said, "whether you knew it or not. I slipped in with you and stayed." He made a motion with his hand like he was a magician. "You are a busy dreamer, Tina. It's only a matter of time before you dream with someone else. Someone I can convince to kill the baby. It'll take time, but I have nothing but time. Time means nothing to me now."

Noble didn't realize that Jamey could enter these dreams too. He knew nothing about dream jumping. Only that he could communicate with her through dreams. She stared at him. "Why would you do that? The Noble I knew on Maui was a friend." She hoped to buy time until Jamey arrived. "My Noble loved me. And I loved him because of his tender heart. That Noble would not try to kill me or my child, to take me from this new life. He'd be happy for me."

Noble grinned. "See what a great con artist I am? That Noble you knew never existed."

She knew better, even if that Noble was nowhere to be seen now.

"Don't think of it as trying to kill you, Sweetheart. Think of it as calling you home." His vacant smile showed he was too far gone to hear what Tina was trying to say.

"I don't want to be with you, or Hank. I'll fight you here, or in the afterlife." She spoke loudly. Jamey had just appeared behind Noble. "And nothing will make me take my own life. I can't imagine you'd think I would do such a thing."

"It's not so hard." He shrugged and stood, pushing the chair away from the table. "It's a fine line between grieving and putting the gun to your head and pulling the trigger. Especially when there's pressure every night to do the deed. Henry saw to that."

"Ah, so Hank did kill you."

"I killed myself, but Hank made life difficult enough to make that happen. And that's what I intend to do to you now. Choose your method, Ti. Because you *will* kill yourself or I'm going to get someone else to kill your baby. I'll eventually get in to someone else's dream and convince them to murder your child. I know you don't want that." He swirled the silver knife in front of her face. "Do you want to get it over with quickly?" In one swift movement, the knife was thrust into her chest, a look of amusement on his face.

Tina doubled over in excruciating pain as Noble pulled the knife out from between her ribs.

"Hello, Jamey. Glad you could join us to watch this. Or maybe even participate." He thrust the bloody knife at Jamey, keeping him from going to Tina who was now on the floor feeling the effects of being stabbed.

But then the pain disappeared and she straightened to see nothing of the knife wound in her chest. No blood. Nothing to suggest she'd just been stabbed. Noble hadn't killed her. She felt fine. Standing, she watched Noble toy with Jamey. She lunged for the gun on the table as Jamey kicked Noble in the face with an impressive ninja move. Noble fell over backwards and Jamey dove on him, holding the hand with the knife against the floor. Lifting the shaking gun, she tried to aim at Noble, but didn't want to risk hitting her husband.

"Will him dead," Jamey blurted between punches and blocks.

She wished Noble dead, but it didn't work. Noble continued to kick at Jamey, his arms held down. "Jamey, move so I can shoot him." As she raised the gun, she felt a pull from behind and was gone. Her eyes opened and she was out of the dream and back in her hotel room.

Shit. Her husband was still asleep in the bed. She had to get back in the dream quickly. One minute up top could be an hour down below. A lot could happen in an hour.

Tina closed her eyes and slowed her breathing, concentrating on getting back to Jamey. But Kai called from the crib. That must've been what had pulled her out of the dream. Her son was awake. Going to him now might be deadly for Jamey. She had to ignore Kai and get back in the dream.

Kai began to fret but Tina took a deep breath and blocked out the sounds of her needy baby. With everything she had, she concentrated on the dream and pushed herself through her consciousness and into her subconscious. A busy downtown street was in front of her, during what looked like a lunch hour crowd. "Jamey!" she yelled into the dream.

Nothing.

Closing her eyes, she imagined getting back to Jamey. It took root and fastened to her thoughts until she felt the pull. Landing for a second time, she was back in the dark room with the table of weapons. No people. Taking a quick inventory, she noticed the gun was missing. She could have been gone for long enough that the fight was over. The knife was gone too. The room was silent, like something terrible had happened and the room was recovering.

Tina ran along the dark edges of the room, looking for a way out. "Jamey?" she called. "Where are you?" With the hammer in her hand, she ran, willing herself to find Jamey. The room was about the size of a basketball court. Finally she found a handle on what felt like a door. She turned the handle and opened the door, looking through the entrance. Inside was black, just like what she was leaving. She called into the darkness. "Jamey?"

Nothing. Where the hell was he?

She stood in the doorway until footsteps sounded behind her. Turning, Tina saw Jamey at the table of weapons with a knife in his hand. "Tina?"

"Chocolate chip cookies are better with milk," Her words wooshed out as she raced to him. "Kai was crying. I got sucked out. It took a full minute to get back."

Jamey was panting like he'd been in a fight. "I've been down here fighting him for a couple of hours. We're playing some cat and mouse game and I'm not sure I'm the cat."

Just then, Tina heard their baby cry out and she had just enough time to grab Jamey's hand before they were both pulled out. They woke in the Granada hotel room, Jamey still out of breath. She sat up and left the bed. Kai was ready to eat, and once she laid down with him, he latched on to her breast immediately. "What just happened in there? Is Noble still looking for you?"

"Probably," Jamey said. "He followed me to different scenes. It was weird."

Tina listened intently.

"I think *you* need to kill him, Darlin'. I cut off his head, stabbed him in the heart, and pushed him off a cliff, and he kept coming back."

Tina gulped. Was she ready for this?

"We'll go in again, once Kai is asleep, and I'll help you. But you need to kill Noble."

If she could feel murderous anger for Rose, she supposed Noble had it coming twice over. "Okay."

They arrived in the dream together. The location resembled a movie sound stage--a long street amongst fake New York brownstones. Standing in the center of the street, Tina and Jamey looked around. No Noble. Not yet.

They ventured out together to look around the area and a half hour later, still hadn't found their prey. Or were they the prey?

"Let's pretend to split up, look for him. See if he shows up. I'll be close," Jamey whispered against her ear.

She agreed. Noble was probably waiting for Jamey to leave the dream.

Very convincingly, Jamey told her to take one side of the street, he'd take the other. "Yell if you see him, understand?"

"I will," she said, knowing this was the plan. Jamey never intended to check the opposite side of the street. He'd follow her.

Tina ventured towards a park at the far end of the street. She opened the black wrought iron gate to enter the grounds, thinking about another dream where she and Noble had talked about how much he missed her in the afterlife. They'd walked in a park like this. That dream was months ago. Remembering his words that day, she continued along the familiar cobbled path, past gardens of blooming roses until she saw a small lake in the distance. A figure stood in the center of a white gazebo ahead. He faced the lake, not looking at her. Even from this distance, she still knew it was him. She walked closer.

He turned and smiled to see her. "Hello, Ti."

"Here I am. You want me to come with you?"

"It's time." He looked at her suspiciously. "Are you going to bring in that husband of yours to try to finish me off again?"

Noble wore a suit and tie, like he'd been to a business meeting. She'd never seen him dressed like this before. "No. I'm here on my own." She approached the gazebo and stood at the bottom of the stairs, looking up at a man she'd once loved as a friend. "Why are you doing this to me?" Tears welled in her eyes.

He walked to the top of the small staircase. "It's not *to* you, Ti. It's *for* you. What you don't know is what it's like beyond. This life you have here is so small compared to what we're going to. It'll be like nothing you've ever imagined. Hank and I want you there with us. We miss you. I've been able to come and go but Hank can't." His expression was deceiving, and she had to remember that.

"I want my life here," she said. "I'm happy."

"You *think* you're happy here. Just wait until you see what happiness is."

"You know how much I wanted a baby. Let me have that." She took the stairs slowly, approaching Noble, knowing Jamey was somewhere close. "I love you guys, but I want this life first." Would he believe her? "Why can't you let me have that if time means nothing to you now?" She stood with Noble, only feet apart. "Why not, Noble?" If this man was determined to kill her child, she'd surrender. But first she wanted to try to reason with him. Then kill him.

"We want you now. Jamey is a distraction. You need to come with us." Noble's expression was soft as he extended his hand for hers.

She took his hand. It was surprisingly warm, but then, this was a dream. "Where are we going?" She tried to seem resigned to the next phase and hoped to God that she could do something to stop this.

"You'll see." They descended the stairs and walked hand in hand towards the lake. "The water seems fitting, doesn't it?" He nodded at her. "You have to drown. It took a while to figure that out, but when the table of weapons disappeared, I realized your suicide would have to be different." He chuckled as they continued walking across the grass to a beach.

"I'm scared." That part was true.

"I'm with you, Ti. Just trust me."

"I do." She nodded.

"Hank is waiting for you. Your brother is waiting too." Noble looked pleased to reveal this tidbit.

Kristoffer? How would Noble know about her twin unless Kristoffer actually did wait for her in the beyond? She shivered trying to hide how the words affected her.

Noble continued talking as they walked to a small beach area. "Hank said your twin brother drowned and that's how you need to go." Noble's expression was one of surrender.

Tina's heart raced as she thought of all the possibilities of how to get out of this. What if Noble was right? What if this was a way to shorten the inevitable, save Kai? She walked into the green lake with Noble's hand locked in hers. "Will we go together?" *Would he let go or hold her under? Where the hell was Jamey? He won't let this happen.*

"Yes." He smiled wistfully.

The water hugged her chest, then her shoulders. If this plan of hers went south, she hoped Jamey would jump in to save her.

"I'll see you on the other side, Tina."

"See you there," she answered, and they submerged, still holding hands.

The lake was murky. Green. Tina was barely able to see Noble even though they were only two arm lengths apart. She kept her eyes open and held her breath as she knew she could. Having snuck four deep breaths before they submerged, she was ready to outlast Noble underwater. As they walked along the lake bottom in what felt like weighted bodies, she fought the panic that pulled at her heart. Noble had to go, that was true. And she couldn't outfight him on land. This was the only way. Drowned him. Outlast him, then surface.

They followed the steep drop off down to the next level and then she felt him stop. She could barely see his shadowy form in front of her, his long hair swirling in the water. She had to make it seem like it was over for her. The only way to do that was to go limp. When she did, he continued to grip her hand firmly. Relaxing all her muscles, she let herself float, eyes open, knowing he couldn't see much in the murk.

Tina knew she had time. She could hold her breath for a freaky amount of time, having a skin diver's lungs. Did Noble know this? Then, thankfully, Noble's hand released. She gave it another twenty seconds, then swam in circles looking for him her arms outstretched but he was gone. Her lungs felt like they would burst. She had to get to the air.

His death seemed too easy but when she surfaced, gasping, Tina had a chilling thought. She looked around. No one. No bubbles on the surface. Nothing. He was dead. In his final moments, in this dream dimension, Noble had assumed she wanted to leave with him. She swam towards shore. Noble had trusted in his own ability to control her. That had been his downfall. His ego. And underestimating her.

Tina swam to the beach where they'd entered the water, moments ago. Then something grabbed her foot and yanked her under. She didn't have time for a breath before she was fully submerged again. Two hands moved up her leg to her clothes, pulling her down and suddenly she was face to face with Noble. Eyes open, a menacing grin on his face only two feet away. Was he already dead in this dimension?

She needed air.

He intended to keep her under but wouldn't that be murder? If he murdered her, she wouldn't be able to go with him, would she? Tina had no intention of testing that theory. Her knee made contact with Noble's groin. Underwater, the action had less impact, but enough to cause him to loosen his grip on her. Tina brought her knee up and with her foot on Noble's chest, gave one huge shove as she straightened her body and shot away from him. She'd given herself enough distance to be unreachable but had to hurry. Turning to the light, she headed up for a breath. He'd see her against the light and would follow her. He might need a breath too. A faster escape waited on the surface. Her swimming abilities were way beyond Noble's. They often joked that Noble and Hank couldn't really swim well, even though they surfed and dove. She broke through, took a breath and started swimming towards land. Noble broke through behind her. He gasped. Good.

She didn't turn to look. Her college swim team training was put to use as she headed to a pile of rocks at the edge of the water. Should she keep going and hope he ran out of steam or get to the shore and start throwing rocks at him? What if she missed? She wasn't a good aim. Neither sounded like a very good plan. She had to concentrate on what to do.

Tina headed for a group of cattails just down the shore. Noble's splashing behind her sounded close. Damn. Near the shore, she dove below to escape his line of vision and eventually came up behind a dense grouping of reeds where she surfaced for a breath. And a look.

Noble swam towards her, head up crawl. Flailing. His excessive splashing indicated his fatigue. She submerged again to grab a rock she'd stepped on. Grabbing it with two hands, Tina moved away from shore a few feet and waited. Her feet made contact with the bottom and with the rock's weight, she was able to stand amongst the cattail stalks. He'd disappeared. Where was he? Then she saw bubbles ten feet ahead, and Noble's arms cut through the water to surface. She moved the rock behind her back, almost dropping it when she moved it to one hand.

Noble dove underwater again and headed for her. When she felt him grab her shirt to pull her down, Tina had a moment of panic like this plan might not work after all. But she kicked him off and when his head broke though the surface for a gasping breath, she lifted the rock above the water line and swung it to hit his head just over his left ear. And again. His hands were on her throat, squeezing. Why didn't he let go? She bashed his skull one more time before her vision took on a blackness around the edges.

As she passed out she thought of Jamey and how devastated he'd be if she died. She lifted the rock to hit the same spot on Noble's head for the fourth time. That did it. She heard a crack, his hands loosened, and blood leaked from Noble's head into the water in front of her face. Noble's eyes rolled into the back of his head.

When Jamey arrived, Tina stood on the beach, wondering what to do.

"I couldn't find you." Jamey ran towards her. "This park didn't exist for me until just now."

"Noble thought we were killing ourselves together." Tina was numb. "I held my breath but he didn't die down there. He chased me and I bashed his head with a rock."

Jamey took off his shirt and draped it across Tina's shoulders. "You needed to kill him. Remember? Don't feel badly, he was already dead. Where is he?"

She pointed to Noble's body floating, face down, less than sixty feet along the shore in a group of reeds.

He kissed her wet hair. "Probably a good sign that his body hasn't just disappeared to wherever Hank is." He pulled her to her feet. "Are you ready to jump out?"

"Should we bury him?"

"Always the compassionate. It's a dream. Remember?"

She did.

CHAPTER 23

Tina and Jamey had a four p.m. flight booked for Houston, then Los Angeles, and on to Maui. Tina just wanted to get home, and Jamey couldn't blame her. Going to Carnation to celebrate Wyatt's return had lost the vote when he and Tina talked that morning at dawn. Jamey would go to Seattle in a few weeks, hash it all out with Pops eventually. Chew the fat, see the twins, answer all Carrie's questions, and have that talk with Pops about Annie.

Tina needed to go home, see Obi, the shop, the house, everything that Jamey thought weeks ago wasn't really his life, but his wife's life. Turned out, he'd missed

Obi with a fierceness that had compelled him to stop and pet everyone's dog in Nicaragua and Mexico. And he couldn't wait to drive around in his truck with that dog again, get back to the business. Go diving with Tina. His expertise and personality was needed at that shop in Lahaina, he knew that with certainty. Reporting to a funky little store on Maui every day sounded like a pretty good career choice for him if he wasn't going back to Afghanistan. Yup, they were headed home.

As they waited for Diego and Annie to join them for breakfast in the terrace restaurant, Kai flapped his arms at the sight of the horse carriages in front of them. Balloons remained tied to the carriages from yesterday's celebration and the streets were littered with confetti, snow cone cups, fireworks garbage, and everything else you could imagine after a celebration has taken over a town. Kai squealed at the sight of a carriage passing close to them, one with Mylar balloons that crackled in the breeze.

They'd made several phone calls after they woke up, one of them to the twins who were anxious about Wyatt's return.

Tina sipped her herbal tea. "What did you say to make the twins cry on the phone this morning?"

"I told them his curls were cut off and Jade sounded like she might cry."

Tina looked at her husband sympathetically. "Maybe all that babying Wyatt held him back socially. He sure seems to have come out of his shell this last month."

"Who knows? Carrie said she was going to focus the twins' mothering on Harley now, where they were more needed." Jamey remembered the conversation with Jade and Jasmine earlier. "Jade said he'd look like a soldier now, and Pops tried to make her feel better by saying that hair grows back." He smiled. "Jasmine said to Pops, 'yours hasn't'."

"Poor Pops," Tina added.

"Oh, he laughed at that one. He's secure in his partial baldness." He's going to your mother's book club tomorrow. Apparently, the men are invited." Jamey raised one eyebrow and smirked.

Tina smiled into her Japanese tea. A loose leaf floating upright reminded her of Mr. Takeshimi once saying it was a sign of good fortune. She hoped so.

"Our parents have found friendship," Jamey said softly.

"Seems so," she smiled. "Those two have been playing a lot of Scrabble and eating a lot of dinners together lately."

"Presumably to get Mr. Boo and Harry, the dog, together. When I asked Pops on the phone if he was having fun, he said, 'Just two old folks flapping jaws, playing cards, watching movies. Liz helped me pass the time while we waited for Wyatt.'" Jamey knew that to be true, but he'd also heard a hint of something in his father's voice that hadn't been there months ago. Probably friendship with an attractive woman was something he'd wanted for years. It wouldn't be bad for Elizabeth either. Tina had said it had been a lonely year for her mother, adjusting to widowhood. In a week filled with surprises, both horrible and wonderful, knowing that their parents were finding comfort in each other's company was good information.

As well as wanting to get home to Maui, Jamey needed thinking time, distance from everything he'd learned about the mother who'd left him. Time to assimilate the facts associated with his mother's disappearance. And he didn't want to upset Pops by suddenly opening his arms wide for his mother, not before he'd had a chance to a have a down and dirty talk with his father about the circumstances of her departure. A text came in from Leilani that said, *Made a friend! We're going for drinks tonight to talk about guys. I won't tell her about my crush on a dive instructor named Jamey.*

He read the text aloud and Tina did one of those half smiles out one side of her mouth, the way she said he smiled all the time.

"Good morning." Annie called, crossing the street with Diego. They mounted the three stairs and crossed to the breakfast table. Annie gave Jamey a quick kiss on the cheek and reached for Kai. She lifted the baby, smelled his head, and smiled.

Jamey stood to shake Diego's hand. "Have you guys eaten yet?"

Diego laughed. "We had our first breakfast at dawn, but we're ready to go again, aren't we, Honey?"

Jamey looked down his nose at Annie. "I thought you didn't come to town."

"Well, I did today," she said smiling at the baby. Kai fidgeted on her lap and took hold of the tablecloth, ready to pull it and all the dishes and silverware off the table. Jamey reached over to free the cloth from the baby's hands while Tina offered Kai a rattle.

Annie gave Jamey a strange look, then spoke. "I keep thinking that you said Tina dreamed of me getting Wyatt out of the restaurant." She turned to Tina. "So you jump dreams too?"

Jamey nodded. "Tina's the better dreamer now. What you haven't heard, and this information is top secret because I don't want the military coming for her, is that Tina somehow inherited dream jumping from me over a year ago."

Annie's eyes were wide. "Oh! Your Uncle Don thought he might have passed it to you."

Jamey stared at his mother.

She looked as shocked as he felt. "He shook your hand after a game of catch one day and told me he felt a jolt of something. It was after that you started to see things. Did Pops ever tell you this?"

Jamey shook his head.

"Maybe he didn't know. It was me who was at the park that day with Don and the kids. You were almost four years old and said after the handshake that you felt all jiggly. Don asked if the shake was too hard and you said no. That night, I saw you in my dream, in a boat across a lake. I asked Don the next day about my dream and he suggested I ask you if you'd been there. You said you had a dream with me, and tried to row across the water to see me."

Jamey hung on every word.

"Soon after, your Dad and I noticed strange things with you and realized that you'd inherited Don's ability." She blinked slowly. "Until now, I had forgotten about that jiggly handshake."

Tina sat forward, as if waiting for more information. Maybe something to tell her how to get rid of the ability.

"Your father and I assumed it was hereditary," Annie said. "I don't think I figured out what happened until years later when I lived in California. One of Diego's nephews had a joy buzzer at a party and I thought about that day and wondered if Don had somehow passed on his ability to you."

Jamey spoke. "Tina's grandmother had strange dreams, said they could share adventures."

"I never tested her claim, but she told me that," Tina added.

Annie shook her head and smiled at Tina. "Your secrets are safe with us. Just know that."

Jamey reached over to touch Annie's arm. "We appreciate that."

"I'm so thankful that you and Tina, and Kai," she added, smiling at the baby, "came to Granada."

No one spoke for a while.

"Do you think that it was pre-ordained?" Annie asked. "That all this--Kevin, Rose, Wyatt and everyone, were destined to be a part of all this?"

Jamey set down his mug of coffee. "I don't know. We stopped trying to figure it out. It makes us crazy to try to determine the rules, if there are any."

Annie nodded at Diego. "Welcome to the family, Honey," she teased.

Jamey smiled at Diego. "I'm the only abnormal of the four kids. Everyone else is boringly normal." He smiled at Tina. "Except me and you, Darlin'." He thought for a moment. "I plan to tell my siblings all about you." he said. "I'm not sure, but I'm betting you'll get some phone calls."

Annie's eyes looked misty. "I guess I could handle some phone calls."

"Maybe even a visit down here. Knowing Jenny, she'll want to get on the first plane to Managua. How would you feel about that?" Jamey wasn't sure.

"I'll have to give that some thought." Annie's words were small, wispy, like dandelion fuzz on a breeze. "I'm planning on spending about as much time in that therapist's chair as I expect Rose will. I heard yesterday's session was a good start for that girl. She admitted that she feels crazy sometimes." Annie turned to Tina. "Thank you for this grandchild. He's a blessing." Annie rubbed her cheek on the top of Kai's head and looked around the restaurant. "How do you get a cup of coffee in this joint?" She passed Diego the baby and left to go look for a waiter.

All that day Jamey's mood was light, his sense of himself rock solid. And all because of one little dream. Until he was discharged from the army and sure that Tina had no connection to Milton, Jamey couldn't tell her about last night's dream. It was damn difficult. Keeping another secret, telling another lie, kept Tina safe. He hated to do it, but he'd hate it more if they ended up in Afghanistan, especially now that they had a son to raise.

The night before, it took a while for Jamey to fall off with thoughts rattling around in his head about Noble, Hank, Rose, Kevin and all the shit that had gone down recently. They'd brought Kai back to bed with them and both the baby and Tina had fallen asleep quickly. Kai's little hand was clenched around Jamey's thumb as his son lost consciousness while sucking. He loved this little dude with everything he had. Lying on his side, staring at his son, he felt himself slip into a dream. He tried to get out, but he'd arrived by the time he realized what happened. How did he jump Tina's dream without touching her?

He'd landed in their hotel room bed, exactly where he was when he fell into the dream. But he knew it was a jump. Beside him, Kai was awake and crying softly, waiting for Tina to offer him her breast. She pulled up her sleep shirt and said something to Kai that sounded like soft, sweet words, but they were unintelligible. Gibberish. The baby beside him grew more impatient until he latched on to the breast. Just then a feeling of relief took over the dream. "Tina?" She didn't respond. Jamey looked around the room but there was nothing beyond the bed. Just darkness. This wasn't Tina's dream. This was Kai's dream.

At first Jamey was impressed and then realized he would be stuck here, unable to jump out until Tina woke in the morning. By that time, Jamey would have been lying in this bed staring at his wife and son for what would be days down here. He could think of worse things to stare at, but still. "Tina?" he whispered again, hoping she was in the dream too. "Chocolate chip cookies?'

Nothing.

He slipped out of the bed but the floor was squishy feeling and he started sinking. Kai's memories of this room didn't go farther than the bed. In spite of his predicament, Jamey smiled to himself. Maybe when Kai finished nursing, Jamey could wake up Dream Tina for some dream sex. Would Kai remember it someday if they fooled around in the bed beside him during his dream? He couldn't take a chance.

He crawled across the bottom of the bed and up beside Tina where he tried to wake her by shaking her shoulder and whispering in her ear. Kai looked up and smiled through his milk-drenched mouth. "Hi Kai," he said. "Daddy's here in your dream. Daddy loves you." Tina didn't wake, and Kai went back to nursing.

He'd never jumped a baby's dream before. Even when Jade and Jasmine were babies he'd promised Carrie he wouldn't try until they were older. He'd go lie down again and wait for Kai to wake. He straddled Tina and Kai, lost his balance, and fell on the bed harder than intended. Then he was pulled backwards and was out. Awake. Lying in the bed, but this time the room looked real. A door, dresser, overhead fan, doors to the balcony.

He'd jumped out!

Kai was sound asleep beside him, still making the occasional sucking noise. Kai wasn't a jumper. Jamey couldn't leave a jumper's dream by himself. Jamey had just jumped in and out of a dream on his own.

He smiled in the darkness of that Granada hotel room. Hot Damn! He was jumping again and it felt great.

***

Their first few hours back on Maui, Tina and Jamey set about getting rid of everything that was ever associated with Noble and Hank.

"Just in case, I don't want to risk keeping their shit around here. Not with a baby to consider," Tina said.

After gathering everything in garbage bags and taking them out to Jamey's truck, they let exhaustion take over and got into bed. "I hate the idea of polluting the ocean," she said.

"What's worse, burning all that junk or dumping it over the side of the boat up north in the deepest part of the channel?" He took her hand in his. "It isn't radioactive waste. It's clothes and sports equipment in garbage bags that will sink. And we're doing this to insure that no trace is left of two evil men who tried to kill you and Kai." He felt her surrender. "I'm sure they're gone, Darlin', but this will be therapeutic for both of us, agreed?"

"Agreed," she said. Obi jumped up on the bed when they got settled. "Maybe I'll even say a few words like *fuck you, Santiago brothers.*"

Tina looked so serious, he tried to not smile at the words of hate coming from such a pretty mouth. Lately, she'd been swearing a lot and he couldn't blame her, considering what she'd been through. "Couldn't hurt." Jamey turned on his side and stared at the profile of her beautiful face. If there was something he was sure of, it was that both Hank and Noble were gone from this world and from their dreams forever. Jamey pulled her in close and rubbed her soft arm.

She looked up at him like she had something serious to say. "Remember how you've always wondered if writing that letter to my parents about Hank's shady motives was the right thing to do, and if you hadn't, Hank and I might still be married and happy?"

He knew what was coming. "I do."

"It was the right thing to do. Don't ever question that."

"Thanks for telling me. I kind of came to that conclusion when we found out Hank and Noble were trying to kill you in your dreams." Obi had passed out against Jamey's legs. Not Tina's legs, but his, and he smiled at the realization. "Obi's glad we're home too. Funny, but he seemed the happiest to see Kai at the airport."

"He's going to love it when Kai starts throwing a ball and running on the beach." She swung her top leg over Jamey's, pressing herself into his hip. Her finger circled his chest. "Let's change the business name to include you. How about Jamey and Tina's Dive Shop?"

"Let's keep it Tina's Dive Shop." He grabbed her hand and kissed it. "I'm okay with the name. And, I'm perfectly fine running what used to be your business." He smirked and Tina nudged him under the covers.

"This is a partnership," she said. "Personally, professionally, and psychically. You are the dream jumper. That's something I do not want. You still hold that position. I'm Robin to your Batman. I'm the student to your professor."

"The Submissive to my Dom," he joked, pulling her in against his erection.

"If that's your way of telling me you're frisky, I have to warn you that I'm exhausted."

"Me too. Okay. Let's have dream sex instead." He could feel her smile against his bare chest.

"I'll imagine a bed like this with total privacy and enough energy to go all night," she said slowly, a prelude to dozing off.

"I'll be there." Even though he wanted to, he couldn't tell her that he was the Dream Jumper again. That knowledge was like poison for them and she was better off not having to keep the secret until the army cut him free. Then he'd gladly spill the beans and take that weight off her shoulders. But this secret kept her safe. Her and Kai.

***

The dream jump that night was a montage of several scenes until they arrived in a premonition that involved Milton.

"Chocolate chip cookies," Tina said.

Jamey nodded. "Better with milk." They stood by Milton's hospital bed, talking to a woman who was obviously Milton's wife. She looked lovingly at him, wore a wedding ring, and her expression was one of fatigue mixed with relief. Milton wore a wedding ring as well. The scene's edges were fuzzy.

The small woman spoke. "He's got a long recovery, but now he has a chance," she said. "I don't know what I would have done if we'd lost him."

Tina looked at her. "Your husband is a fighter. And he loves you very much."

The woman nodded. "Lloyd said you work to find abducted children." Her eyes filled with tears. "We don't talk about little Julia, but I know that means a lot to him. And to me."

Jamey hugged Tina to his side. It was true then. Milton had lost a child to a heinous crime, his hard crust guarding a heart that had been broken in the worst way imaginable.

Tina spoke. "When he gets back on his feet, we want you both to be our guests on Maui. Take some time for yourselves. We have a big house and a guest house out back if you want privacy. Only thing is you have to tolerate a dog and a baby, but you're welcome to come stay with us."

Before Milton's wife answered, they were gone. Sucked into another dream. Tina was pulled backwards first and because they held hands, he followed with a jerk. The journey seemed longer than usual, but within three seconds, landed on a familiar beach on Maui. Molokai loomed miles off Fleming Beach, just below the Hawaiian burial ground and Dragon's Teeth. The surf rolled in to the long beach as Obi jumped at the edge of the water. Jamey put his arm around Tina's shoulders and they watched another version of themselves walking up ahead.

"Think they can see us?" she asked, against his shoulder.

"I don't think so. I remember being in this dream once before, and I don't see another me, where I watched it before." He pointed up the beach, just below the ground cover that paralleled the sand.

Tina looked over at him. "When were you in this dream?"

It wouldn't hurt to tell her the truth. "It was just after we found Hank's body. Before you got pregnant."

Tina stopped and looked at him, her head slowly tilting to ask for more information.

"I knew there was a possibility of having this child, but the future isn't secured just because we see these dreams." He pointed to the threesome up ahead. "It was when we were brand new and I didn't know if you'd keep me on." He smirked.

She took his hand and kissed his knuckles. "Oh, Baby. I was wondering how to keep you on after you saw how messed up my baggage was." She looked ahead to a group of picnickers, then back to Jamey. "Do you see my mother and your father over there with Jade and Jasmine?"

"I do."

"And look how big Kai looks. How old do you think he is, eighteen months?"

"You're the expert." He remembered that Kai was able to speak a few words like Obi and Dada. "If the twins are here, it might be next summer." His daughters looked older too, age more measurable in children. Jade grabbed a Frisbee and both headed off to the surf.

"Let's get closer." Tina started forward, pulling him with her. "I want to hear what we're saying."

Jamey knew what they were saying, but walked with her. At the end of the beach, Pops poured Elizabeth a drink from a pitcher and together they laughed at Jade and Jasmine jumping around in knee-deep surf.

"Obi Wan Kenobi," the older Tina shouted. "Get back here, you old turtle hunter."

Kai thought this was funny from his perch on his father's shoulders. "Obi, Obi," he said.

Jamey and Tina moved closer to hear.

The older Tina turned and walked backwards, smiling up at the little boy. "You love Obi, don't you, Kai?"

"Mama Up!" The boy reached for her and she lifted him off Jamey's shoulders to set him on the sand.

The child was the spitting image of Jamey, right down to the slightly lopsided smile. Tina and Jamey watched their boy carefully navigate the uneven terrain of the beach, his arms held out from his sides for balance. He squatted to pick up a stick. "Dada." It was a present for his father.

"Thank you, Kai," Older Jamey said, the collection of sticks in his hand growing.

The older Tina took Jamey's hand and she twirled under his arm, into his hug. "My father would've loved Kai. I wish he'd lived to meet him."

"Me too, Darlin'."

"Lucky for my mom, I finally understood how fiercely a mother will fight for her child's well-being. Without that, forgiving her would've been difficult."

"I can't imagine what she went through when Kristoffer died." Obi dug for something in the wet sand at the edge of the surf.

"What if Kai is a jumper? What'll we do, Jamey?"

"He'll use it for the greater good, like us." Jamey stopped and looked into her eyes.

"No war." Tina said.

"Maybe he'll help us look for missing kids." They watched Kai follow Obi along the sandy shore.

"Do you miss it?" she asked.

"Jumping? Not when you bring me along." Jamey ran to catch the boy, playfully sweeping him into his arms, and setting the child on his shoulders again.

When Tina caught up, she linked her arm in his, looking pensive. "I love finding kids, even if it means putting them to rest."

"You use your gift well."

"And you use your gut reactions well." She poked him in the ribs. "And I love your guts, James." He laughed, and as they moved in to kiss, Kai grabbed a fistful of both parents' hair and yanked hard.

This was where Jamey had left the dream the last time˜. The pain of having his hair pulled must've woken him. Jamey, the jumper, turned to his wife as they walked behind their future selves. "Think this is next summer?"

Just then the older Tina lifted Kai off Jamey's shoulders and set him on the sand, holding his hand. She turned to face the couple behind her. "It's September, and we can see you, as well as hear you. You are see-through and barely there but we hear you perfectly. Right Jamey?"

"I'm trying to ignore those eavesdroppers behind us, to tell you the truth." He turned around and looked at the couple standing behind them. "Wow, Tina," he said. "Look how flabby I was from all that Nicaraguan beer. I'm glad I started working out again."

The younger Jamey looked down and had to admit, he'd gotten a bit soft in the middle but not flabby. "Hey Man, I just spent three weeks looking for Wyatt."

The two couples smiled at each other as Kai leaned down to pick up another stick in the sand.

Tina, the jumper, spoke to her older self. "I don't lose this ability, do I?"

"Not in the next year," Tina said. "But it's okay. Look at it this way—we find missing kids."

The younger Jamey nodded. "What about Afghanistan? Do I go back?"

"Negative. Milton has the locator taken out and grants you, me…I guess…a discharge. I just came back from Virginia, as a matter of fact. They have someone better in Sixth Force. Someone who can mind walk, it's called." He looked over at his wife and son who were digging in the sand. "Milton and his wife stayed with us a month. He's retired now." Older Jamey locked eyes with his former self. "There is nothing better than this life here on Maui, Dude."

"Hey, let's have a foursome," the younger Jamey said, and they all laughed. "I wonder if Pops and Liz can see us all out here talking." It didn't seem like anyone noticed the anomaly. "Freaky shit," Jamey shook his head. "I doubt we'll ever know all the secrets of dream jumping and I hope we stop trying to figure it out."

The future Jamey answered. "We do. Once Milton retires and guarantees my discharge, things lighten up. Dream jumping isn't so bad when it's not for the military. We do good work for missing kids. This next year is fantastic, but I can't tell you all that."

Tina asked the other Tina about her mother and Pops and while they were talking, Jamey leaned in and whispered to the older Jamey. "I still got it?"

He nodded. "As good as Tina. Long distance too. I'm just getting ready to tell her now I've been discharged." He nodded to his wife.

"Wow."

Tina broke through. "Here comes Jade and Jasmine. We better clear out."

She hadn't heard the exchange between both Jamey's about his ability to dream jump on his own, which was Jamey's intention. His Tina was safer without that knowledge for now.

The older Jamey put his arm around his wife's shoulders and nodded to the younger couple on the beach. "We are freaky ass weirdos. All four of us." They laughed and the older couple turned and started to walk away.

Before they got too far, Jamey stopped and called over his shoulder. "Don't just stand there, you two. Go wake up and start living."

The End

Thanks for reading. If you enjoyed this book series I would greatly appreciate a simple review on Amazon. I'm a struggling author, hoping to make a mark in this crowded market. Even just saying it was very entertaining, or suspenseful or that you enjoyed the book, works fine.

Thank you,

Kim

Novels by Kim Hornsby

Necessary Detour

Girl of his Dream

The Dream Jumper's Promise

The Dream Jumper's Secret

The Dream Jumper's Pursuit

Dream Come True

Rocky Bluff

Find out more at Kim's Website:

www.kimhornsbyauthor.net

The story continues three months later...

DREAM COME TRUE

Chapter 1

James Dunn stood in the snow in his front yard in Carnation, Washington and watched his childhood home burn. Orange flames licked the side of the old two-story home, heading from the back to the front of the house and up. "Pops!" His father stood in the front window of the bedroom he'd slept in his whole life. Why the hell wasn't his dad running down the stairs? The house wasn't completely overtaken by the inferno. "Get out of there!" he yelled to the old man in the window, waving his arms.

Pops shook his head, as if it was too late. But it wasn't. He could still get down the stairs. And then Jamey remembered that the hall from Pops bedroom ran the length of the house at the back and the fire appeared to have started in the kitchen. The back of the house where the kitchen had been was completely engulfed in flames, crackling and finishing off the gathering place for the Dunn family for forty some odd years.

He pointed to the window. "Open the window. Jump!" Pops could slide down the roof of the front porch outside his window and only fall about fifteen feet into the snow. "Do it!"

Pops showed that the window didn't open and then Jamey realized that his father had painted the window shut a few months ago when he'd decided to cover up the blue bedroom for a "nice neutral and masculine tan."

"Smash it!" James yelled. Why in hell didn't Pops do something. "Come on, Man. Get out of there." Jamey's voice cracked. If Tina was in this dream, she could take away the fire, leap up to the window, smash the glass and rescue Pops. She had the ability to change the dream because this whole fiasco started as her dream. She'd be wondering what happened to him, where he went. He wondered himself. Maybe he could call her into this branch of the dream. "Tina! Get over here."

Pops stood at the window shaking his head.

Jamey ran to the porch, stood on the railing and tried to shimmy up the corner post to the grab the gutter. How had he ever gotten to the roof this way in his teenage years, it was so slippery? He couldn't get any traction. He jumped down and ran to the garage at the back of the house, a building not attached to the blaze. Finding the ladder hanging at the back of the garage, he hoisted it down and ran it outside, hitting Pops' truck several times along the way.

By the time he got to the front of the house, flames had engulfed the front rooms but it looked like Pops' bedroom would be the last to go. He still stood at the window, his face a blank mask of nothing. Jamey extended the ladder, locked it in place and placed it against the roof outside Pops' window. Just as he got to the top of the ladder and was about to step to the roof, flames invaded Pops' room. He could still save his father. He jumped onto the slippery, angled roof, half crawled his way to the window and when he looked up, what he saw made him stagger backwards.

It wasn't Pops at the window. The person who'd been watching him was a young woman with a skeletal face and stringy hair, laughing to see that the trick had worked. Now James would burn to death.

***

Tina floated among the decrepit ruins of the sunken ship. Before falling asleep, she and Jamey had decided on a wreck dive and she'd imagined a wrecked pirate ship at thirty-five feet under, somewhere in the Caribbean. Who knew if such a place existed beyond her mind, but as Jamey always said, "Darlin', if you can imagine it, we can go there in a dream."

If anyone had told Tina two years ago that she'd have this vivid dream life, she would've laughed in their face. Until Jamey, she hadn't believed in paranormal mumbo jumbo. A business major, Tina had been influenced by her traditional upbringing with two very conservative parents and hadn't even heard of most of this shit before Jamey came back into her life and revealed he was a psychic freak. Then the mumbo jumbo became her life—entering other people's dreams, sharing lucid dreams, even telepathy, which Jamey called hyper-intuition as a way of soft-peddling a "strange-ass ability." It was all Jamey's doing. He'd brought the strangeness into her life.

Tina kicked through crystal clear, turquoise water, across the deck of the pirate ship, Jamey back there somewhere. She was the dive instructor with the most experience, the boss underwater.

Pulling herself through a doorway on the schooner, she floated down the stairs to what looked like the ship's dining room. A long wooden table and benches dominated the room. As ordered, the visibility of the water was extraordinary, the fish plentiful and the exploration of this ship fascinating. A large candelabra dominated the center of the dining table, an ornate chair with carvings of mermaids at one end.

When she turned to Jamey to point out the chair, he wasn't there. Had he not followed her? She kicked herself up the stairs to the deck, but Jamey was nowhere to be seen. That was strange. He couldn't leave a dream without her. She controlled this ability now, not him. Where was he? If he'd woken, she would've too.

Tina took the water from the dream and stood on the deck. "Jamey?' Where'd you go?" she called into the dream.

No answer.

Where the hell was he?

The ship wasn't so large that he wouldn't hear her. "Jamey?"

Nothing.

She glanced over the railing to see that the vessel now rested on a sandy bed in what used to be a picturesque bay. Then, she heard an anguished cry from her husband.

"No!" Jamey's voice sounded very far away.

Tina ran to the bow's highest point. Aside from that one word, the dream was deathly quiet around her. "Jamey!"

Footsteps sounded on the wooden stairs and seconds later, Jamey emerged from the doorway.

Tina jumped down from the higher deck and ran towards her husband. "Where were you?"

"We need to end this." His face had that shut up and follow my lead look. "I'll tell you what happened when we jump out." He still wore his scuba gear but had removed his regulator from his mouth and his face mask. "Now!"

She didn't ask why they needed to leave. Didn't have to. Jamey was the expert dreamer. They joined hands, ran to where they'd arrived in the dream, and on Jamey's "1, 2, 3…" jumped into the air.

The trip back to their prone bodies in their Maui bedroom was less than two seconds from the moment they jumped. Tina opened her eyes still holding her husband's hand from when they fell into the dream, probably only minutes earlier. She sensed something was wrong. Terribly wrong.

Jamey bolted upright. "I was taken into another dream."

That was impossible. "How?"

"I don't know. But, Pops' house was on fire. Burning to the ground. It was snowy and Pops was inside, trapped in his bedroom. I kept yelling at him to jump out the window, into the snow, but he wouldn't." Jamey turned to her, his eyes skittish with emotion. "He just watched me, nodding, like this was his time to die. He didn't even try to escape. I got a ladder and when I reached the window, he turned into a ghoulish woman." He covered his face with his hands and let out a strangled sob.

Tina slid over to wrap her arms around him. "Was it a proph?" They'd taken to calling premonitions this, shortening the word prophetic.

"I couldn't tell. Everything was on fire. I don't know." Jamey was rattled, a state she rarely saw with her confident husband, the ex-cop and soldier. "The Christmas tree was in the window."

Tina wondered if Pops had his tree up yet. "If everything was bright, maybe it was a normal dream." Normals were innocent. Prophs were easy to tell with pale colors and fuzzy edges. "Probably just a bad dream, Jamey." She hadn't seen her husband this upset since she went into labor with Kai nine months earlier. "Your dad wouldn't just let himself die inside a burning house."

Jamey's breathing was labored. "You're probably right. But who the hell was that woman?" His eyes darted around the room. "She looked young, but dead and she laughed like she'd caught me in a trap."

"Maybe nothing," she offered. "I wish I'd come with you to this dream." How had he left her dream on his own? "Call Pops to see if he's doing fine."

"Yes, I will." He got out of bed to retrieve his phone from the dresser top.

In another two weeks, she and Jamey would head to the mainland with Kai to spend Christmas in snowy Carnation, Washington. Maybe Jamey was just worried about his father and it came through in his sub-conscious, causing him to have bad dreams. After all, that's what dreams were supposed to be—the hindbrain not shutting off during sleep and amusing itself with all your memories and emotions while your front brain shut down. "How did you enter a different dream?"

"Not sure."

Tina waited while Jamey dialed his father's number, her cheek resting on the back of her husband's shoulder. For over a year, she'd been leading these dreams they called Fantasy Fun Time, as a joke. Jamey had never left one in the middle. Her timing of the dream was his timing like he was attached to her. She'd shared probably a hundred dreams with Jamey ever since he'd unknowingly passed a thirty-four-year-old ability to her in the dive shop over a year earlier.

"Pops, you okay?" Jamey said. It was three hours later in Carnation, but still too early for a leisurely phone call. "Sorry I woke you."

She studied Jamey's gorgeous profile in the darkness of their bedroom, his jaw tense. Pops was used to years of middle of the night calls, simply to check in. He didn't need details.

"Just a bad dream, I guess." Jamey mumbled to his father. "Don't get your Christmas tree until I get there, okay?" After they hung up, Jamey turned to Tina. "He hasn't got the tree yet. Either I drifted from your dream or the new dream was still part of our diving dream. Regardless of whether the dream was a proph or not, I have a very strong feeling that Pops' house is going to burn down." He took a deep breath. "I need to get to Carnation. See what's going on. I'll leave as soon as I can get a flight out."

She nodded, knowing two things. Jamey wasn't an alarmist and her husband was rarely wrong about dreams.

To Be Continued...

Find this novel at Amazon Books

Acknowledgements

To my relatives who live in Nicaragua

To my cousin, Rob Martin, and his wife Jill, who live on Mombacho and have those noisy monkeys to contend with on a daily basis. Thanks for taking me hiking in the jungle, fixing me delicious meals, taking me sightseeing, and at the end of the day letting me sit on your deck, stare at the view, and be a part of your family. My time in Nicaragua has made me a happier person. Thank you Rob for being my Nicaraguan research go to, and for proofreading this novel for accuracy.

To Leroy Martin, Ana and Anaise, who operate El Camello in Granada, one of the yummiest stops for lunch, dinner, or late night drinks. Thanks for all the free meals and for inventing avocado fries!

To all the lovely Nicaraguan people on Mombacho who have so little but always have a smile when the truck drives by your house.

To the Nicaraguan Children's Foundation who do wonderful work for the small villages and children of southern Nicaragua. And to Veronica Castro at San Juan del Sur Spanish School who made our mission possible.

To Eliza Tector who answered the call to go to Nicaragua and carried fifty pounds of crayons all over the country before we got to the tiny school to drop them off.

If you ever go to Nicaragua, think about taking an extra duffel bag full of children's clothes and school supplies.

~

I wrote this novel during NaNoWriMo, National Novel Writing Month, a wonderful way to get the bare bones of a story on the page in one frenzied month. Thanks to all the folks at NaNoWriMo.

To my writing community who validate me, encourage me and guide me to be a better writer—Laurie Rowell, Alec Rowell, who plot stormed with me for this one, Christine M. Fairchild who lends and ear and a pen whenever I need her, Anna L. Walls, who edits and critiques, Alicia Dean, who does so much for so many, including me, and Lori Leger who always answers the call so patiently.

And to my beta reading team who drop everything to read. Courtney, Ilsa, Lisa, Diana, Marie, Nancy, Terri, Lu, Mary, Jen and Cath. I treasure your opinions and your support of this unknown author. Thank you! To my friends, Catharina, Eliza and Lynn. Just because. You epitomize friendship.

No book can be written without the love and support of my sweet husband, Roland, who accompanied me to Nicaragua to research the local beer. He makes it possible for me to pursue this dream. And to my gorgeous teenage kids who I crazy love because they are mine and because they are both writers.

And, to all the parents of missing children whose story didn't end happily, I am so very sorry for your loss.

Mombacho Coq au Vin

Ingredients

12 slices bacon, sliced into 1/2-inch pieces
5 large skinless, boneless chicken breasts, rinsed, patted dry and cut into 2 inch cubes
2 teaspoons salt
1 teaspoon freshly ground black pepper
1 onion, finely chopped
20 small pearl onions, peeled
1/2 cup minced shallots (2 large shallots)
1 head garlic, cloves separated and peeled
1 pound button mushrooms, wiped clean and halved or quartered if large (should match size of pearl onions)
1/3 cup all-purpose flour

2 teaspoons tomato paste
3 cups dry white wine, California Chardonnay
1 1/2 cups rich chicken stock
1 teaspoon dried thyme
2 bay leaves
1/2 cup heavy cream

Directions

Preheat oven to 350 degrees

In a Dutch oven fry the bacon until crisp and all of the fat is rendered. Using a slotted spoon, transfer the crisp bacon bits to paper towels to drain.

Season the chicken pieces with the salt and pepper. Brown the chicken pieces in the hot bacon fat, until golden on all sides. Transfer the chicken pieces to a large plate and set aside. Remove all but about 4 tablespoons of the bacon fat from the Dutch oven. Reduce the heat to medium-high and add the chopped onion, pearl onions, shallots and garlic cloves. Cook until soft, 5 to 6 minutes.

Add the mushrooms and cook for 7 minutes longer, or until they've released most of their liquid and have begun to brown. Add the flour and tomato paste and cook, stirring constantly, for 1 minute. Slowly add the wine and stock, stirring constantly. Add the thyme, bay leaves reserved bacon and chicken. Bring liquid to a boil, reduce the heat to medium, and cook the sauce at a gentle simmer for 15 minutes, until liquid is slightly thickened. Bring the sauce to a boil and cover the pot. Place in the oven and cook for about 1 1/2 hours, or until the chicken is very tender. Transfer the chicken pieces to a serving dish and cover loosely to keep warm. Return pot to medium-low heat. Skim any fat from the surface of the cooking liquid and increase the heat to medium-high. Add the heavy cream and cook until the sauce has thickened slightly and coats the back of a spoon, about 15 to 20 minutes. Taste and adjust the seasoning if necessary. Return the chicken to the Dutch oven and cook for a few minutes to heat through, then serve over wild rice with mango chunks.